the Orchard

OTHER BOOKS AND AUDIO BOOKS

BY KRISTA LYNNE JENSEN

Of Grace and Chocolate

a novel

Krista Lynne Jensen

Covenant Communications, Inc.

Cover image: *Cherries* © Sunnybeach, courtsey of istockphoto.com

Cover design copyright © 2013 by Covenant Communications, Inc.

Published by Covenant Communications, Inc.
American Fork, Utah

Printed in the United States of America
First Printing: April 2013

19 18 17 16 15 14 13   10 9 8 7 6 5 4 3 2 1

ISBN-13: 978-1-60861-145-4

For my sister, Shelli. I love you forever.

Acknowledgments

"The glory of friendship is not the outstretched hand, nor the kindly smile, nor the joy of companionship; it is the spiritual inspiration that comes to one when he discovers that someone else believes in him and is willing to trust him."

—Ralph Waldo Emerson

THE ORCHARD TOOK A FEW weeks to draft and a few years to get to print. This story was my first novel, my first publishing contract, and my first lesson in patience as a writer. I'm so excited to finally share this book. As writers, we learn that tension and suspense add thrill to our stories. I'm totally thrilled.

To my ladies in the 2007–2008 Cody Third Ward Writing Club: Carla Parsons, Norma Rudolph, Janet Card, Arlene Brimhall, Sue Severns, and RaNae Daniels. Thanks for believing in me.

Many thanks to Samantha Millburn, my editor at Covenant and a blissful newlywed. You guide my sword. Thanks to Covenant for taking a chance on a new writer who didn't have a clue.

Thanks to my alpha readers for their valuable feedback and endless encouragement in writing this book: Carla, Norma, Janet, Rebecca Sorensen, Richelle Larson, and Debby Anglesey.

Thanks to Maija for her hospital expertise and to Randy Tayler and Marion Jensen for their corny-joke input. You make Twitter a happier place.

Thanks to my friends in WordPlay: Melanie Jacobson, Abel Keogh, Kate Palmer, Julie Wright, and Becca Wilhite; it's so great to have you around. To the Bear Lake Monsters: Robison Wells, Josi Kilpack, Marion Jensen, Margot Hovley, Chris Miller, Nancy Allen, Jenny Moore, and Cory Webb—I just love you guys. Thanks for embracing my dorkiness.

Annette Lyon and Sarah Eden, I'm trying to be you. Only me.

Thanks to my grandma Dorothy Graesser, who gave me my first romance novel. Happy ninetieth birthday, Grandma! And thanks to my parents, who practically *are* a romance novel. I love you.

Braeden, Jacob, and Maren, thank you for the many hugs and kisses and the laughter. And the dancing. Never forget the dancing. Brandon, thank you for the Magnum Double Chocolate ice cream bars and for seeing me. I know your heart.

To my daughter Chelsea and her new husband, Matt, I wish you every happy moment that flits your way, all the strength to endure the tough things, and all the love you can give each other and share with those around you. Thanks for being my joy.

"Half the sum of attraction, on either side, might have been enough . . . and when acquainted, rapidly and deeply in love. It would be difficult to say which had seen highest perfection in the other, or which had been the happiest: she, in receiving his declarations and proposals, or he in having them accepted."

—Jane Austen, *Persuasion*

Part 1

Chapter 1

April 2008

"I feel colorless," she whispered to the sunset.

Alisen Embry, at age twenty-three, had climbed a tree. Again. She wasn't focused on the aged branches supporting her body but on the sloping view before her: the rows of carefully pruned treetops stretching down the hill, the roofline of the big house dark against the dusk, the silhouette of the boathouse and dock melting into calm, rippling water. Fading sunlight shot straight across the tiny waves, and she imagined the lapping sounds this far up in the orchard, this far up in the old cherry tree. A breeze caught her hair, and a few curls escaped the ponytail at the back of her head, feeling their way across her face and catching on her mouth. She absently pulled them away, tucking them behind her ear.

This was her place. These were her cherry trees. That was her house and her dock. Sort of. How many times had she sat in this very spot, watching the day close, breathing in the air around her, listening to sounds of home?

A car whooshed by on the highway just twenty yards behind her.

She swallowed.

How could they leave this place?

She knew the answer to that question: she would leave this place if it meant keeping it.

Her gaze narrowed toward the house. She knew her father was there, probably making his way to his leather club chair with his *GQ Magazine* in hand and reading glasses tucked neatly into his shirt pocket.

Alisen had always struggled with the idea of her mother, intelligent, easy-mannered Anne Riley, falling in love with handsome, egotistical Keith Embry. How he had fallen in love with her was never a question. Anyone who knew Alisen's mother loved her. But a person had to earn Keith's approval.

His acceptance. And somehow, Anne had succeeded both in winning his heart and tempering his superiority.

But even as a young girl, Alisen had asked her mother why she had picked *him*. Anne saw the reasons behind her daughter's question. Keith could be aloof, abrasive. She had sighed with a smile, and her simple answer was that she hadn't. Love had picked him for her.

Only days after Alisen had asked the question, Anne Embry had fallen off a ladder in her carefully nurtured orchard and broken her neck—and the hearts of those closest to her.

The funeral had been a blur of faces and words and pats on Alisen's shoulder. She'd stared at the portrait of her mother surrounded by roses and ferns and tried to figure out how she would not touch that face ever again, not hear that voice ever again. It wouldn't make sense to her thirteen-year-old mind.

But the questions that came after the funeral hit harder.

Her father had shut himself away for days and left Aunt Rachel, his wife's sister, to take care of Alisen and her two sisters. When he'd finally emerged looking perfect and unruffled, they had gone to him, looking for assurance and comfort. Looking for their father. Elizabeth, the oldest and so much like Keith in most ways, reached him first. And although he pressed a hand to Elizabeth's cheek and shushed little Amanda as she dissolved into hysterical tears, it was his actions toward Alisen that had sealed the changes in her life forever.

She'd waited for the acknowledgment, no matter how slight, that he was still her father and that things would be all right. Her insides were already a hard knot, constricting if she tried to breathe, not letting her exhale. The tears rolled from her eyes like someone hadn't turned off the garden hose completely. Hesitating and coming no closer, he'd allowed his gaze to come to her face. For just an instant, she'd seen open pain, but he'd quickly closed it up and hidden it somewhere she could never find. In his appraisal, Alisen had felt for the first time just how much like her mother she was: her dark waves of hair, her round blue eyes, and the natural rose of her cheeks and mouth. But Alisen had felt colorless.

He'd held a hand out toward her, palm down, closing his eyes . . . and had turned away.

Alisen wiped the tears from her eyes with the back of her hand, and the fire of color above the trees in front of her came into focus.

A faint star caught her eye to the south, and she knew it was not as bright as it would be when darkness completely took over the sky.

She looked around as though someone might see her here in the dark, a fully grown woman perched in a tree, and wondered if she was too old to make a wish on a star. *Obviously not too old to climb trees.* She closed her eyes.

Star light, star bright . . . Her thoughts trailed off. She opened her eyes.

With a sad smile, she deftly climbed down and dropped to the soft orchard floor, spongy with mulched tree limbs.

Darkness was not a problem. Alisen knew every tree, every path, dip, and mound down the hill. As she reached the lower boundary, the glow from the house threw the branches into sharp contrast. Buds were just beginning to form and would soon swell to bursting. The orchard would fill with fragrance and become a playground for humming bees, bouncing in frantic joy from limb to limb. The scent always brought reminders of things sweet and bitter.

She strode around to the front of the house, ignoring the dock. The Embry home might have better belonged somewhere in the Mediterranean or Central America, not there in Montana. The red-tiled roof and white stucco played along with the grand charade, as did the giant clay pots and ornamentals. All the patio lights glowed above each arched window and entry. The effect was stunning. But so was the electric bill.

"Let him have a few more nights of neighborhood envy." Word of their situation would travel fast in the lake community. She hoped people would be kind.

She walked past the deeply carved mahogany door and followed the brick path past a large, silent fountain, then around to a side door.

There, waiting as though by appointment, was Jane, the stray orange-and-white tabby who, years earlier, claimed their place as her own. Alisen pursed her lips, remembering her father's reaction when the cat's first introduction was a pounce on his unsuspecting lap and a rub right into his black, cashmere sweater.

"Naughty Jane," Alisen whispered and smiled wryly as she opened the door to the long, narrow mudroom, the only room the cat was allowed in.

Purring rose around Alisen's legs as she scooped cat food into a dish and filled the water bowl. Alisen crouched down and rubbed Jane's neck. The purring grew louder.

"We should have named you Motor," Alisen observed.

She let Jane finish her meal, closed the door behind her, and made her way upstairs. A mirror hung at the top of the landing. Several large mirrors hung on the walls around the house so a person could check their appearance before continuing to another room, another activity. Alisen resented them.

Vanity. The word made her cringe. It was the reason they had to leave. The reason they had to buckle, to cave. Putting on appearances, keeping up with the "Joneses," holding their place in social circles. It had all come with a high price tag.

She paused at the mirror. By the world's standards, she was an adult. She felt it and had felt it for some time now. But sometimes she felt thirteen again.

She passed the mirror. She knew how she looked. Tired.

She had been beautiful, had even felt it. She had been loved the way a girl wanted to be loved, and dreams had pulsed through her like sweet water through parched limbs. Now she just felt worn. Maybe after this mess with the finances was straightened out—maybe a change would be good. A fresh start. She straightened her shoulders and went to find her father.

He sat in the living room, just as she had pictured.

"Dad?" She tucked her hands in her pockets.

He took his reading glasses off, not really looking at her. "Yes?"

"I wanted to remind you of the meeting we have with Mr. Shepherd in the morning."

After learning of the dismal state of their affairs, Keith had nearly shut down. He remained stoic and cool but indecisive and withdrawn. They all had to walk the fine line of directing important decisions and not pushing him over the edge.

"I'm aware of the meeting. I'll be ready to go at eight forty-five. Remind Elizabeth, will you?" He turned back to his paper.

The coolness between them had increased lately. She felt his pride being assaulted at every suggestion she made. But she had already met with Aunt Rachel and John Shepherd. They had approved of her plan, and John had promised he would outline everything to the last detail so her father could have no choice but to see it was the best way. She wondered if it would be enough. Keith Embry, if anything other than vain, was stubborn.

She climbed another set of stairs and passed another immense mirror as she walked to her sister's room and knocked.

"Yes?" came the bored reply.

"It's me. I needed to talk to you about tomorrow."

"Come in."

Elizabeth was sprawled across her silky brown bed, just closing her laptop, wearing dark skinny jeans and a form-fitting sweater. It was just barely eight o'clock, but Alisen had exhausted herself in the orchard, and

Elizabeth looked freshly made up with her long golden hair brushed to a smooth sheen. A pair of strappy copper heels sat on the floor, and Alisen wasn't sure if they were waiting to be worn or had just been taken off.

Elizabeth worked in fashion merchandising, traveling all over the world, staying in plush hotels, dating beautiful men she never brought home. She was home more often now but could take off in a moment's notice without saying more than "Back in a week."

Elizabeth turned her face to her younger sister and waited as if Alisen had interrupted an important style show.

"I just spoke with Dad." *I guess you could call it that.*

Elizabeth raised one eyebrow.

"He asked me to remind you of the meeting tomorrow. We'll be leaving at eight forty-five." Elizabeth drew her lips together in disapproval, but Alisen ignored it. "I think this could save us from having to give up the house."

"I'm not sure why you've been secretive. Dad deserves more respect than that."

"Elizabeth"—Alisen kept her voice even—"this isn't a secret. If it had been, you still wouldn't know about it." Elizabeth looked affronted, but Alisen continued. "I was talking with Rachel when the idea came, and since Dad wasn't around, we immediately called John and ran it by him." *And we have to be careful with Dad so he doesn't have some kind of breakdown*, she added to herself. "We have to act quickly. You know that, don't you?"

Elizabeth hesitated then nodded. "Of course I do. I don't want to lose this place either."

Alisen looked down at the plush carpet. "And I show Dad every respect owed him. I think after tomorrow, he'll appreciate this and see it's for the good of everyone. Including him."

"Well, we'll see." Elizabeth was already picking up her cell phone. It was her dismissal.

Alisen wasn't quite done. "I'm going to bed. Please let the cat out before you leave tonight."

Alisen heard a mumble of sarcastic joy from her sister as she shut the door behind her. The corner of her mouth twitched upward. She leaned against the door with her eyes closed then headed up the hallway to her own room. She paused at Amanda's old room.

It hadn't changed much. Hot pink and orange and zebra stripes. The Black-Eyed Peas and Jonas Brothers smoldered at her from their places on the wall. But Amanda had married last Christmas. Amanda, who at nineteen had become a pretty, pouty girl, had fallen in love with one of the neighbors-turned-friends at the fruit stand. Greg Stewart came from a respected family, was in his final year of dental school, and was ready to enter a busy practice in town. Keith and Elizabeth had insisted on making a good public showing of the Embry name and had spared no expense for the wedding.

Alisen closed the bedroom door and moved on, even more in need of a shower and sleep. She wanted to be through with this night already and to be on with it. What *it* was, she had only a vague idea. But the sooner, the better.

Feeling heavy, she entered her room. A sense of peace greeted her, though she was barely aware of it. The soft green walls and white furnishings soothed her subconscious mind, and splashes of red in the lamp, the pillows, and the frenzied floral painting on the wall cheered it. She pulled herself over to her mother's old trunk at the end of her bed and sat down, brushing her hand along the dark wood. On the wall hung a small painting in a gilded little frame: a bowl of cherries spilling out onto a warm wooden table. It was a simple, ordinary offering. Alisen didn't know the artist's name, but she'd always been grateful to whoever it was.

She remembered the day her mother had come across that painting. They were running errands in the tourist town of Bigfork, north of the lake. She and her mother had ducked into an antiques store for a quick perusal. Her mother had browsed intently.

"What are you looking for?"

"I'll know when I find it."

A few moments later, her mother's hand reached out as if it had known all along and brought back with it the painting of the cherries.

"There. I found what I was looking for."

"How did you know?" Alisen was amazed.

Her mother looked mysterious and excited. "I *didn't*."

The clerk at the store wrapped the painting in brown paper, and Alisen cradled the sacred bundle all the way home.

Then her mother had surprised her further by ceremoniously walking up the stairs with the painting held in front of her and continuing toward Alisen's room. Alisen's eyes had widened, and she had dared to hope. Her mother had stopped and motioned for her to open the door. She had swept across to an open wall, took out a nail and putty knife from her back pocket, and, using the handle of the putty knife as a hammer, installed the painting on Alisen's very own wall.

They'd sat on the edge of the bed and surveyed her mother's handiwork.

"Sometimes, when you don't know what you're looking for, that is when you find exactly what you need," her mother had mused. Then she'd leaned into Alisen's ear. "But you have to be looking."

Alisen had grinned, and her mother had caught her up in her arms.

Alisen came out of her reverie, her arms wrapped around herself. She got up and walked over to the painting, brushing a little dust off the frame. "What am I looking for this time, Mom?"

She tilted her head to the side as if expecting to hear an answer.

Chapter 2

Ten years before, after the bleary fog of her mother's funeral had lifted, Alisen had been struck by a fear so paramount she took it straight to Aunt Rachel. She was convinced that if left to itself, the orchard would run wild and her mother's love for it would have been a waste. And that was an impossible reality. To put the caretaking entirely into a stranger's hands seemed wrong. So, of the few requests that she'd made regarding her mother's things, she had dared to ask for help with this one.

Rachel had waited outside the den with Alisen until invited in by Alisen's father and John Shepherd, who, aside from being an old college friend, was also Keith's financial advisor. Rachel had quietly prodded Alisen into the room, where she stood opposite Mr. Shepherd. Alisen presented her plan, determined not to let the tears persuade them but rather her purpose. Her father had not turned in his seat but gave a brusque nod to Shepherd, who told her he thought it a fair proposal and would make the arrangements.

So the orchard was Alisen's. A local man, semiretired and trustworthy, was hired to oversee Alisen's training and safety. Jay Whitney had older sons to work his own extensive orchards and considered the time spent at the small Embry orchard a bit of a break. Most of Alisen's mother's usual laborers returned, and during the growing seasons of the next ten years, after school, weekends, nights, and mornings, the orchard became Alisen's refuge.

Elizabeth had no interest in orchard work, but Amanda would often tag along, chatting and asking endless questions. In the spring, Alisen would go over the lists with Jay, making plans for improvements and learning the books. Bouquets of blossoms filled her room with the scent of her mother. In late July and August, the bright little fruit stand on the main road attracted smiling tourists, eager as Alisen handed them their bags of dark sweet, Rainier, and tart pie cherries. In the fall, the girls raked and burned leaves but not before jumping into the piles. Even in winter, Alisen's footsteps traced patterns in the snow around the trees.

By the time she was sixteen, Alisen had saved enough money for a good used vehicle. To Elizabeth's dismay—her own pearl Porsche Cayman S dazzling on the road and in the driveway—Alisen's old Ford F150 was big, powerful, and red. And Alisen had just enough pride in it to add to the driver's side door, in small, elegant, white vinyl lettering, *Embry Orchard*, with twin cherries underneath.

While the orchard had mended a portion of Alisen's heart, after all these years, it had become a piece of her as necessary as oxygen. Steady and trusted, sustaining her as she nurtured it. And as John Shepherd had finally revealed the family's financial state to Rachel, Elizabeth, and Alisen, the orchard was where Alisen's first concern had settled.

The news had been bewildering. The Embry family had always enjoyed wealth. Keith and Anne had both come from affluent homes, and Keith had been independent of his parents since their divorce when they'd granted him access to his bulked-up trust fund. Keith's law firm did well and handled a large portion of Montana. But when Anne was alive, she made sure they lived within their means, and her self-sufficiency and moderation kept Keith in check. Now, ten years after the death of his wife, Keith Embry had run his fortune into debt.

John Shepherd had tried to warn his friend, had tried to show him the numbers, but it had come on so gradually—but now so fully—that Keith hadn't listened until it was too late.

Alisen had not panicked. She had found resolve. She would not lose her mother's orchard.

She could not.

* * *

The meeting was going as Alisen had expected, and John Shepherd's office had never felt so confining.

John shook a handful of paper at Keith. Numbers. "But don't you see? If not this, then you will lose everything. The house, the cars, riding lessons and horses, travel—collection agencies aren't the ice cream man, Keith." John was a broad, tall man with a good crop of silver hair on his head, and he had a couple of years on Keith. His pleading, if not exactly firm, was still affecting his friend. Though what effect, exactly, was still to be determined.

Keith paced back and forth, throwing his hands around. "But leave the lake house? Where would we go? What would people say?"

Alisen hadn't seen him so agitated in years. She reminded herself to breathe as she felt the weight of this being her idea. At least he was reacting instead of turning to stone.

"Sensible people, real friends, will see that you're doing the right thing in taking action for your future," Aunt Rachel said.

Her words brought a look of disbelief from her brother-in-law, but then Keith sighed and nodded. They were getting somewhere.

Elizabeth spoke up for the first time. "Dad? Haven't you always wanted to live in the city? This could be your chance—"

"I'm not sure a drastic relocation is necessary or that living in a city would be good for the financial situation either." John rubbed his chin, directing an apologetic look at Elizabeth.

"I can't leave the firm," Keith said.

"No. Now would not be a good time for that. But I wonder, would you consider a town in state, Kalispell, perhaps, where you could still meet with respectable people, enjoy some culture, and not only find but afford housing and living expenses within the ranges you are to be . . . confined to?" He said this last part with hesitancy.

After a heavy pause, Keith asked, "What about the investments?"

"You know we can't touch those," John sympathized.

Alisen felt it was her turn. She held her breath. "Dad?"

Keith slowly turned to look at her.

She plowed forward. "With the rental market the way it is on the lake, the demand is high, and with what I can bring in from the orchard"—at this her father raised an eyebrow—"we feel you could afford smaller but respectable housing and fair living expenses and still have enough left to pay the debts. We'll have to sell the boat." Keith closed his eyes. "And downsize the cars. It may be a few years, but when it's done, we would still have the house. And our dignity." She swallowed then gave him another option. "Or we could use the trusts Mom set up for us."

His eyes opened and, in a rare moment, locked on Alisen's.

"No." His response was quiet and firm.

Alisen didn't push it further. Though she hadn't asked her sisters, if she'd had enough, she would buy the house herself. Elizabeth remained quiet.

Keith turned, his eyes drawn to a picture on the office wall, a painting of the lake, a sailboat navigating its way across glittering water.

He turned abruptly to John, who started at the movement. "*What* kind of people would be renting the house? I wouldn't want just anybody willing to slap down money."

"Of course you can dictate your wishes on that part, but trust me, Keith, we would find only the best people. We probably wouldn't even need to advertise. We can find good renters through word of mouth who can be vouched for by friends and associates."

And with Keith's nod, that was it.

On with it, then.

* * *

They found a renter quickly, and by word of mouth, as John had said. Alisen gathered with the family on the veranda, and John shared what he knew. He had found a perfect renter for the place, and the family could be in at the first of the month.

"Their names are Marcus and Hannah Crawford, a couple with no children, but they have family ties to the area. He's been a professor of agriculture, Environmental Studies, I think he said, for some years at UM in Missoula, and before that, I believe he was a farmer."

"A farmer," Keith exclaimed.

Alisen detected the glance he flicked in her direction.

"Yes, a very successful farmer. I believe he spent time in some international something-or-other. Expert in his field. That's why he's been teaching at the university." He continued. "It has always been a dream of theirs to live out here on the lake, and now they find themselves with the means to do so."

"And what is the woman like?"

Alisen kept herself from rolling her eyes.

John answered. "Lovely woman, educated, obviously devoted to her husband. She is a teacher as well. Literature, I believe."

Keith nodded, his look distant.

Stay with us, Dad.

"They understand the terms of the orchard and agreed to allow Alisen to manage it as she always has. Mr. Crawford offered his services, of course, as he leans toward that kind of thing. They even offered Alisen her room at the house, which I thought very gracious of them, but I assured them all that had been arranged and Alisen would be staying with Rachel and Amanda at times." He looked at Alisen and added, "I hope that was all right."

Alisen gave a slight nod, keeping her eyes on Jane's tail swinging back and forth as the cat sat on the veranda wall.

At this pause, Rachel decided to add her news. "I've been looking, Keith, and I think I've found a place for you in Kalispell."

Keith turned his attention to his sister-in-law. "You have, have you?"

"I was curious. I have a friend who owns a condominium in a very desirable area. It's on the golf course and is part of the country club community. She e-mailed me pictures of a condo a neighbor is renting out, and I have to say, I was very pleased and could easily picture you there, Keith, as well as Elizabeth, when she isn't in New York."

"And the rent?" John said, keeping them on track before anyone got their hopes up.

"Very, very good." Rachel raised her eyebrows in delight. "I was tempted myself."

John arranged an appointment for Keith to meet with the Crawfords. As the gathering broke up, only Alisen remained in her chair, looking out over the lake but not really seeing.

She had been very still during the discussion. At the names mentioned, her heartbeat had quickened and then had seemed to quit altogether. She'd found it difficult to breathe and hard to focus on the conversation, though she had heard every word.

Hannah Crawford. Was it possible?

Jane came over, purring, and rubbed against Alisen's legs. Alisen absently opened her arms, and the cat leapt onto her lap.

"Oh, Jane, he could be here," she whispered. "Oh no. No, no, no."

Her hand raked through her hair as the memories came flooding over the dam, which had, Alisen noted, crumbled far too easily.

Part 2

Chapter 3

May, Four Years Earlier

Alisen grabbed her cap and flung it in the air with everyone else. High school was over; confetti, streamers, and beach balls filled the air above her; and Alisen, while searching for her family in the crowd, thought of her mother waiting with a big grin, arms open wide. She let the image float for a second then concentrated on finding her father and sisters. Friends called her name and wrapped their arms around her, smiling into digital and cell phone cameras. The atmosphere was that of sudden freedom after long imprisonment. Alisen gave in to the energy of the occasion as a beach ball bounced off her head. Her family would find her eventually.

At home, things were more subdued but pleasant. Earlier in the week, her father had approached her and, expecting her to want a new car like her older sister had been so insistent on, asked what model Alisen would be interested in as a graduation gift. If Alisen had ever surprised her father before, she was sure this one topped it.

It wasn't a Porsche, a Jetta, or even a Prius. Alisen's request had been simpler than that.

She stood on the dock, admiring her graduation present: a new, dark green, polished and perfect rowboat waiting in the water, tied with a big, red, floppy bow. A set of oars, two life jackets, and a small but heavy anchor rested inside. She smiled as she reread the words on the rear right-hand side: *BOWL OF CHERRIES*. It was corny, but she loved it.

As much as she wanted to take her new vehicle for a spin around the lake, now was not the time. Behind her, a small gathering of friends and family waited. She hadn't wanted the big, loud party Elizabeth had given herself years earlier. This was just a quiet gathering on the lake with a table of good food and drinks. Amanda had put together a couple of CDs of Alisen's favorite songs, and they played in the background.

She heard footsteps on the dock. Rachel walked toward her, beaming. Alisen studied her aunt, the most influential woman in her life now. Rachel was not as tall as Alisen's mother had been but had the same dark waves of hair, though cut short and layered all over. And instead of cornflower blue, her eyes were a soft brown. Alisen could see her mother in Rachel's smile and hear her in her laugh.

Rachel had married twice, once for love and once for money. Her love had died young, and her money had run away with someone else. She was wary of marriage now and had declared herself indefinitely single. When Alisen's mother died, Rachel had moved to the lake, finding a condominium close to town. Alisen didn't know what she would do without her.

She beamed at her aunt and gestured to the back of the boat. "Was this your idea?"

Rachel glanced at the lettering. "How did you guess?"

"Thank you." She gave her a hug. "I love it."

"You deserve it, honey." Rachel glanced over Alisen's shoulder at the little boat. "Well, you deserve much more than *that*."

Alisen pulled back and looked at her aunt, who rolled her eyes and mouthed, *A rowboat*?

Alisen laughed.

Rachel's gaze drew to the fine chain around Alisen's neck. "Is this new?" She fingered the half-carat diamond set in a round bezel.

"Yes. Elizabeth gave it to me just before graduation."

"Is it silver?"

"White gold."

"Well, now, that's more like it."

Rachel glanced one more time at the rowboat and shook her head with a smile.

From beyond the dock, they heard someone call, "There's the graduate!"

Jay Whitney and his wife, Bobbi, waved from the yard. Alisen waved back, and she and Rachel walked from the dock arm in arm to greet the guests. She glanced up toward the veranda, guessing her father and Elizabeth would make a polite appearance below and then retreat into the house for the evening.

Alisen found Jay at the food table. He set his plate down and crushed her in one of his bear hugs.

"How's my girl doing? Nice set of wheels over there at the dock." He winked.

She grinned. He knew she'd turned down a sports car. He'd always wanted a sports car.

"So, Miss Diploma, what are you going to do with all this time on your hands?"

"Time?" She smirked at his teasing. They were in early-summer maintenance mode and had just heeled in three new rows of young trees. She had plenty to do.

"I'd like to get some of those PVC crates."

He pursed his lips. The PVC crates were expensive but lower maintenance. "The old ones'll do for a few more years."

She shrugged. "I know. But I leave sorting and mending the crates and picking baskets until I'm rushing like mad to get them done."

"You don't need to do it by yourself." Jay's face brightened. "Hey, that reminds me. My nephew's coming tomorrow, and I wanted to bring him by the orchard. He's in an undergraduate program at UM. Environmental Studies. He's looking at smaller operations like yours. Only been around us bigger fellows." He stuck out his already large chest.

Alisen smiled, amused. "Why would he be interested in that?" She was proud of her little orchard, but it didn't usually attract men who wanted to make actual money.

"I'll let him explain it to you. He's pretty enthusiastic about it. Always been an impulsive kid. And I figure he'd be happy to mend the crates for you while he's here."

"I wouldn't make him do that on his vacation."

Jay lowered his voice, talking out of the side of his mouth. "Well, he's going to be here all summer, and to be honest with you, he's kind of a pest."

At this, his wife, who was talking to another woman behind Jay and was apparently keeping up with her husband's conversation as well, turned and jabbed him in the ribs with her elbow. "Jay! Be nice."

Jay chuckled and amended his statement. "Don't get me wrong. I have plenty of things for him to do at my place, and he's a hard worker, but . . ." He caught another glance from his wife. "Anyway, it would be great if he got to know some of the kids around the lake too." He turned around to his wife. "Is that better, dear?"

She shook her head and sighed toward Alisen then turned back to her conversation.

"So," Jay continued, "I'll bring him by after church tomorrow, if that's all right, and introduce you, and we can show him around the place. Okay?"

She nodded. Alisen knew Jay attended church with his family every Sunday for three hours, no less, and tomorrow wouldn't be work, just a visit. He called it his *holy day*. That's how it had been since they were thrown together in her crazy scheme, and she respected it. She'd noticed through the years that he didn't smoke or swear the way some of the laborers or her father's associates did, and she asked him once, after going to an uncomfortable party her junior year, if he drank.

"What, orange juice?" he had teased her.

"You know what I mean." She had already been fairly sure of his answer but was surprised at the intensity of it.

He had looked her right in the eyes. "I never have, Alisen, and I never will. I've been asked to drink many times—in high school by guys on the football team and as an adult—but I never did see any good come of it, any improvement for taking a drink. So why do it? If it doesn't feel comfortable, that's your warning." Then, as if realizing the seriousness of his tone, he had pulled back and grinned. "Orange juice tastes better anyway. I would guess." He'd winked and walked away.

Alisen turned and looked at her boat again. Her thoughts shifted to the memory of her father's face when he had hinted that she should take a walk down to the dock that morning. She remembered his face from the veranda above as she'd found her canoe, squealed, done a little spin and jump, and then called up to him, shielding her eyes from the morning sun. "Thanks, Dad!" She hadn't been sure, but she thought he had looked . . . pleased. She would take that.

* * *

The following morning, Alisen stirred in the white down comforter and stretched, reaching her hands far over her head as she yawned. She opened one eye and looked at the clock. Ten twenty-two.

Her head came off the pillow, and she blinked at the clock again. She couldn't remember the last time she had slept that late. And she had slept so well. She let her head drop back onto the pillow. The sun was already bright through her curtains, and the fabric swayed with the breeze from the open window. Sliding out of bed toward the balcony doors, she let herself outside.

While managing another stretch, her gaze drifted down to the dock. Her rowboat sat waiting, rocking occasionally with the waves. She made a quick decision, whirled back inside, and showered, dressed, and ran downstairs, nearly colliding with Elizabeth, who held two suitcases and a designer handbag. Elizabeth rolled her eyes and muttered something about "boat girl."

As Elizabeth's car roared up the road toward the airport, Alisen made her way down to the dock. Carefully, she unfastened the big bow from around the middle of the boat, taking it dripping to the garbage can in the boathouse. She came back and set the extra life jacket on the dock. She put on the other life jacket, adjusting it a bit so it fit right, then eagerly untied one end of the boat and stepped in. During this delicate maneuver, she saw sudden movement out of the corner of her eye. She let out a scream and jumped back, only to lose her footing. She tripped backward as she waved her arms and landed with a cold splash in the frigid lake.

She came up sputtering and chilled—and thankful Elizabeth was already gone. She pulled herself up dripping wet to peek over the side of the boat.

What she had initially taken for a snake slithering in the bow was the tail of a small cat, flicking back and forth as the animal lay curled up. The cat meowed at her apathetically.

Alisen narrowed her eyes. "Good morning."

The orange-and-white tabby got up and approached Alisen. It paused, looking Alisen over with a sweet little face and round eyes. It seemed to make a decision and stepped over to lick the drips off of Alisen's face.

The rowboat could wait.

Alisen went back to the house, and after she'd toweled off and changed, she walked out onto the veranda with milk sloshing in a dish. She set it down in front of the cat and stayed there, cross-legged, stroking and petting until the milk was gone, going over possible names in her mind, saying a few out loud, looking into the little face to see if one fit.

"Tiger. Nutter Butter." She paused. "Snakey."

Hm. She was trying too hard. Something simple.

"Jane."

The cat finished a last lick of her paws, climbed into Alisen's lap, and started a contented, staccato hum. Jane closed her eyes and fell asleep.

"Naughty Jane." Alisen sighed. She leaned her head back against the glass door and closed her eyes as well.

Chapter 4

The white pickup veered sharply to the right and headed off the drive. It bounced its way along a row of popcorn trees and followed a dirt path opening up to a clearing in front of the storage buildings. The scent of fading cherry blossoms filled the cab. Jay pulled up next to a red Ford, put his own Dodge Ram in park, turned off the ignition, and grabbed his cell phone.

"Hey, sweetie, it's me. Yeah, we just pulled up. Okay, see you in a bit."

Derick watched his uncle put the phone away.

"She saw us pull off the drive from the house. She'll be up in a minute." Jay was already out of the truck and shoving the door shut with a bang.

Derick took in his surroundings. Jay had told him the story of this girl, how at age thirteen she'd lost her mother, been practically disowned by her father, and asked for her mother's orchard to somehow heal the hurt. And, according to Jay, it had worked. He had talked about her like a proud parent.

So as Derick looked around, it was with piqued interest. They had parked in a wide pale-dirt circle in the center of the hillside orchard. They faced a large outbuilding with a couple of small sheds on the side and a few odds and ends piled up. Behind those, a large stand of pine trees ran all the way down the slope to the north side of the house. Beyond that was the lake, blue and shimmering.

As he opened his door and stepped out, Jay gave a loud greeting, and Derick heard a pleasant reply. Derick rounded the front of the truck, looking down to straighten his shirt.

"Derick."

Derick's head came up.

"I'd like you to meet Alisen!"

Derick stopped midstep. His mind took in the chocolate waves swinging loose across her forehead, falling behind her shoulders in the sun. His mind processed the eyes as blue as the lake, framed in dark lashes. His gaze was drawn to her mouth, her lips turned up in a half smile. He blinked, and the girl turned her face up to Jay, who stood with one arm around her as he looked amusedly at Derick. Derick's mind told him he looked like an idiot.

He collected himself, swallowed, straightened his shoulders, and stepped forward, hand outstretched.

"Hey. I'm Derick Whitney."

She hesitantly looked at the outstretched hand then brought hers forward and took it. "Alisen Embry."

Her hand was warm and strong. He almost held it too long. But he let it go and watched her stick her thumb in the back pocket of her jeans. Her smile widened, and Derick's Adam's apple got stuck.

He slowly turned his gaze to Jay, who seemed to be having a hard time keeping his chuckle inside. Derick stared at him and pressed his mouth in a straight smile.

You could have warned me.

His uncle's stifled grin responded to the unspoken chastisement. *Where's the fun in that?*

* * *

Derick, Jay, and Alisen meandered through the entire orchard, and although Derick kept finding himself watching her in his peripheral vision, she'd been so easy to talk to that he felt much more at ease. After all, he'd talked to girls before. He'd talked to a lot of girls. Why should she be any different?

But she was different. Instead of talking about movies and music, he asked her questions about water consumption, irrigation and drainage, chemicals, soil content, harvest numbers, and climate control. On a few occasions, she turned to Jay for answers, but even then it was only to confirm her guesses. Derick was impressed.

As they walked, she spoke with confidence, but a vulnerability lay behind her eyes as she reached absently to run her hand along tree limbs and finger leaves. Often, he caught her looking at him longer than the moment required, and her quick smile as she looked away encouraged his own.

They reached the base of the orchard, where the slope of the hill leveled toward the circular driveway and the house, and he stood facing the lake. More pine trees bordered the far side of the drive to his left, stretching all the way back up to the main road. Derick glanced at the house on his right and stopped himself from making the whistle wanting to escape his lips.

He looked instead out at the lake. A distant ski boat towed a wakeboarder, leaving a white trail in the water. The boarder attempted a jump with a twist and bit it. Derick wrinkled his nose in sympathy.

Jay's cell phone rang. "Smoke on the Water." He put a finger up as he answered and turned away to take the call.

Derick smiled after his uncle. "Jay tells me you're taking over the orchard after this summer. That's impressive."

Alisen watched Jay walk away. "I guess. He insisted I was ready last year, but I wasn't so sure. He says there isn't much left for him to teach me." She sighed. "I'll miss him."

Derick looked again to the orchard, the trees scattering blossoms here and there like snow, and the pines, tall and swaying in the high breeze.

Derick turned, catching Alisen watching him again. She looked down with a smile, and he cleared his throat. He gestured toward the lake. "It's beautiful here."

She pressed her lips together and nodded. "Where are you from?"

"Washington. Southeastern Washington. The desert part."

"Washington State?"

He nodded.

"There's a desert part? I thought it was all evergreens and rain."

He grinned. How many times had he had this conversation at school? "Most people think so. But it's dry where I'm from, all brown and windy. If it weren't for irrigation, things would be pretty desolate."

She tilted her head to the side, considering.

"Have you ever been there?" he asked.

"I was just trying to remember. My mother and I flew to Washington once for a cherry festival somewhere. I was pretty small; I don't even remember where it was."

"Probably on the west side if you remember evergreens and rain."

"I do." Her voice became wistful, and she looked down. "She was excited about getting ideas for the festival here."

He watched her for a second, fighting the urge to lift her chin. His heart kicked up at the thought. He tried to redirect his focus, but she had some spent blossoms in her hair he hadn't noticed before, and he almost reached to lift them out. He shoved his hands into his pockets and continued talking. "Well, the great thing about the Tri-Cities, where I'm from, is the orchards and vineyards. They're all over. We're about a month ahead of you for the cherry season."

"But I thought you said it was a desert."

"It is, away from the irrigation. See, the Columbia River flows right through the center of it, and the Snake and Yakima rivers meet up with the Columbia there, and the rivers divide the three cities: Richland, Pasco, and Kennewick. So, Tri-Cities."

"I see," she replied, her expression amused.

He tried to hide his own smile. "The irrigation comes from the rivers, and with the long, hot summers, you can grow just about anything. Orchards and vineyards are everywhere. Even in town, although not so much anymore. The farmers are moving farther out and selling their land to developers."

She watched him intently. He kicked the ground.

"It has its beauties. They have really great sunsets." His head came up, and he looked around. "You probably have great sunsets here though, right?" He grinned.

She grinned back. "I couldn't imagine a better sunset than here at the lake."

"Well, I'll have to see one or two while I'm here."

They both stood there, taking turns looking around and at each other.

Derick heard a soft meow.

"Hello," he said to the small engine suddenly making figure eights around his lower legs. "Is he yours?"

"That's Jane. She's new around here too." Alisen glanced at a small rowboat tied to the dock. She shook her head. "I *found* her this morning."

"Is that yours?" he asked, gesturing toward the rowboat. *Of course it is. It's their dock.*

"That's my rowboat." Her grin grew into a wide smile as if she had told a good joke, and color rose in her cheeks. She bit her lower lip and looked back at him.

"Hey!" It was Jay. Derick had almost forgotten his uncle was there. "Have you taken the boat out yet?" He walked toward them, rubbing his hands together. "Did she tell you? It's her graduation present."

"No, she didn't." He looked at Alisen, eyebrows raised. "Congratulations."

"Thanks." She ran her fingers through her hair, and the stray blossoms flitted to the ground without her noticing. She sighed, exasperated. "I tried to take it out this morning, but I got a little"—she paused and looked over at the cat, now stretched out full length in the midday sun—"sidetracked."

Jay turned to Derick. "Hey, that call was the bishop. He wants me to meet him out at the Anderson place to give someone a blessing."

"Oh. Okay." He felt a twinge of disappointment. "Do you need any help?"

Jay shook his head. "He also wanted to know if I could meet with him afterward to go over the calendar and some budgeting issues. I wondered, if it's okay with you, Alisen, if Derick could stay here a little longer while I go. The Anderson place is out this way, and the meeting would be pretty boring." He slapped Derick on the back. "Maybe Derick could help you with the boat."

The disappointment floated away.

* * *

Alisen searched the back of the boathouse, where she had flung the other life jacket. She felt a little self-conscious as Derick waited while she rummaged around.

"Ah-ha."

She turned to him, holding up the life jacket and a waterproof bag. He smiled back easily, an open grin showing a small crease at each side of his mouth.

"Great," he said and glanced at the silver speedboat next to them. "Umm, nice boat."

She shook her head. "I guess. It's my dad's." Her shoulders raised, and she sighed as she looked at the bullet built for water. "His pride and joy. I'd offer you a ride, but it's too much machine for me." She gestured to the door. "You can see where I stand on watercraft."

He laughed, and they left the boathouse.

"Here," she said, handing him the life jacket. "This should fit you. I'll get us some food."

He took the life jacket, shrugged, and pulled it on. She noticed the lean muscles on his forearms move under his tanned skin, his long fingers grabbing the buckles and pulling them toward one another as he looked down, concentrating. He paused and looked up.

"Yes?"

Hazel eyes ringed in emerald green waited patiently for her reply.

She flushed. "Oh, um, I'll be right back."

He looked back down and continued adjusting, a small, crooked smile on his lips.

When she got to the side door, she glanced back just as he cinched up the waist belt.

Get a grip. He's just putting on a life jacket.

Her brisk heartbeat wasn't listening.

She took two stairs at a time, reached the kitchen, and threw the bag on the counter. Standing at the fridge, she grabbed two bottles of soda and some food from the party last night. She filled the bag and glanced out the window over the sink.

Derick waited at the rowboat, crouched down, giving Jane a good scratch on her neck. She could see his mouth moving and wondered what he was saying. Jane leapt away after some other amusement, and Derick took his own small leap into the boat. He walked to the fore end and turned around, placing his hands on his hips. Suddenly, he looked right up to her window, and their eyes met. He'd caught her. She could do nothing but lift her hand in a weak wave. He broke into his open grin and motioned for her to come down.

She backed away from the window and shook her head at herself. *Get. A. Grip.*

* * *

Alisen sat with her face to the breeze. It really was a beautiful day. The lake could be cold and choppy this time of year, but at the moment, it was great to be a boat owner. Derick had offered to row, and after this morning's attempt and subsequent cat adventure, she decided to let him.

So she sat with her hands resting flat on the seat, listening to the oars dip into the water.

Their conversation had been easy, but this silence was easy too. Fairly. The tension between the two of them was not an unpleasant one. And, she had to admit, watching him row was better than watching him put on a life jacket.

"What are you smiling about?" he asked as he pulled.

She raised her eyebrows. He had caught her again, and she decided to avoid the question. "Why did you come see the orchard today?"

"It's research," he answered.

"Research for what?"

"An idea I have for what I want to be when I grow up." He grinned at her.

"You want to run a small orchard and a fruit stand? You know, it pays but not that well." She grimaced, and he laughed.

"No. Actually, my family has a pretty big farm in Washington, and we have some fruit trees but just enough to grow for ourselves and share with the neighbors."

"What else do you grow?"

"Onions. Have you heard of Walla Walla Sweets?"

She had.

"Those and potatoes, corn, mint—"

"Mint?" she interrupted him.

He leaned forward and raised his eyebrows. "Mint." He pulled back on the oars. "It smells great all season."

"Hm." She tilted her head to the side, imagining an entire field smelling of mint. "So what does that have to do with my little orchard?"

He looked amused for a second before he continued, and she wondered what he was thinking. She thought it was something good.

"Well," he took another pull at the oars, "my brother-in-law, Marcus, is involved in a global research group that works with third-world countries, desolate areas, and high-altitude areas where growing food is a problem. Most of the people who live in these environments are undernourished, undereducated, and don't have the means to better themselves; they either have to rely on food brought in, which is expensive, or they subsist on what they can pry from the earth's dry hands. There are people out there, mothers who can't feed their hungry kids, husbands who want to provide for their families, grandparents who see the struggle and wonder why. Real people."

Alisen's eyes scanned the shores of the lake, all the big homes with slides at the ends of their docks, patios of furniture and umbrellas, American flags waving on poles next to boathouses filled with jet skis and paddleboats, and refrigerators full of food.

Derick followed her eyes and stopped rowing. He lowered his voice. "It's all right, you know."

She met his steady gaze, those remarkable eyes gentle. "Why do you say that? It seems so unfair."

"This is a promised land." He shrugged. "Things grow well here in an incredibly high percentage of the continent. We were born here, so we should feel blessed, but what we do with this blessing makes all the difference." He broke into a smile. "And that is what I want to do."

"Explain." She leaned forward, truly interested.

He leaned forward as well, resting the oars in his lap. She watched, fascinated as his demeanor intensified.

"I'm studying a system of irrigation, soil amendments, terracing, raised beds, and so on, and applying them to varying environments and high-nutrition crops or whatever is needed in a particular region." His eyes were suddenly on fire, and he spoke a little faster. "And I want to put together a corporation to distribute, train, and help the people learn it for themselves all around the world. So they can help their own people." He paused and took a breath, seeming a little wary of his own intensity.

They were a foot away from each other. She didn't break her gaze, and his eyes held hers as her breathing stilled. He swallowed and blinked.

Then softly, he said, "I would be working on a smaller scale, small acreages, hillsides, and so . . . coming to your little orchard . . . is research."

He leaned back and began to row again. His passion lingered, and he seemed to be putting some of it into the oars. Then he turned the boat toward shore and headed for a little public beach.

"What are we doing?" She was still a little dazed from whatever had just happened between them.

"*We* are going to have a picnic." His face opened up into that smile she was really getting used to. "All that talk about food made me hungry."

* * *

"How long have you been at UM?" Alisen popped a grape into her mouth.

They were perched on a picnic table facing the water. What was left of the food lay out on the flattened bag between them.

"Well, two years all together." He acknowledged her surprised look. "After my freshman year, I continued another semester through the summer, then I spent two years in South America. I only just got back last Christmas, in time to get into the spring semester."

"So," she pursed her lips in thought, "you were doing research for your brother-in-law while you were there?"

He chuckled. "Not exactly. Though being there certainly did strengthen my determination, and I was able to gather a lot of data and contacts. But my main purpose in going was to preach the gospel of Jesus Christ." He threw a pretzel in his mouth and chewed, giving her time to process the information before he looked at her.

He finally glanced sideways.

She looked mildly incredulous. "Really? You were . . ."

"A missionary." He held his palms open in a welcoming gesture. "For The Church of Jesus Christ of Latter-day Saints." He waited, not having a clue how she would react.

"Hm." Her face relaxed. "Well, that's different."

He nodded. "Actually, there are about 60,000 of our missionaries out in the world right now."

She lifted her face in surprise. He was once again drawn into her startling blue eyes, intelligent and searching.

She took a long, stray curl from her shoulder and started playing with it in her fingers, looking back at the water. "Do you get college credit or a scholarship from your church to be a missionary? I mean," she paused as if searching for the right words, "what made you decide to do that?"

She looked absently at her lock of hair, and he studied her profile—her nearly black lashes, her straight nose, the curve underneath meeting her upper lip. She leaned forward as he did, her elbows resting on her knees. She brushed the tip of her curl along her lower lip then dropped her hair and rested her chin on the palm of her hand, slender fingers curving up her cheek. She looked at him expectantly.

Had they really met only today? Just hours ago? He found himself wanting to tell her everything about the gospel, to fill her up with it so she would be bursting with understanding and light, so he could take her hand and stand beside her and look into forever.

Whoa, whoa, *whoa*! He was getting way ahead of himself. And if experience had taught him anything, that was the wrong way to go about it.

Start simple and answer her question.

He quietly cleared his throat. "Why did I decide to serve a mission?"

She nodded once.

"Well, the Church asked me to go, and at first I went because I knew it would be a great learning experience for me, that I would grow and get to try new things. But later, after I was in Bolivia serving the people, serving the Lord, I realized it wasn't about me. It was about the people I was teaching and seeing the changes in their lives take place through the Spirit of Christ. It was about making others truly happy. The only way I mattered was if I was the instrument in sharing that happiness."

Had he said the right thing? He watched her expression. She looked thoughtful and a little forlorn staring out at the lake. He was about to apologize when she started to speak, carefully.

"You forgot about yourself by thinking of others, and that made it even better than you thought it would be." She turned to him and raised her eyebrows. "Is that right?"

His mouth spread into a slow smile. She smiled slowly back.

"I couldn't have put it better myself."

She nodded.

He could tell she was still thinking, so he got up and started putting the remains of their picnic away. She sat for a couple minutes longer, then she got up and stretched her lean arms out before they both turned for the boat. He tossed the bag in then turned to help her, but she was closer than expected, and he faltered, catching his breath. She took his offered hand. He paused for just a moment, feeling his heart swell up at the connection, and met her eyes. His mind worked as the color rose in her cheeks.

It's beautiful here.

He looked down at their hands and stroked the top of hers with his thumb, just once. He brought his eyes up again, and she was watching him, waiting for his next move. Her eyes flickered to his mouth. He thought of kissing her, thought she might want him to kiss her, but the idea of it being too soon won out. She smiled, starting his heart racing again, and he wondered if she'd read his mind.

He willed himself to step back, and he helped her into the boat.

* * *

It was a longer ride home.

Only because Alisen insisted on rowing. The results were a zigzag path across the water, a few circles going nowhere, and lots of laughter. It was directly after her grip on one of the oars slipped, the wide end of the oar slapping against the water and sending a sheet of spray all over Derick, that Alisen surrendered one oar.

"I'm. So. Sorry," she said as he shook his hair out.

"That's all right." He grinned. "I needed to cool off anyway." He winked at her as he took the other oar.

"I really have done this before," she said, an apologetic smile on her face. "I guess it's just been a long time." She grudgingly turned around in her seat and faced the same direction as him.

"Okay, you take the right side; I'll take the left." She liked the chuckle in his voice.

"Right." She was determined.

It was better after that. Handling one oar was much easier, and they kept an easy rhythm. She concentrated for the first little while but then was able to allow her thoughts to drift.

Internally, she shook her head in wonder. She was not the kind of girl to fall easily, to let her guard down. She had almost *kissed* him. Right there when he was helping her into the rowboat. She'd never kissed a boy first in her life. She wasn't going to start just because Derick Whitney was older; self-assured; refreshingly sincere; hot; and, she could be wrong but, totally flirting with her.

Suddenly, she was suspicious. Had Jay planned this? She wondered if he would be waiting for them when they returned or if they would have more time before Derick had to go. Would he come back tomorrow? Or would it be later in the week? She knew he was helping her with the crates. She wished the pile was huge, but it wasn't. Maybe she could find more from neighboring orchards.

The way he spoke about his plans for the future, so determined and hopeful, she was caught right up in them. She imagined herself traveling, helping with the plans, with growing things. And when he talked about being a missionary . . . At first it puzzled her when he started talking about religion. That wasn't something she made a part of her life. When she was little, her mother insisted they all go to church on Easter and Christmas. But after . . . well, Alisen hadn't been since.

But when Derick spoke about it, it seemed such a part of who he was, and she liked who he was, that it wasn't uncomfortable to listen. And what he had said about forgetting what he wanted and thinking of the people who needed him struck a chord. It had turned her thoughts to her father.

"Alisen?"

She liked the way his voice sounded when he said her name. "Yes?"

"What are your plans this fall? Will you stay here with the orchard?"

He was thinking of the future. Was he thinking about a future that might include her?

Stop getting ahead of yourself. You barely know him.

"I'm starting school here at the community college, studying business. Jay thinks it would be good to get more of that in my head."

"Mm-hm."

She thought a minute. "Derick?" She liked saying his name.

"Yes?" Was he smiling? It sounded like he was smiling.

I wish I could face him. "Jay said something earlier that made me curious."

"Yes?" Definitely smiling.

"He said he had to go give someone a blessing. And you offered to help him. What did you mean? I guess I could see a religious leader, you know, bestowing a blessing on his congregation or whatever, but this didn't sound like that."

"Hm." He paused.

"I'm sorry. Am I not supposed to ask about that?"

There was a quiet chuckle. "You can ask me anything, Alisen."

She turned around, the earnest sound in his voice prompting her to see his face.

Chapter 5

ALISEN ASKED HIM MORE QUESTIONS, and Derick tried to give her simple, direct answers. She asked about blessings and prayer, and she was clearly surprised when Derick referred to God simply as *Father*. She confessed that she often shared her thoughts and questions with her mother. And that she hoped, but was never sure, that she was heard. Derick assured her that she was. She had looked hopeful.

Derick kept her hand when he helped her out of the boat and onto the dock. It had felt natural to keep it, and that had surprised him. They walked through the orchard, quiet now, and he was very aware of the warmth of her hand in his. The heady scent of cherry blossoms swirled around them as the breeze followed them up off the water. A scattered white carpet had formed, and they followed its path.

Alisen broke the silence. "Tell me about your family."

His smile was quick. "Well," he ran a hand through his hair. "My parents run the farm. My dad likes to fish and play on the water. He had us all waterskiing before we started kindergarten. My mom is a great cook and used to barrel race in the rodeos." His smile grew wider. "She actually grew up here in Montana. My older brother and his family built a house on the farm. They'll be taking over when my parents retire in a couple of years. My parents will go on a mission together after that. And," he paused and squeezed Alisen's hand, "my big sister is married, and she and her husband live in Missoula. I lived with them last semester. They're out of the country for a few months now though."

"You're the youngest?"

"You could say that. After my sister, Hannah, was born, my mom had complications with a few pregnancies. She thought they were done. It was really hard for her because she'd wanted a big family." He brightened. "Then I showed up."

Alisen grinned.

"Hannah and I are fourteen years apart. She was always after me about something. When I was nine, I started calling her my '*old* sister.'" He grinned. "But we're pretty close. She and Marcus couldn't have kids. I stayed at their place a lot and she'd boss me around like a mom. It was good for both of us." He grew quiet. "I think she's proud of me, so far."

Alisen searched his face, curious.

He looked off, laughing nervously. "I'm sorry; I don't mean to sound conceited."

She shook her head. "No, you don't. I just don't think I've met anyone so at ease with himself."

He chuckled again, shaking his head. He had her fooled.

They continued their walk in silence, shoulders nearly touching. Jay called Derick's cell phone to let him know he'd be there soon, so they sat down under a tree near the clearing to wait. Alisen leaned against the tree trunk, and Derick sat near her, resting his arms on his propped-up knees.

Jane found them and rubbed along Alisen's legs, moved to Derick, and nudged his hand with her head, then wandered off. Derick moved his hand to Alisen's, and she took it as a small wrinkle appeared between her brows.

Finally, Derick spoke. "What are you thinking?"

Alisen answered, looking directly into his eyes. "I was remembering something my mother said when I was little."

"What was that?"

"She said, 'Sometimes when you don't know what you're looking for, that's when you find exactly what you need.'" She paused. "But she said you have to be looking." She looked away, and he noticed her blush. She said quietly, "I didn't realize I was looking."

* * *

The ride home was quiet only for a few minutes. Then Jay started. "So . . ."

Derick looked at him out of the corner of his eyes, eyebrows raised, waiting.

"Did you have a good time?" Jay watched the road, but Derick saw a smile fighting at the corners of his uncle's mouth.

He looked down and rubbed both hands through his hair, blowing out a breath. "Mm-hm."

"What'd you two do while I was gone?" The smile fought harder.

Derick frowned. *Oh, nothing really. Took the boat out. Talked about the orchard. Introduced her to the gospel. Fell hard.* "Got to know each other," he lamely offered.

"Looks like you were getting along all right." The smile won as Jay still watched the road.

Derick hadn't been able to completely hide the grin etched into his face as he had walked to the truck after Jay pulled up, and he suspected Jay had a good idea as to how they had gotten along. He probably had no clue though about how deeply Derick was feeling about this girl.

This girl who looked at him with a deeper sense of belonging than any other girl had looked at him before. This girl who absorbed the spirit of his words as though she was dry earth and they were cool water. This girl who had, in a single afternoon, made him feel as though he had a particular place in this world, and it was by her side, and if there was anything happy, it could be found only with her.

Jay interrupted his thoughts. "I'm going to give you a warning though. I may be protective of that girl, I may think of her as one of my own, but you, Derick Whitney, are impulsive. You always have been. And even though that girl's father has estranged himself from her, God help him, I don't think he would hesitate to tie you up and drag you a few times around the lake behind that pretty boat of his if you so much as hurt one hair on her head."

Derick swallowed, considering the warning. Jay said no more.

Derick's mind went back to the last several hours. Was he getting ahead of himself?

* * *

Alisen found herself at the dock but couldn't remember the walk down. Her mind was swimming. It had started out as such an ordinary day. She looked at Jane, asleep in the rowboat.

No, it didn't. I slept in. I found Jane. Or, Jane found me. Then I met him, *and he drilled me on everything I could know about my orchard, and to my own surprise, I could answer. And we took the rowboat out.*

No, this day had started out very *un*ordinary.

She pictured his warm eyes, so earthy and alive, looking into hers until she thought her heart would dissolve into a million little hearts shimmering around inside her. She remembered his laugh echoing off the water and the sound of his voice, gentle but so sure, as he told her about things she had never considered but that felt so right.

Alisen looked down at her hands. She could still feel the way his strong fingers had wrapped around hers. She sighed.

There had been other boys, of course. But those who had pursued her in high school had left her feeling so . . . old. Like she was the adult. She hadn't liked that feeling of inequality and somehow felt like it was her fault. They had been nice, attentive, and fun, but her feelings had never gone deep. Or was it that maybe her feelings were deeper, beyond their reaching?

And then there were her father's associates' sons.

Ugh.

Boys so full of themselves and their cars, just waiting to get her alone so they could give her the attention they thought she so obviously desired from them. Twice she had stormed out of a boathouse, once from a car, and once from a stable. She had finally refused to attend another one of her father's business functions.

Her fists had balled up, and she shook her head, looking up the road the way Derick and Jay had gone. Her hands relaxed.

It had been so different with him. She felt equal to him, well, except for the rowing. She would have to work on that. And she felt he cared about her in a way that went beyond . . . beyond what? Beyond anything she was right now, like where she had been and where she was going, who she would be. She smiled and shook her head again. It was like there had been a puzzle piece missing right next to her.

And it was Derick shaped.

* * *

She stood at the kitchen sink peeling an orange when her father's car pulled into the circular driveway. She hadn't even thought about where he or Amanda, for that matter, had been all day. Her father got out of the car and disappeared under the entry below. The door opened, she heard him throw his keys into the wooden bowl on the entry table, and then she listened to his footsteps make their way up the wide stairs leading to the living room and open kitchen. She returned to peeling her orange.

"Alisen."

He said her name so seldom it sounded strange to her every time he used it.

"Hello. How was your day?" she asked. Harmless enough. She didn't even look up from her orange.

"Fairly good. I took Amanda over to the stables, then she headed over to the Watson place to stay for the week. Something about a comedy at the Playhouse tonight and shopping in Kalispell tomorrow after school. They're breaking in a new horse at the stables. I spent a few hours at the office working on some things. Then I, uh, played a few holes of golf with Darrel and John."

She'd stopped peeling her orange at the word *playhouse* and watched her dad finish his day's summary. He leaned back casually against the opposite side of the bar, his back to her. This was not the strange part. The strange part was that he was still talking, giving details, that he was still in the room.

Her mouth hung slightly ajar.

He continued. "You were still in your room, or Amanda would have said good-bye this morning."

"Oh," was all she could think to say. Would this unordinary day ever end?

Her father turned, eyeing the orange, then looked up at her. His eyes widened, and he placed both hands on the counter.

"What?"

"It's nothing. Well, you just look, like—" He stopped and looked at her orange again. He turned back around, and she wondered if he was done or if he had any more unfinished sentences.

"I was thinking that since the other girls were gone, that, uh, we could just go get something to eat."

It was a complete sentence, but she nearly dropped her orange. "You mean you and me? Go to dinner?"

She watched the back of his head as he nodded.

She was wary but mildly encouraged.

He turned and looked at her out of the corner of his eye. "You'll need to change."

She looked down at her work clothes. "Of course."

She wrapped the peeled orange and put it in the fridge for later then made her way past her dad, thinking this day could not get any stranger. Then, at the thought of the day, she grinned, and she found herself practically skipping to her room.

She showered and changed into a light cotton skirt, T-shirt, and thin cardigan, then drew the front of her hair into a clip on the side and put on mascara and lip gloss. She pulled out some wedge espadrilles and tied them up her ankles. Turning in the mirror, she watched her skirt swish around her knees. Her cheeks were rosier than usual. She liked it. She wished Derick could see her like this instead of her usual T-shirt and jeans.

Grabbing a little straw purse, she headed downstairs.

The sun sat low and heavy in the sky as they drove, and she fiddled with a button on her sweater. She was trying to remember the last time she had been out with her father alone. Nothing came to mind. Nothing. She moved her hands and fiddled with the beads in the centers of the straw flowers woven into her bag.

What was this? Did it mean something? She thought again of the pleased look on his face when she had seen her rowboat for the first time. Was this some sort of attempt to change the course of their relationship, to get to know her after almost six years of ignoring her?

Weariness hovered around her, and she wanted to sleep so she could wake up and it would be tomorrow and she would see Derick again. She'd felt happy with him. Light.

She sat up straight and released a silent sigh. The truth was, her father was making this effort, and she wanted to see where it led. She would give anything to have a relationship with him. But years of neglect made her suppress anything but the tiniest hope. She had learned to find happiness without his love. It was a survival mechanism. But she never stopped wondering what it would be like to win his approval. And that was painful, knowing that even this might just be nothing.

She glanced at the man next to her. He was tall, still trim, and broad across the shoulders. And perpetually tan, which made her suspect he visited a tanning bed regularly. He had lines across his forehead and at the corners of his brown eyes, but the silver in his wiry blond hair at his temples and sideburns looked like sun streaks, adding youth instead of taking it away.

The only similarity she could find between him and herself was in the mouth somewhere, the fullness, and the square chin. When she was a young teenager, when she noticed her chin starting to square off, she had stood in front of the mirror with her hand across her nose, a dividing line between the upper and lower portion of her face, and thought she could see her dad that way. She'd thought maybe if she'd looked more like him, like Elizabeth, then maybe he would—

His phone rang, and she brought her eyes to the window. They were coming into town now and were headed for a newer restaurant above one of the art galleries.

Her father pulled into a parking space as he hung up his phone. He came around to open her door, and she found herself nervous as she walked by his side. He held the door for her, and they climbed the stairs to an open, airy dining space. People were seated out on a balcony overlooking the quaint main street lined with colorful hanging flower baskets. A host led Alisen and her father to an inside table near a large window.

As they looked over the menus, her father shifted his to the side and watched her fingers drum on the tabletop. He raised an eyebrow, and she paused. Looking somewhat amused, he set his menu down and folded his hands in front of him.

"So." He cleared his throat. Was he nervous too? "What kind of day have you had?"

She blinked at the question. *What kind of day?*

"I, um." *It's been amazing, astounding, startlingly glorious and breathtaking, somehow deeply spiritual and absolutely exhilarating.* "I took the rowboat out."

"Oh." He did look pleased. "How was that?"

"It was . . . perfect."

"Good. I hope you didn't have any trouble."

She remembered the circles in the water and gave him a small smile. "No, nothing I couldn't handle." She swallowed and nodded. "And I, uh, found a cat."

His eyebrow shot up again, and the corners of his mouth turned down. He looked like Elizabeth.

"It's just a little cat. She was curled up in the boat this morning." She paused at his unchanged expression. She tried her own. She looked right into his eyes and lowered her chin. "It's too late, Dad. I already named her."

She thought she detected a hint of a smile. "All right," he said, and the subject was closed.

The waitress came to take their order.

Their conversation continued haltingly and sparingly. The food came, and a silence settled in while they started in on their dishes. She was ravenous.

"Darrel's daughter, Bree, is going to Yale this fall. You remember her, don't you?"

"Umm, yes. The one with all the hair." She gestured as if clouds were billowing around her head, and her father smiled at that.

"Yes, the one with the hair. You know, it's still not too late to apply to some bigger universities. I could pull some strings here and there."

She looked at him thoughtfully and proceeded with caution. "Thanks, Dad, but I think the business courses at FVCC will be adequate."

"I agree that they would be adequate, if all you wanted to do was run a little orchard in a little town and make a little profit." He pushed some food around on his plate and took a bite.

"That *is* what I want to do." She had thought that was clear.

"I'm just asking you to think about the big picture here, to broaden your options. It's a big world out there, important people to know, money to be made, and you could do a lot more than babysit cherry trees."

Her food stuck in her throat, and her eyes stung. She took a sip of water and swallowed what felt like a rock. She looked down at her plate, feeling the tears fill her eyes, willing them to stay put, to shrink back. She had no qualms about continuing her education. She was a good student and loved to learn, but the orchard was her life, her passion. She felt her cheeks getting hot.

"Alisen." His voice was rough but quiet. "I didn't mean it that way." He glanced around the room.

She shook her head with a little jerk and dabbed her eyes with her napkin.

"I just meant that I see potential in you, and you wouldn't want to waste that."

She pulled her head up and looked at him. "You . . . see me?" she asked.

He blinked at her and swallowed. "Yes. Of course I do."

She took a deep breath and let it out slowly, raggedly, unable to hide the fraction of a smile.

"Will you just think about the school thing?" he asked, picking up his fork again.

She looked at him steadily and took another breath, softer this time. "I'll think about it."

Chapter 6

ALISEN LOITERED IN THE LOWER northwestern corner of the orchard and checked the bee boxes. The road wasn't visible from this part of the orchard, but she still found herself frequently glancing in that direction.

A yawn pushed its way out. She had fallen into bed physically and emotionally exhausted, but sleep had not been restful, even after the longest day she could remember. She'd shoved the conversation with her father out of her head and focused on seeing Derick again, but it hadn't worked completely. Strange dreams about attending big universities where she couldn't find her classes haunted her, and when she'd finally find a class, Derick was her professor. He would ask her about the orchard, and somehow her father would find out and send her to a different college; then it would repeat all over again. She sighed.

"Would you happen to know where I could find a good rowboat guide?"

She spun around at the mellow sound of his voice, and a smile spread across her face as she took a deep breath. "Derick."

He held a hand out to her, his eyes asking her to take it. She did. "Are you busy?" he asked.

"No." She looked down at her shoes. "I was just hoping you would show up soon." Her heart thumped, and she wasn't tired anymore. She peeked at him. Sunlight seemed to filter through the colors in his eyes like it filtered through the leaves.

He motioned up the hill. "Let's walk, then."

* * *

Again, he watched her as they walked. This time, he didn't have to concentrate on questions about the orchard. She had pulled her hair back, the ends tucked up, and a few loose curls floated around her face and neck. When he'd found her down by the bees, he thought she looked a little sad, staring away at nothing. But now as he watched the natural blush in her smile, she seemed so ready to . . . be happy. He felt a small satisfaction, a hope that he'd had something to do with the change. He squeezed her hand in his.

"Were you set on working today?" he asked casually.

"Umm, I did have some things to get done, but you might persuade me otherwise." Her eyes danced.

He chuckled. *That was easy.*

"I talked to Jay, and he agreed you deserve a little vacation, you know, just graduating and working hard the last, oh, six years in this place." He gestured to the surrounding trees then stopped walking and lowered his voice. "And I'd like to get to know you, so—" He glanced at her.

She raised her chin, looking up at him with a question in her eyes.

He gave her a self-conscious smile. "What?"

She brought his hand up and wrapped it in hers. "It's just that—" She moved her thumbs along his knuckles, seemingly unaware that he was about to come undone at the touch. "I mean . . . can you—" She fumbled for words as she opened his hand and laid his palm against hers. "I'm just—" She blew out a breath of frustration. "Are you just as blown away by this as I am?" she finished as she laced her fingers between his, her clear blue eyes stunning him into his own speechlessness.

He swallowed. *Steady*, he told himself. "Yeah."

She beamed. Then she abruptly turned to look up the hill, and her eyebrows drew together. "Wait a minute. So Jay knows—"

"That I'll be spending as much time here as possible," he finished for her and grinned.

She threw her arms out and lunged into his chest.

"Whoa." He regained his balance, and his arms, which had come up in surprise, wrapped around her. She pressed her cheek against his shoulder, and he was very aware of his pounding heart, which she must easily hear and feel.

"So I guess that's all right with you?" As he spoke, his breath made her curls tremble against her neck.

She gave a little nod and flushed.

Derick placed his hands on both of her arms and gently pulled her away. He looked at her squarely.

"Jay had a few . . . conditions." He attempted a serious look, and she mirrored it. He struggled to hide his smile. "First, we have to get to know as much about each other as possible." He paused, nodding gravely. "And, second, you have to take the week off so we can get started right away." Alisen blew her serious look with a big smile and started bouncing on the balls of her feet.

"And condition number three." He composed his face and steadied her bouncing. "He made me promise that I would never hurt you. He made me swear. And I usually don't swear, Alisen."

She took in his expression. He was asking her to believe him.

"Okay," she answered.

His smile returned. "Okay." He took her hand, and they started up the hill again.

They reached the clearing, where they found Jay studying a clipboard. He looked up at the sound of their approach, glanced at their hands clasped together, and shook his head. "I leave you alone for a few hours, and look what happens."

Derick gestured toward Alisen, holding her out at arm's length. "What could I do? I had absolutely no choice."

Jay nodded and chuckled. "Well, she sure does make everything look good. Even you." He winked at Alisen.

Alisen grinned at the attention and moved closer to Derick. "Are you sure about the week off, Jay?"

"Sure. What's to do? Just gotta keep these things warm and dry, right?" Derick knew he was understating the attention a cherry orchard required this time of year. "Listen, you two go have fun while you're young." He waved them off with a grin.

Derick pulled Alisen around her truck to his old Camry.

"Is this yours?"

"Mm-hm," he replied as he pulled out his keys. "Old Reliable."

"Where are we going?" She glanced down at her clothes. She had dressed for orchard work in jeans and a T-shirt but still looked great. She looked over Derick's clothes. Just the usual. Faded jeans, broken-in polo shirt.

"You'll be fine; trust me," he said, opening the passenger-side door. She ducked in.

Derick walked around to the driver's side, got in, and put on his seat belt. He faced her. "Ready?" he asked with a mysterious smile.

She reached for her seat belt and clicked it in place. "Ready."

* * *

Swan River was known for its beauty, abundant wildlife, and walking trails. Bear-proof garbage receptacles stood at the trailheads, and anglers, kayakers, and photographers frequented the river. Today, Derick and Alisen were hikers. They descended steep wooden stairs from a parking area above the riverbanks then followed a trail into the shade of evergreen and deciduous trees. Shrubs and small flowers had been coaxed into bloom by streams of sunlight here and there.

"Mmm. Smell that." Alisen lifted her face, inhaling. "I love that smell."

Derick placed his hands on his hips and took a breath. Pine and sweet air above, water and old leaves underfoot. He nodded his head, looking at the narrow, winding trail disappearing over a fallen log and into the woods. "C'mon." He motioned with his head.

After a couple of miles, one foray off the trail to examine a moth the color and pattern of tree bark, and some tricky spots where the trail fell completely away above the river, they came down to a small beach. A large boulder leaned out over the water, and Alisen headed straight for it. Derick followed, and they sat side by side, watching the river go by. Derick brought out two water bottles and a bag of dry-roasted peanuts from the backpack he'd slung on before they left the car. He offered her the open bag.

"Thanks." She threw a few peanuts into her mouth.

He watched her for a minute. "Can I ask you a question?"

"Isn't that what we're supposed to be doing? Asking questions, getting to know each other?" She squinted up at him as the sun moved toward the center of the sky, making a flourish with her hand. "Ask away."

Could she be any more appealing?

"This morning, when I found you, you looked . . ." He reflected. "You looked a little sad." Alisen's eyebrows came up. "What were you thinking about?"

She pursed her lips and looked at the river, the sound of rushing water filling the silence. She shrugged. "I was thinking about my father." She took a drink.

"That made you sad?"

"I don't know if I was sad, really." She faced him, smiling, but it was there—sadness. "Did Jay tell you anything about my father?"

He shrugged now, taking a turn to look at the water, feeling a little guilty about the discussion Jay had had with him about her family. "He told me a little, about how he treated you after your mom died. How he just sort of let go of you." He winced, hoping he hadn't said something wrong.

She nodded. “That’s a good way of putting it.” Her eyes were subdued now. He was sorry he’d brought it up, but he’d been wondering since he found her that morning.

A soft smile returned. “I look so much like my mother. I think her death, it hurt him so much. He couldn’t stand to even look at me.” Her voice became a whisper. “I could see it, even that young.”

“But,” he ventured, “he’s your dad, the parent, the only one you have left here.”

“I know, and the older I get, the more I see how wrong it was. But back then, when I glimpsed the—” She paused, searching for the right word, “the despair. It was awful pain. I knew he couldn’t look at me. And I didn’t want him to have to . . . Even though I wanted more than anything else for him to hold me and tell me everything was all right because he still had *me* and I was like Mom.” She blinked, and a tear rolled down her cheek. She brushed it away.

Derick tried to understand how a father could disregard his own child. His hand found hers and enfolded it.

She shook her head. “I don’t know. Wouldn’t you want a reminder?” She wiped away another tear and blinked her eyes a few times. Then she surprised him and smiled again. Her eyes glistened, bright and fluid.

“I had Aunt Rachel. She took me in; she helped me get the orchard.” She leaned her head to the side. “My mother’s death without the orchard would have been like your Tri-Cities without the rivers. Desolate. It saved me.”

He nodded, trying to imagine.

Alisen looked out over the water. “Mom would bring us here, and we’d sit on this rock. She would tell us stories.”

“What kind of stories?” Derick suddenly felt like he was sitting on sacred ground. He put his free hand on the rock, feeling its warmth and imagining a group of little girls piled up here in his place, listening to a woman with dark wavy hair.

“Fairy tales, love stories, nursery rhymes, and camp songs, stories of her and Dad.” She looked back at Derick. “Good stories.”

Will we be a good story? Derick couldn’t help thinking it.

“Elizabeth would get so upset if the story didn’t end the way she wanted it to, and Amanda would sulk through a story until Mom got to the one she wanted to hear.” Alisen shook her head, smiling at the memory. “Cinderella. Always her favorite.”

"And what was your favorite?"

"Oh." Her eyes searched the past as she thought. "I loved them all. I loved the sound of my mother's voice changing tempo and pitch, the silly or wicked voices she would give the characters. Sometimes I'd lie back on this rock and close my eyes and listen while the story played out in my mind like a movie." She paused, lost in the memory. He waited with a small smile to hear what she was thinking. "It was hard to picture the stories of her and my father though."

"Why was that?" He watched her cautiously. He was learning quickly that her father was a volatile subject.

"My father is, and you may have already guessed this for yourself, a very selfish person, very"—she sighed—"vain. He's very careful and guarded with his appearance and affection. I guess it was just hard to picture him doing some of the things my mother would share. The stories were so happy."

"Hm. So, is that what you were thinking about this morning?"

She shook her head. "Actually, no." She gave a little exasperated sigh. "This is something new and different."

"What?"

She looked at him. "Well, you remember yesterday." A huge smile spread across her face, and she bit her lower lip. Another little habit he noticed with pleasure.

He lowered his chin and looked at her. "Of course I remember yesterday."

She moved closer to him on the rock, and he lifted his arm around her shoulders as she leaned into him. It was such a comfortable movement, as if that was what his arms were for. She reached for his free hand and took it in both of hers, absently playing with it again as she related the way her father had astonished her with the invitation to dinner, the puzzling conversation, and her overemotional reaction to his simple request.

She shook her head again. "I just don't know what to think. I mean, I know what I would like to think, but I'm not sure I can let myself think that. You know?" Their heads were close together, and she turned hers to look at him. "It was just the oddest end to the best day." She looked at his mouth and smiled. She met his gaze and then shrugged. "And then I had crazy dreams all night and didn't sleep well." Her voice quieted. "And that is what I was thinking about when you found me this morning."

He'd had enough of two things: her father's mind games, which, whether they were intentional or not, angered him and had his defenses up, and he didn't want to feel that way right now; and Alisen being so close, playing with his hand, turning her face up to his, opening herself up to him so honestly. His arm around her shoulder constricted, pulling her up to him.

His mouth met hers, and the salt on her lips accentuated the sweetness of her skin. She responded, her hand tracing his jaw, his neck, then she reached around and fingered his hair. He stopped kissing her and brushed her eyelashes and cheekbones with the tip of his nose.

"Alisen?"

"Yes?"

"Thank you for telling me."

"Derick?"

"Yes?"

"I'll tell you anything."

Her lips found his again.

He was a little light-headed when they left the rock.

Chapter 7

THE WEEK FLEW BY. THEY explored her own home county as if she didn't live there and visited places Alisen hadn't been to in years.

Jay set up a trail ride on horseback, and unlike the rowboat, here Alisen had some experience. Amanda had dragged Alisen along to her first riding lessons, and although Alisen hadn't found the enthusiasm for it that Amanda had, she had a basic understanding of horses. She understood that they were big and she was not.

Still, the ride inspired her to see her sheltered world in an unexpected light. They stopped as Derick pointed, and watched a small herd of deer bound noiselessly through a pasture just behind a massive, lazy Brahma bull. When the bull turned his head around just as the last deer gave a final kick in what looked like mockery as it went over the fence, Alisen couldn't help laughing and wondering what else she'd missed without someone like Derick to point it out to her.

They went to town and walked the boardwalks in the rain, ate ice cream, and peeked into art galleries. And Alisen took Derick into the antiques shop where her mother had found her painting. When she told him the story, her face lit up with delight in the mystery of it, and he kissed her right there in front of the same smiling clerk who had wrapped up the painting years before.

They took the boat out again, of course. Jane joined them, jumping in deftly as they left the dock. The cat watched the water over the edge, her head twitching back and forth. Alisen's rowing had improved, but she preferred it when they each took an oar.

Their conversations about Derick's faith continued. Alisen found herself drawn to the idea of a spiritual family existing before this life with sisters and brothers who knew and loved her, who might cross her path at any time here on earth. Like Derick. She pictured her own family and wondered how they fit into that broader picture.

The most meaningful subject, though, was how she could return to live with Heavenly Father after this life. Derick gently explained his beliefs in what happened after everyone died, carefully referring to Alisen's mother and opening to Alisen the possibility of seeing her mom again someday. She swallowed the tears hope pulled from inside her and felt she would burst with longing.

At the end of each day's geographical, mental, and spiritual exploration, Derick would bring Alisen back to the orchard and they would walk down through the trees or drive down to the house to sit on the edge of the dock and prolong their good night. He had seen a few sunsets on the lake now.

"You haven't met my father."

"No."

"We don't keep track of each other much during the week."

"Mmm." Derick didn't push the issue, but Alisen knew a meeting with her father was inevitable.

* * *

On the last day of that dreamlike week, Derick stowed away the extra things in the boathouse while Alisen tied up the boat. She sat at the end of the dock, her feet hanging over the edge, and he watched her a moment before joining her there.

When he approached, she turned at his footsteps. He sat down, and she leaned her head on his shoulder. They sat like that for a minute, watching the sun and clouds start the show.

"What is your favorite time of year?" Alisen asked.

He looked at her and decided. No contest. "Summer. Yours?"

"Fall. But early fall, when the orchard is still green but things are just beginning to turn and the cherries have all been picked and it's still warm but the air feels crisp at times, and then you catch that first scent of brush being burned and you want pie."

"What?"

"You can get great jumbleberry pie at this little place on the way to Kalispell. It's best warm with ice cream." She blinked at him.

He laughed at her, but she continued the game of question and answer, one they had been playing all week.

"What is your favorite sea creature?" she asked.

"Mermaid."

She lifted her head and looked at him sideways, but he stuck to his answer. "By far." He ignored her look. "You?"

"Porcupine fish."

He muffled a laugh and tousled the back of her silky, loose hair.

They sat in silence for a few minutes, letting the sun sink and the sherbet colors smolder, reflect off the water, and fade, making a vast, dark space for stars. The automatic light at the back of the boathouse clicked on with a hum, followed by the exterior lights on the main house.

"That was better than last night." Alisen looked up at him and smiled, relaxed. "I think sunsets have improved since you arrived, Brother Whitney."

Derick pulled her closer to him. "I would have to agree."

Just then, headlights turned down the long road behind them, and Alisen and Derick turned to watch. The lights illuminated the dock and paused before turning into the circle drive. The car was black and shiny and had the potential to go very fast.

Derick looked at Alisen, who bit her lip.

The car stopped, and her father got out, stood for a minute in the dim light looking toward them, then folded his arms. He turned to the Toyota parked next to him. After another pause, he placed his hands in his pockets and began to walk in their direction.

Alisen's grip on Derick's hand tightened. "Well, here it goes."

"It'll be all right," Derick assured her. But he was calculating how he felt about this man and the manners he'd been taught and the feelings he had for Alisen and her future, their future, versus the suddenly fierce protection he was now feeling for her.

Don't blow it.

They both stood and walked toward Keith Embry without being able to see the man's expression because of the lights behind him.

They reached a point where the dock met land, and the light from the boathouse encircled them.

"Hello, Alisen." Keith nodded at his daughter and turned to Derick. "Good evening." He nodded again.

Derick nodded back. Then Keith looked expectantly at his daughter.

Derick heard her quiet intake of breath. "Dad, this is Derick Whitney. Derick, this is my father, Keith Embry."

Derick brought his right hand forward. "Sir."

Keith looked him over, his eyes resting on Derick's left hand holding Alisen's. His eyes drew back up. Derick kept his hand extended toward Keith.

"Dad, Derick is Jay Whitney's nephew."

Keith turned his head abruptly to Alisen and then slowly back to Derick. He extended his own hand and shook Derick's firmly, locked eyes, and let go.

"He's here for the summer," Alisen offered, "working for Jay. He's been helping out here at the orchard too."

Derick suppressed a grin.

Keith looked back and forth between the two of them, scrutinizing. He stopped at Derick again. "Where are you from, then, Derick?" He folded his arms, and one hand came up to his chin.

"Washington State, sir."

Keith's eyebrows came up. He nodded slowly. He glanced at Alisen, then his gaze shifted up to the orchard.

Suddenly, his face relaxed. He dropped his hands into his pockets. "Well," he looked at Alisen, "don't stay out too late." He nodded to them both. "Good night."

They watched him turn around and head up the path to the front entry.

"Good night," Alisen called.

The front door closed.

Alisen turned to Derick and put her arms around his neck. He held her for a moment before she released the breath she'd been holding.

She pulled her head back, relief in her eyes. "Well, we got that over with."

He looked thoughtfully up at the house and wrapped his arms tighter around her waist then looked down at her hopeful expression. He gave her a grin and kissed the tip of her nose. She smiled and laid her cheek against his shoulder.

But Derick looked back up at the house. He glanced at the orchard as her father had done. Then it clicked.

Keith Embry had bristled. Derick had felt the animosity in his appraisal, his grip. It reminded Derick of the Discovery Channel shows. The old bull elk defending his territory from the young, challenging bull. But then Keith had looked at his daughter and the orchard and had let it go.

Keith doesn't consider me a threat.

He didn't believe his daughter would leave the orchard. Not for a kid from another state visiting on summer break, working a summer job. But Derick knew something else: Keith didn't know his daughter very well.

* * *

Keith sat in his club chair, reading lamp on, waiting for her. He could hear her coming up the back stairs from the utility room. Why didn't she use the front door? He heard the other car make its way up to the main road.

Hm. This was something Keith had not considered, not with Alisen. It seemed too distant; he had been too distant. He'd only begun thinking of how to fix the gaping hole he had created between them. He felt it was finally time. He could use his influence, steer her in the proper direction, make sure she had the right connections, try to make up for . . .

"Dad?"

"Alisen."

There was a pause and then, "Are you all right?"

"Yes, I was just waiting for you."

"For me?" She stepped farther into the room.

"Yes. I wanted to ask you about something."

"Oh." She waited, her lips pressed in a straight line, her eyes looking around the room.

"I wanted to know how you would feel about a trip to the park tomorrow? We could pick up Amanda on the way out."

Her eyes widened in surprise. "Oh." She furrowed her brow and swallowed.

"Do you have other plans?" He waited.

"Umm, not really." She looked around the room again. "It's just that . . ." Her eyes came back to his. "Glacier National Park?"

He nodded slowly. He could see she was torn. He could see she was considering. He let her.

"When would we leave?"

"Early, six a.m. We could have breakfast there. I ordered a basket from Pop's."

"You did?"

"It's in the cooler in the garage." He felt a small smile coming on at her baffled expression. He was going to win this.

"Umm." Her fingers brushed her hair back off her face. Then she blew out a breath. "Okay. That sounds . . . good." She shrugged and stuck her thumbs in her back pockets.

Her posture needed some help too, Keith noted. He smiled. "Good. I'll see you in the morning, then."

She turned and headed for the stairs up to her room.

"Alisen."

She stopped and turned again. "Yes?"

"Good night."

She stared at him. "Good night," she answered quietly.

He listened to her footsteps retreating to her room then pulled out his cell phone and dialed.

"Hello, Carly? Keith Embry. How are things at the diner? Good. Listen, I need a favor. What would it take to get a breakfast to go delivered here tonight?"

* * *

She dug her cell phone out of her jeans and dialed. She could hear her own heartbeat as the anticipation of hearing his voice flooded her. She was such a goner.

He picked up. "Hello, Alisen."

Peace settled all over her. "Hi."

"I'm glad you called. I've been thinking about something."

"What?"

"You."

Alisen smiled and rolled her eyes.

He chuckled. "It's something I wanted to ask you earlier, but we were interrupted." He paused. "I was wondering if you would come to church with me on Sunday."

"Oh," she said in surprise.

"I just thought you might—"

"Okay."

"Really? You'll come?"

"Of course I will. I want to." She really did. "What time should I be there?"

"I'll pick you up, but we can talk about it tomorrow."

Her eyes turned down. "I can't tomorrow."

"You can't?"

"I, uh, we're going up to Glacier tomorrow."

She waited.

"Who is 'we'? You and your father?"

"I guess, and Amanda. I'm sorry."

"No, that's all right. I've been spoiled. But how are you feeling about this?"

"A little weird. I'm really glad Amanda will be with us. It will help with the, uh, weirdness."

He chuckled again, and she closed her eyes and sighed, wanting him close.

"Do you know when you'll be back?"

"I don't think it'll be too late. It's just over an hour's drive."

"I have something for you."

"For me?" She grinned.

"It's just a little something. I wanted to give it to you tomorrow. Do you think you could call me when you're almost home? I don't care if it's late."

"Sure. I would call you sooner than that, but I'm not sure how cell phone reception is in the park."

"I understand."

"So I'll see you tomorrow, then?"

"Count on it."

* * *

Amanda stayed true to form and kept up a steady narrative of her week during the trip, which was a very good thing. Alisen tried to keep up with her report of her stay with Lucy Watson and her cute older brother as well as the generous details about the play in town; the shopping in Kalispell; the time at the stables; the movie she had seen; the restaurants they had tried; the party Lucy had attempted to have, complete with who showed up and who got sent away when her parents came home early; and especially the new car Lucy was getting for her seventeenth birthday. It was all chatter from the backseat of her father's SUV, and Alisen vowed to be forever grateful to Amanda.

Her father pulled off at a picnic spot, and they carried the basket and cooler to one of the tables.

"Dad, is that orange juice?"

"Yes, and there's a thermos of coffee here somewhere. It looks like we have apple juice as well." He looked at Alisen. "What would you like?"

"Orange juice, please."

He handed it to her, and she noticed how the lines of his eyes crinkled when he smiled. Had she noticed that before?

They ate a pleasant breakfast. Any passerby would think they were a close-knit family on one of many outings taken together in the mountains. Alisen's mind scrambled to remember if they had ever done this, or anything like it, since her mother's death.

They visited areas of the park that sparked memories. Good memories. Alisen's father bought them all matching ball caps with the park's insignia at Amanda's insistence and Alisen's shock. They saw deer, elk, and a couple of eagles circling up high. They walked to waterfalls and viewpoints, and her father pointed out anything he thought the girls might have missed.

She'd forgotten—the peaks rising out of beautiful forests, sparkling rivers fed by melting glaciers; it all seemed new to Alisen, who couldn't help but see it now from Derick's point of view; this was something God had created for His children. She had a few quiet moments throughout the day to consider, and in those times, she felt it. Heavenly Father loved her enough to surround her with such majesty—alongside the difficulty.

But in all the beauty, Alisen couldn't get past six years of neglect. *Why couldn't we have been doing this all along?* She knew why but didn't understand it. Through her thoughts, she could come to only one conclusion: she hadn't been important enough as an individual for her father to try, to push past his pain to love her. The thought made her slow to embrace her father's attempts. As they ate dinner at the lodge, she felt a pull to get home, as if Derick were her source of gravity.

They seemed to inch along the highway. While Amanda turned her steady flow of conversation to a riding camp she and Lucy wanted to attend this summer, Alisen turned her thoughts to Derick. She replayed their week together in her mind, staring out the window, glad to have been facing away from her father when she caught herself smiling several times. Once, she even breathed out a little laugh and tried to disguise it as a yawn. The yawn turned genuine though, and she closed her eyes.

The sun had just gone down when she opened her eyes. She had slept until the ignition turned off.

"Alisen, we're home."

She sat for a few more seconds, trying to wake up, her father's voice strangely mixing with her dreams. She had been dreaming of all of them. Her father and mother and her sisters. They'd been walking on the trail at the river, and Alisen kept running ahead. Her father was calling her back, stern. It wasn't sad or scary or even happy, really. Just a place somewhere between memory and imagining.

Her father was already getting out of the car.

Then, with a little gasp, she remembered. She got out of the car and ran into the house, past her father, and up the stairs, pulling out her cell phone.

* * *

Derick smiled as he pulled up to the house. Alisen waited on the low brick wall that surrounded the fountain. He had never seen the water on before, but it was flowing now. As soon as he stepped out of the car, she was there, arms around his neck, pulling him to her with a big smile.

Her damp hair fell in feathery waves, shiny in the porch lights, and she smelled like coconut and orange and cedar. He wrapped her in his arms, his fingers in her hair, the soft skin of her face next to his. Inhaling deeply, it was all he could do to say something, anything.

"Whoa." *Eloquent.*

She pulled back and grinned. "Hello."

"Hi." He reached for her again. "Wow, you smell great."

She let him pull her. "I missed you."

"Apparently I missed you too."

He kissed her.

He pulled away and looked at her from arm's length. "Did you just shower?"

She grinned up at him impishly. "Mm-hm."

He paused. "That's dangerous." He shook his head at himself.

She looked at him slyly. "I'll remember that."

He found his bearings and led her over to the wall she'd just been sitting on. He pulled her down next to him.

Jane made an appearance and affectionately rubbed Derick's calf before she was off again.

"How was your trip?" He'd been wondering most of the day.

She pursed her lips in thought. "It was pretty good." She shrugged her shoulders. "Better than I thought it would be. It was good to have Amanda along. I don't think she stopped talking the whole way there. Dad seemed relaxed enough." She looked up at the house. "I think it was good for him to be doing something for us that involved more time than money." She looked at Derick. "Does that make sense?"

He nodded.

"Still, I can't . . . I don't know what to think. I feel like I have to be careful."

"Then be careful." He brought her hand up and kissed it. "I'm glad you had a good time though."

She nodded her head and looked up at the stars. "I'd forgotten how beautiful the park is. I mean, we have so much natural beauty right here, and you start to take it for granted, but then you go to the park, and the scale of everything—it's incredible. You feel closer to God there. I mean, Heavenly Father. It's hard to imagine not thinking that way before." She glanced to the house. "But I guess people do. They just don't know, do they?"

Derick found himself looking at her, holding his breath.

He had to ask. "What don't they know?"

She turned to him and answered simply, eyes open and honest. "The truth."

His mouth turned up in a smile. He looked up at the stars, and her eyes followed. Then he looked back to her, and she met his incredulous gaze. The water splashed quietly behind them.

It's too soon. "Alisen Embry." His voice was rough but soft. "I love you."

Her fingers came up to her mouth, a smile forming as she looked into his searching eyes. "I always wondered how that would sound."

He swallowed, feeling the weight of his words hanging out there. "How'd I do?"

She pressed her hand over his heart, her eyes never leaving his. She nodded. "You sounded like you knew I loved you too."

They stayed that way for a time, fingers entwined, as the night moved on without them.

* * *

"I wanted to give this to you."

They stood by the car, and he held out a small, dark book.

"We used this book with the Bible to teach the people about Jesus Christ."

Recognition lit her face as she took it from him.

She leaned back against the car as she read the cover. "The Book of Mormon?"

He leaned next to her. "Mormon was an ancient prophet here in America. He compiled the writings of his people into this book."

"Oh, I see." Thumbing through the first few pages, she stopped when she saw handwriting. "What's this?"

"It's my testimony. A letter to you about the way I feel about the things I believe."

She started to read, but he gently closed the book.

"I don't want you to read it while I'm here." He smiled down at her faint pout.

She looked up at him. "Okay."

"I want you to read it for yourself. Not for me. Promise?"

She nodded.

"One more thing."

"Hm?"

"You remember our talks about prayer?"

"Yes." She had thought a lot about those talks and had even thought about trying, but she felt inadequate somehow.

"Do you think you could say a prayer before you start to read?" He saw her hesitation. "It doesn't have to be long."

"What should I say?"

"Just talk to Heavenly Father, tell Him how you feel, ask Him for the help you think you need." He sensed her apprehension. "Like when you talk to your mom." She relaxed a little. "Then close in the name of Jesus Christ."

"And I say amen?"

"Yes." He smiled broadly.

She returned it.

He caressed her arms and looked her in the eyes. "I do love you."

"I know." She took a quick, deep breath. "How did this happen?"

"I blame Jay," he said. She grinned, and he kissed her good night.

Chapter 8

Late July

Keith steadied his club, looked once more at the hole, then swung. He smiled in satisfaction and turned to raise an eyebrow at Darrel, who looked at the ground, shaking his head. John laughed, slapping Darrel on the shoulder as Keith retrieved his ball.

"Looks like you're buying, Darrel." Keith took out a handkerchief and wiped the back of his neck. "And I'm going to be really thirsty."

They still had seven more holes, and the mid-July sun was kicking out the heat. They gathered their clubs and began the walk to the next hole. Keith regretted their decision to skip the golf cart.

"So, Keith, how are the girls?" John pulled out a water bottle and took a draw.

"Good. Elizabeth just got back from a tour of Europe. Milan, Prague, Paris. Who knows what she does, but she seems to do it well." He heard the strong hint of pride in his voice. "And Amanda's been off at some riding camp all summer, so I don't have her endlessly whining for a new car for a while," he said, though he was secretly looking at the models he knew would look great in his driveway.

"And what about Alisen?"

Keith shot him a glance. John knew that was a loaded question.

He shrugged. "Alisen is great." Keith adjusted his visor. "We flew to Denver for that Broadway show you suggested. We, uh, spent a couple days in San Francisco when I attended that law convention. I convinced her to apply to a few universities, and we've toured some campuses. Things are . . . coming along." He furrowed his brow.

"But?"

"What do you know about the Whitney family?"

"Jay Whitney? He's worked for you the past few years."

"You know I haven't had much to do with that. That's been Alisen's thing. Besides, you're the one who hired him." He hadn't meant to sound accusing.

John placed his hands on his hips. "Yes, I did hire him, because he was an honest, hardworking man who knew a lot about running an orchard. I trusted him right away." He wrinkled his brow. "Why do you ask?"

Keith sighed and ran his fingers through his hair. "Alisen has been spending a lot of time with a boy—Jay's nephew, here for the summer."

"Is that all?" John chuckled with relief. "I thought you were going to tell me he was skimming money or something."

Darrel obviously didn't see any humor in the situation. "The Whitneys are *Mormons*."

The mild hostility in Darrel's voice brought Keith's and John's heads around. Even Keith was puzzled at Darrel's words.

"Is this kid a Mormon?" Darrel asked.

Keith shrugged his shoulders, shaking his head. "I don't know."

"I'll tell you right now, Keith, you do not want your daughter mixed up with that group. A bunch of fanatical churchgoers brainwashed to worship their prophet like he's Jesus. Like a *cult*."

Darrel's face was turning red, which wasn't unusual since he had a hot temper and high blood pressure. Keith would have laughed, except Darrel's words concerned his daughter and were filled with alarm.

John, however, wasn't moved. "Now, Darrel, the Whitneys are very respected in Polson and in the orchard community. You know that."

"Yes, but you don't know what goes on at home, behind closed doors, how their religion affects everything they do, what they eat, what they wear. They don't sneeze on Sunday if their prophet tells them not to." He turned to Keith. "They have polygamists, Keith."

"Jay Whitney is not a polygamist, Darrel." John threw his hands up at his friend, rolling his eyes.

But Keith's eyes narrowed. "How do you know about Mormons, Darrel?"

Darrel wiped the sweat off his lip. "My niece went and married one. The guy brainwashed her, baptized her, moved her to Utah, and my brother never saw his daughter again. They couldn't even go to the wedding 'cause it was in their *holy temple*." He stopped for a second then murmured, "Who knows what goes on in there. Sharla was devastated. We've broken off all ties." He looked Keith right in the eyes. "I'm telling you," he repeated, pointing his finger with every word, "you *do not* want Alisen mixed up with a Mormon."

John shook his head and rolled his eyes again.

Keith looked down, his hands in his pockets, his mind working. His jaw felt tight. "I don't know, Darrel. I was really just concerned that the kid was a nobody, you know, no future, unconnected. A farmer, of all things." The thought still made him livid. "I've been hoping it's just a summer thing."

"Has he gotten her to go to church with him?"

Keith whipped his head back to Darrel. Without warning, anger filled his chest. Maybe it was his concern for his daughter. Or maybe he was looking for a reason to hate Derick Whitney for interfering with his plans for Alisen. Either way, he couldn't concentrate on the rest of his golf game and ended up with the drink tab.

* * *

"Hello?"

"Rachel, this is Keith."

She could hear the anger in his voice. "Yes, Keith, what's wrong?"

"You know that boy, that *Derick* Alisen's been seeing?"

"Well, I would hardly call him a boy, but yes, I've met him several times."

"What do you think of him?"

She paused, thinking her answer through. Something was wrong, and she felt she needed to be careful. "Has something happened?" Her concern was for Alisen.

"Not yet. Maybe, I don't know."

It wasn't like Keith to be so agitated.

"Well, frankly, Keith, I would like to know what this is about before I answer you."

There was a pause, then, "I'm concerned about Alisen, that's all."

Rachel listened to these words with deeper understanding. She was aware of Keith's attempts to mend things with Alisen and knew the confusion it was causing her. Alisen vacillated between hope and distrust, and Rachel didn't blame her. Alisen would be excited and dazed by her father's attentions and apparent efforts, and then fear would throw up a cautionary barrier, and she wouldn't know how far to let him influence her. This, of course, sent Alisen readily into the arms of her young man.

"You are concerned about Alisen? Or your *plans* for Alisen?"

"Rachel, I think this boy is the wrong influence."

Ah, that was it. Money.

"I've never seen her so happy, Keith."

Another pause. "He has her going to some church."

"Some church would do you good, Keith."

He was getting frustrated; she could feel it. "I think this thing is getting too serious, Rachel. What has she told you?"

Now, at least, she could say something.

"I agree."

"You do?"

"I agree that it is serious. From what I have observed, and from what Alisen has expressed, she is in love with this Derick." She decided to continue. "And I think she is too young to be feeling as strongly as I think she feels. It has me worried."

There was a sigh of relief on the other end. "Rachel?"

She knew what he would ask. "I'll talk to her."

She hung up the phone and sighed. She continued watering her plants on the patio then sat down on the wrought-iron bench.

It had made her wary to see Alisen's obvious attachment to the young man. Alisen was not yet nineteen, after all. Of course she enjoyed seeing her niece so happy, so, well, loved by a man, and he was such a good-looking young man too. But looks weren't everything, and from what she could tell, Derick was a dreamer, just starting out, not even a degree under his belt. Just a plan and good looks. Alisen deserved so much more. She hadn't even had a real relationship with anyone else, only a few silly boyfriends in high school. She had never even been away from home.

"I'll talk to her," she whispered to the plants.

* * *

Derick finished the week early at Jay's and was helping Alisen at the fruit stand. They spent the afternoon selling bags, boxes, and crates of cherries, as well as jars of honey and bars of soap from the local beekeepers. It was hot, sticky work, but six thirty came quickly.

"Want to help me put up the sign?"

He grinned and threw his fists in the air. "Yes."

They placed the big painted plywood sign over the front of the stand.

Embry Orchard Closed
Daily Hours 8:30 a.m.–6:30 p.m.
Cherries, Honey, Soap

Then they got into Derick's car and drove down to the house.

"How about we go for a swim? Did you bring your trunks?" Alisen asked.

"Of course." Derick looked up at the house as he put the car in park. He had been inside a few times, had spoken with her father a few times, had the feeling he wasn't welcome a few times. "I'll change in the utility room and wait out here."

She sighed and nodded her head.

Derick knew things were getting better with her father, but there was definitely a strain when it came to him dating Alisen.

They went in the side door, and Derick held it open as Jane came shooting through. He went into the small bathroom to change, and Alisen scooped out some dinner for Jane. Derick came out as she set the water bowl down.

"That was fast. I'll hurry." She paused just a moment to roam over his bare abs with her eyes then laughed at his smile as she ran upstairs.

Derick walked outside with a towel over his shoulder, following the path to the circular driveway. He stopped at the garage. A shiny pearl sports car sat in one of the bays. Another Porsche. He didn't remember seeing that one before.

He continued down to the end of the dock, where he sat and waited, looking out over the lake. It was especially calm, and the water looked great. His stomach growled. Lunch had been a long time ago.

Footsteps sounded along the dock, and he started to say something about dinner as he turned. But it wasn't Alisen.

This girl was tall; blonde; tan; and wearing, well, not much and sunglasses. He quickly turned back to the lake.

Who is that? Amanda? He glanced sideways. *Nope, not Amanda.* This woman could not be in high school.

Then it dawned on him. *The other sister. Elizabeth.*

Alisen had mentioned Elizabeth was coming home.

"And who are you?" She pulled off her sunglasses.

He pushed himself up to stand and focused on her eyes. Elizabeth Embry looked like her father. And she knew it looked good on her.

He cleared his throat and almost held out his hand but thought better of it. He folded his arms instead. "I'm Derick. I'm just, uh, waiting for Alisen."

"Alisen, huh?" She eyed him from head to toe and back up again, holding the tip of her sunglasses to her mouth. Her hair swung around as she looked back up to the house then back to Derick. She shrugged.

"So, *Derick*, what do you do?" She bent down to remove her sandals, and he suddenly had nowhere to look. He concentrated on the sky.

"Umm, I'm a student at UM, but I'm working here." She flipped her hair as she looked back up at him. Eyes again. "For the summer."

She perused him like a purchase she was considering. "Hm. Too bad."

Stepping away, she pulled off what he was surprised to see was a cover-up of some sort. He put his hands on his hips and turned to face the lake again. He sincerely hoped she didn't remove any more layers.

There was a splash, and she was in the water.

He exhaled, and his shoulders sagged with relief.

"Hey, Derick," she called from the water, "come on in." She executed some backstrokes. "The water's amazing."

"I'll just wait for Alisen, thanks." He watched the house.

"Suit yourself."

After a few more minutes and no sign of Alisen, Elizabeth swam back to the dock. "My sister seems to have forgotten you." She started to pull herself up the ladder, out of the water. "What a shame."

"Maybe I'll go see where she is." He quickly turned toward the house but halted.

Alisen was already coming down the dock but had stopped, her mouth open. Derick threw out his hands in a helpless gesture then threw them back toward Elizabeth, who had finished her climb out of the water and was walking his way. He kept his eyes on Alisen as Elizabeth reached for his towel, still tossed over his shoulder. Alisen's eyes widened as Elizabeth toweled off then threw the towel back over Derick's shoulder, sideswiping his face. He looked up at the sky as Elizabeth slipped her sandals back on, using his shoulder to balance herself, then picked up her article of clothing and sunglasses and started walking toward Alisen.

"Nice, um, swim-thing, Elizabeth. Did you find that in France?"

Derick could hear them but still looked up, hands on his hips.

"Spain. Nice, um, friend, Alisen. Did you find him in the orchard?" Then she called, "Thanks, Eric."

He lifted his hand high to acknowledge the thanks, but he still stared at the sky.

Elizabeth paused and said, just loud enough for him to hear, "Too bad."

He waited until he thought it was safe then slowly brought his eyes back down to rest on Alisen, who watched him, shaking with silent laughter.

"Now we know," she said between gasps, "what you would do if you ever met a mermaid."

He threw off the wet towel, sprinted up the dock, grabbed her up in his arms like a baby, and sprinted back down to the end. Alisen squealed the whole way, and he threw her into the lake. Then he dove in after her.

Later, they stretched out on a blanket on the dock, eating sandwiches and chunks of watermelon.

Derick was propped up on his elbow. He spit a black seed into the water. "A little birdie told me your birthday is next week."

A grin popped onto Alisen's face, and she nodded her head quickly, chewing a bite of sandwich.

"And you'll be nineteen?"

Again, a quick nod.

He whistled low. "That's old. Practically twenty."

She nodded, slower this time. She swallowed. "Before you know it, I'll be twenty-one."

Derick sighed and shook his head. "Well, I guess we'll have to do something extra special, seeing as how your youth is about to fly away."

Alisen sat up on her knees, eyes dancing. "What are we going to do?"

He looked at her. She was wearing one of those two-piece swimsuits that covered her front, then tied in the back like an apron, the shocking purple electrifying her eyes. The orchard work and the summer sun had made her lean and brown. Her wet hair had begun to dry, and curls were starting to flutter around the edges, lit up by the lowering sun behind her. He forgot what he was going to say.

Alisen leaned forward a little, her eyes on his, inviting him to come back into focus. "Hello?"

Slowly, he smiled back at her. "You don't even know, do you?"

"What?"

His voice was low. "How beautiful you really are."

She looked down, a deeper blush forming in her cheeks. "Sometimes I do." She looked back up at him, her smile wide. "Now, can we talk about my birthday? Please?"

* * *

Later, alone in her room, Alisen smiled to herself. Rachel had always made sure Alisen's birthday was not overlooked, but the celebrations were always tainted with the fact that Alisen's father distanced himself from them. Of course, there would be a gift, and he would be there, sometimes, in the background as she blew out her candles. But there was no enthusiasm, no gleam of excitement, no "Happy birthday, Alisen," no comfortable way to say thank you, no "I love you," or even a hug from her father. Never that.

So the idea of a birthday with Derick, no matter how simple or extravagant, thrilled Alisen inside and out. She knew without a doubt that all those missing elements would be there from him.

"I'd like some of it to be a surprise," he'd said. "But if you could be ready, all dressed up," he winked, "at two p.m. next Friday, I would be so happy to help you celebrate the day you were born."

A giggle found its way up from inside her. She was going to love turning nineteen.

Chapter 9

Alisen stood at the kitchen counter, chopping vegetables for a quick salad. Her father came in and leaned back against the counter beside her, his arms folded.

She glanced up. "Hi, Dad."

"Alisen."

A corner of her mouth came up. Always so formal.

"Are you . . . on your own tonight?"

She knew it was his way of asking if Derick would be showing up anytime soon.

"Yes, I am. Derick put in a full day today and is spending the evening with Jay's family." She could feel him tense up when she said Derick's name and thought she saw out of the corner of her eye that he was shaking his head. "I was going to eat and read a good book." She smiled at herself.

Her dad shifted his weight. "I'd like to talk to you about your birthday weekend."

She stopped chopping and looked over at him. "Birthday. Weekend?"

He cleared his throat and continued. "Yes. I'd like to do something over the weekend to celebrate your birthday. It's not every year you turn nineteen."

She resumed chopping, her brows knit together. *Or fourteen or fifteen or sixteen*. She sighed. "What did you have in mind?"

"New York."

She stopped chopping again.

"*New York*?" She looked at her father incredulously. "*City*?"

Her father raised one eyebrow and grinned.

But Alisen was already shaking her head. "I can't go to New York that weekend, Dad." She began chopping again. "I'm sorry, but I have plans."

Her father straightened himself to his full height, taking a deep breath. He held it. "With Derick?"

She knew he was trying to maintain whatever emotions were stirring inside him.

She thought carefully. "Derick is taking me out Friday." She finished the cucumber and started the tomato. "But I have plans on Sunday as well. Not birthday plans." She hesitated. "I have church plans." She looked up slowly. "But I would like it if we could do something on Saturday. I really would."

A muscle twitched in his jaw.

"*Church* plans."

Her eyes remained steady. "Yes." That Sunday would be her final lesson with the missionaries. It was the date that had worked for everyone, including Jay, who was hosting the lessons in his home. "This is a special meeting I don't want to miss."

Her father was silent, and she started a green pepper.

"Alisen." He exhaled slowly. "I don't like this."

"I know, and I'm sorry. But we could do something on Saturday, couldn't we? We could go to New York another time?"

"It's not that. I don't . . ." He wavered. Then he seemed resolved. "I don't like how involved you are in this church, how devoted you seem. Really, Alisen, *three hours a week*? What could you possibly be doing for three hours? And you want to give up a trip to New York for some meeting?"

She tried to keep herself from smiling. That wouldn't help. "Listen, Dad—"

"No, Alisen." He struggled to maintain his composure. "I want you to think, to consider that maybe, maybe you're being brainwashed."

No, smiling definitely did not help. "Dad." She shook her head and tried to respect his concern. "Who have you been talking to?"

He pulled his head back abruptly, but she continued. "I'm happy going to church. I'm happy believing the things I'm taught there. And no one is forcing me to believe. I just feel it for myself." She smiled at him then.

He inhaled sharply through his nose. "How is that possible when you hang on that boy's every word, when you follow him around like a lost puppy, when you spend *practically every waking moment* wrapped around *his little finger*?" His anger came on so fast it frightened Alisen, and she stepped away from him.

Her eyes started to swim. "Don't you want me to be happy, Dad?"

He breathed heavily and closed his eyes. He turned, placing both hands on the counter. His shoulders came up and dropped. "Of course I do." His voice rose again. "But not if it means *alienating* your family."

Her chin came up, and she squared her shoulders. "I am sure, Dad, that if I ever alienated a member of this family," the tears spilled over, but her voice was steady, "you would be the first to recognize it."

Neither of them moved. She could hear the big clock on the living room wall tick. It was as though an invisible force held them in place, and she couldn't even move to wipe her tears. One fell over her lips, and she tasted the salt.

Haltingly, her dad lifted his hand from the countertop and placed it over hers. Alisen held her breath at the touch.

"I'm sorry, Alisen," he said quietly, roughly.

Alisen slowly allowed the quiet sobs to come, giving in to the feelings of loneliness his only touch in six years sent pouring out.

* * *

She lay on her bed, staring at the ceiling. The Book of Mormon lay open just beyond her fingertips. Several weeks ago the missionaries had challenged her to be baptized, and she had accepted. She had not, however, committed to a date. She wanted to make sure her family knew, that they understood her desire for this, that she could at least have one of them there to support her, or tolerate the idea, anyway.

Here and there she had dropped references to the Church, made it clear that she was attending, and even tried once to have the missionaries come to her house. That had been a disaster. The elders had come early. Elizabeth had unexpectedly answered the door and amused herself by turning her flirt on the poor young men. Then her father had appeared, stonily telling them they had been mistaken, that it was not a good time, and that it never would be.

But Alisen had thought, for a moment, that the conversation in the kitchen was taking a direction where she could tell her father her intentions, that he could feel her happiness in her words. But his anger had come so strong, so fast. She had no idea where it had come from or how long it had been simmering. And she had struck back.

She still couldn't grasp her father's apology. Overwhelmed, she had run to her room.

When she had finally stopped crying, she rolled off her bed to her knees and prayed to her other Father. She had poured out her heart to Him like she never had before, talking to Him like He was in the room. She had spoken about her father, about her mother, about Derick, about the orchard. She'd wondered about her future and what she might do to change things, what she might do to have things remain the same. Finally, she'd sensed a peace settle around her and felt that at least He had heard.

She reached once again for her book and opened it to Derick's letter. She had read it so many times she could see the words when she closed her eyes. Her fingers traced his handwriting, and she felt emotion sting again. Her father's words crept into her ears like a faint echo. *You hang on that boy's every word.* She breathed the echo away.

Alisen thumbed through the thin pages, skimming passages she'd already read and then resting the book on her chest. She stared at the ceiling.

Mom, you know this is right, don't you?

* * *

"Rachel?" He looked at the clock. Ten forty-seven p.m.

"Yes, Keith?"

He switched the phone to his other ear and rubbed his forehead. "I hope I didn't wake you."

"No, I was just getting a little reading done. What can I do for you?"

"It's about Alisen." He paused. "I think I've been going about this the wrong way."

He could feel her intuition kick in. She'd heard the regret in his voice. Slowly and clearly, she asked, "What did you do?"

He growled, "I got after her about going to church and, uh, accused her of alienating her family."

Silence.

Suddenly, Rachel's elevated voice filled the line. "Keith Embry, you have finally done it. After all these years, I'm going to say out loud what I have been thinking all along." She made sure he heard every syllable. "*You* are an *id-i-ot.*"

He had no reply. So she went on. "Did you know I was meeting her for lunch tomorrow? Did you know I was planning to have a nice chat with her about all this? Did you know, that now, knowing my niece, I will comfort instead of criticize, listen instead of speak, encourage instead of prune? Oh, you are such a . . . such a *man.*" She spat the word into the phone.

Still, Keith had nothing to say.

He heard an exasperated sigh from her end. "You're right about one thing," she offered.

He was afraid to ask.

"You've been going about this the wrong way." She paused. "*Idiot.*"

* * *

Alisen looked in the mirror. She had finally gone shopping yesterday and now had everything on. Her dress was a soft, brushed, raspberry silk with an open mandarin collar, fitted princess seams, and softly gathered cap sleeves. Her hands brushed down her hips, where the slim dress fluidly curved to a gentle flounce just above her knees. She brought up a foot to look at her shoe. Three delicately thin pale-beige straps wrapped around her newly pedicured foot and connected to a two-inch heel.

She had teased her hair just a little toward the back then made a deep part and swept her bangs across her forehead. A few pins held her curls up here and there, but most of her hair fell loosely down her back. Her lip gloss matched the color of her dress and the growing blush in her cheeks. And her smoky brown eye shadow and mascara emphasized the blue in her eyes. She fingered the diamond at her throat. She didn't wear jewelry often because of her work in the orchard, but she did love this necklace. There had been a moment of softness in Elizabeth when she had helped her put it on the morning of graduation.

She inhaled, and her lips formed an O as she breathed out.

Things had been strained like never before between her and her father, but talking to Rachel at lunch the other day had helped, and Alisen noticed an effort on Keith's part to back away and leave her to her choices. And now, it was her birthday.

Alisen took one last look in the mirror, front and back, and turned for the bedroom door, anticipation fluttering in her chest. She grabbed a champagne-colored silk clutch on her way out.

As she moved down the hall, she heard Elizabeth's voice.

"Wait."

Elizabeth came to her door, which had been open as Alisen had walked past. Elizabeth leaned against the doorway with her arms folded and crossed one ankle in front of the other. She held up a finger, pointed down, and twirled it in the air.

Not knowing what to expect, Alisen slowly turned around in place. She stopped and looked at her sister.

Elizabeth pursed her lips and nodded. "He's not going to know what hit him."

A slow smile spread across Alisen's face.

Elizabeth turned into her room and said over her shoulder, "Be good, little sister." Then she murmured, "Don't do anything I'd do."

* * *

Derick pulled up to the house and parked. He glanced up at the veranda, the main windows reflecting sky. He angled the rearview mirror so he could check himself and ran his fingers through his hair then over his freshly shaved jaw. He took a deep breath, drumming his fingers on the steering wheel, then got out.

Butterflies. Why was he nervous? He had seen her all summer, practically every day. But his stomach muscles were tense, and his breathing was just a little off.

He came up to the big curved door, rang the doorbell, and put his hands in his pockets. It felt like he stood there for a long time. Finally, the door opened, and Keith stepped into the doorway. The man's eyes narrowed.

Derick stuck his hand out as usual. "Sir."

Keith didn't even look at his hand this time. Derick still held it there, thinking that if Keith did speak, his words would be laced with threats. Sincere threats. Maybe involving a boat. Derick did not look away, nor did he say anything more.

From what Alisen had told him, Derick had a good idea where this hostility was based. The Church had been brought into it. Derick could tell from Alisen's questions that Keith had been talking to some people with a skewed idea of what Mormons were. Suddenly, Derick had become the worst kind of threat.

Then, to top it all off, Alisen had told him about her dad's plans to take her to New York for her birthday, something that, in the past, he would never have even thought to attempt. And Derick had undermined it—in her father's eyes, anyway.

So there they stood, Keith glaring, Derick waiting. Keith finally stood aside, and Derick dropped his hand and came into the house. Keith began to climb the stairs to the living room but stopped abruptly. Derick's eyes were already on the reason, and his mouth hung open.

Alisen stood at the top of the stairs, drawing the hostile air from the room like a flame. Her eyes shifted a little uncertainly between both men below her, but her expression remained radiant. She descended a few steps toward her father, rooted in place, and turned to look at him.

"Bye, Dad." She gave him a small smile then continued past him down the stairs.

Derick's eyes hadn't left her. His mouth still hung open. Alisen laughed softly as she brought her fingers up under his chin and pressed his mouth closed.

He swallowed. "Are you ready?"

She grinned and nodded. He stepped back to let her pass through the door, instinctively placing his hand at the small of her back.

As Derick reached back inside to close the door, he glanced up toward Keith. He stood, fists clenched, knuckles white, but instead of looking at Derick with hatred, he was staring after Alisen, and the look on his face caught Derick completely by surprise.

It was a look of anguish.

* * *

Alisen gawked. She didn't even know they had these in town. Her smile trumped her look of disbelief though. Derick was obviously pleased with himself. He stood with one hand toward her and one hand on the buggy. She looked to her right again, at the matching white horses and the driver sitting up front, also watching her with a pleased smile. As cliché, as corny, as this was, she had never done this, and it thrilled her.

She took Derick's hand and stepped into the seat. He followed, nodding to the driver, who gave a sharp whistle and tapped the reins. A laugh escaped Alisen as the horses jerked forward and threw Derick and her back against the leather cushion.

Derick had cleaned up for the occasion. His new haircut left a faint tan line where his hair had begun to curl over his neck. The collar of his shirt opened casually above his thin navy sweater vest, and he'd rolled up his sleeves, but pressed stone khakis replaced his usual jeans. He put one arm around Alisen's waist and pulled her close, flashing a smile.

The two of them leaned forward, watching the vibrant streets go by; then, as the buggy turned up a hill leading off the main street, they settled back in the seat. The climb was steady, and then the view opened up to the valley beyond. They passed homes nestled back in the trees on their left and a hill gently sloping down on their right. A car passed them on the left and gave a couple honks. Kids waved from the backseat. They waved back.

"I can't believe you did this. This, I did not expect."

"So you like it?"

"*Yes*, I like it. It's the kind of thing you see in the movies or when you visit historical cities and you want to say, 'Oh, yes, let's do that,' but you don't because you're afraid of looking silly. But you just led me right up and helped me in, and here we are in this horse and buggy, with you looking like that." She gestured to him with a wave from his head to his feet.

"And you looking like that," he added.

"And the world looking like this." She laughed, motioning to the pastoral view.

He watched her with an amused, relieved expression. His gaze warmed.

She lowered her lashes and smiled. "I just feel very . . . celebrated."

That must have been enough because he nodded then leaned toward her and whispered in her ear. "Happy birthday, Alisen."

She turned to him, so close, and whispered back, "Thank you."

The buggy wound slowly down and around then followed a path along the Swan River, meandering at the edge of town. They had nearly made a complete loop. They crossed over a bridge leading to a small park with big trees spreading their branches out in canopies. People were gathering there, making their way from parked cars or walking over from the main street. A crescent-shaped amphitheatre rose out of a green hill, with a large half-round stage backed by high wooden walls.

The buggy pulled up to the sidewalk and stopped. Derick jumped out and kept Alisen's hand after helping her down. They waved good-bye to their driver and walked toward the theatre to join the small crowd of people laying out blankets to sit on. But Derick led her past the grassy seating to a knoll just above.

"Oh," Alisen softly exclaimed. There, on the lawn, sitting on a white wicker love seat with a blue ticking cushion, was a sign that read *Reserved: Alisen & Derick*.

"How did you do this?" Her eyes were wide, blinking.

Derick shrugged. "I know some people." He motioned to the seat.

She sat and pulled him down next to her. "What are we watching?"

He answered with some importance. "A community theater summer performance of *Barefoot in the Park* by Neil Simon."

She gasped. "I've always wanted to see that one."

"Really?" He seemed genuinely surprised. "I only hoped it wasn't a tragedy."

"Nope, not a tragedy. And yes." She looped her hands around his elbow. "Really."

The crowd began to quiet down, and then applause broke out as the characters took their places on stage. Alisen nestled in against Derick's side, and the play began.

* * *

"Whose boat is this?" Alisen carried her shoes as she followed Derick down the dock, then Derick helped her into the ski boat. She took the seat across from the driver's as Derick expertly untied the boat, hopped in, and pushed it away from the dock. He started the engine and carefully maneuvered it out into open water. Then he looked at Alisen with a grin.

"I told you. I know some people."

She laughed. "I'd like to know your people."

"You will." He gave her a meaningful look.

It took her a moment to blink. She looked over the lake. "Where are we going?"

He grinned. "You'll see." He looked her over. "I'll take it easy so the wind doesn't muss you up."

In just a short time, Derick had the boat angling toward a long dock leading to a low building with a wall of windows facing the lake. A deck stretched out from the wall, and a portion of it ballooned out into a seating area with tables and umbrellas. Several other boats, and even a couple of kayaks, were tied up along the dock. A few groups and couples sat scattered among the tables. Alisen could hear music playing as Derick maneuvered the boat into an open space, secured everything, then held out both hands to lift her to the dock.

He paused as she got her balance. "Have I told you how gorgeous you look?"

She nodded. "A few times." She suppressed a smile. "But I don't mind. At all." She bit her lip, and he kissed her.

He held her steady while she slipped her shoes back on. A host led them to a small table at the edge of the deck. Alisen's eyes darted around instead of focusing on her menu.

"Are you all right?" Derick asked, though she couldn't seem to lose the smile on her face.

She nodded. "I just want to take it all in. I want to make sure I remember this."

"I hope you will." A breeze came up. "Are you warm enough?"

She reached across the table and took his hand. "Yes, I am." She picked up her menu. "And I'm hungry."

He laughed.

The sun balanced on the horizon as they finished their meal. Strings of lights and glowing Chinese lanterns hung around the perimeter of the deck and reflected on the water. The waitress brought a dish of sorbet the color of Alisen's dress and set it in front of her. As the waitress walked away, Derick brought out a single candle, placed it in the sorbet, and lit it with a lighter from his pocket.

"Now, I'm not going to sing." He grimaced, and she laughed. "But you can certainly make a wish." He looked at her expectantly.

She leaned forward and closed her eyes. Then she opened her eyes and softly blew out the candle. She brought her eyes up to Derick, who seemed mesmerized by her simple act.

Please make my wish come true. Oh, please, oh, please.

As they shared the sorbet, Alisen noticed a few couples moving to a space beyond the tables, a small dance floor under a canopy of miniature lights. The couples moved together with the soft music. She looked at Derick questioningly.

Derick leaned toward her. "Once a month, this place has a Full Moon Night, with dancing and music as the sun sets and the moon comes out."

She watched the dancers, enchanted. She searched the violet sky blinking with new stars and found the moon casting light off the water.

"Alisen, would you like to dance?"

She smiled.

He pushed his chair out then pulled hers out for her. He led her to the dance floor and placed his hand at the small of her back. She brought a hand up to his and placed it on his chest, folding into him. They began to dance, swaying in time to the music, and Alisen felt his heart beat beneath her fingers.

Nat King Cole crooned, "My sweet embraceable you."

"Derick."

"Hm?"

"I don't want this to ever end."

He looked into her eyes and promised, "It won't."

But a look of worry flickered across his face. He pulled Alisen a little closer.

Please don't let this end.

Chapter 10

ALISEN MADE HER WAY UP the stairs, suspended between reality and dream. Her hand came to her neck, her little finger touched her mouth, and a smile followed a sigh. It had been the best birthday of her whole life.

Sorry, Mom, it's true. Even better than the zoo.

She swayed back and forth to the music in her head as she reached the top of the stairs and walked toward the hall. Even in the dark, she felt blissfully content, remembering the soft glow of the evening.

Then she heard a door. The den.

"Who's there?" Her father's voice sounded in the dark.

"Dad?"

She heard something drop on the floor. She could make out her father's figure in the doorway across the living room. The low light from his desk lamp in his office barely illuminated his silhouette from behind.

She moved toward him slowly. Her father took a few steps her way, but something was wrong. He leaned too far to the right and bumped into the small table there. Alisen put her hands out where she stood as if to catch him. A lamp wobbled then tipped over and rolled with a thud to the carpet.

She heard him breathing heavily, raggedly.

When he spoke, his voice came out rough, full of sadness. "Anne."

Alisen froze. Something was wrong, but she couldn't move. She hadn't heard her mother's name from her father's mouth in a very long time.

"Anne?" He sounded so remorseful, so tired.

"No, Dad, it's me, Alisen." She tried to keep control of her voice, though emotions were starting to tear her calm, no, her *euphoria* to pieces.

"Where have you been?" Anger tinted his voice now.

The light from the full moon through the large windows gave everything a blue cast. Her father supported himself on the table, shoulders hunched as he looked at her. His eyes were sunken, swollen, but watching her painfully.

"Where have you been?" he repeated.

"My birthday. I went out for my birthday."

His face crumpled, and he brought up a hand to his eyes. His shoulders started to shake. "Gone so long."

Alisen trembled now. She'd never seen her father like this. Never anything like this. He was so controlled. She held out her hands again.

"I'm here now, Dad." She went to him and placed her arms around his shoulders. He smelled heavily of scotch. "I've always been here." Tears came to her eyes.

He brought a hand up to her arm and hung on.

"I'm *so sorry*. So sorry. Sorry." He was weeping.

She opened her mouth to assure him, but he continued in a jagged whisper, "If I'd helped you. If I'd helped you in the orchard." His voice cracked.

"Dad, you didn't know."

"No!"

She jumped.

"You asked me." His voice suddenly became helpless again. "You asked me to help. Shorthanded." He was breathing raggedly again, slumping to the floor. "You asked me, and I didn't." He sat on the ground, sagging against the wall, Alisen's arms still around him. "And you fell." He swore. "You fell off that ladder."

Alisen froze.

"You fell. And I wasn't there. I didn't help," he whispered. "I didn't. I didn't. *I didn't.*"

Alisen's tears flowed freely now, and all she could do was hold his shoulders and comfort him as a parent comforts their child.

* * *

"Rachel?"

Rachel cleared her throat, fumbling the phone to her other ear. "Yes? Alisen? What's wrong?" She was waking up now, adrenaline kicking in.

"I'm okay. We're okay. It's just—well, Dad." She sounded strained, on the verge of tears. "He's had too much to drink. Elizabeth's not home yet, and I can't help him by myself."

Rachel's hand came to her mouth.

"I was going to call Derick, but . . ."

"No. You were right to call me." She thought quickly. "I'll be right there."

"Hurry."

* * *

"Derick?"

"Good morning, birthday girl. How'd you sleep last night?" He leaned back in the kitchen chair and stretched.

She didn't answer right away. When she did, her voice was small and wavered. "Uh, not very well."

He leaned forward again. "Why? What's wrong?"

"I, uh." She sounded like she had been crying. "My dad . . ."

Derick felt his shackles come up. "What did he do?"

"*Nothing*. Nothing." She sniffled. "He, uh, was drunk last night when I got home."

Derick froze. There were a million things that could come after that sentence, and none of them was good for Alisen.

He braced himself. "Did he hurt you?"

She made a sharp cry, or was it a laugh? "No. No, he didn't. He, uh . . ." She paused to take a deep breath. "He thought I was my mother."

Derick stood, but she continued. "Derick, he—" She took another breath, but Derick couldn't breathe at all. "He feels like it was his fault she died."

He slowly sat back down and let that sink in. He thought of the years Keith couldn't even look at his daughter, the tortured look on Keith's face when he saw Alisen yesterday. Alisen, looking so much like her mother. He remembered the glares of hatred when Derick had done nothing more than fall in love with the man's daughter. *Who looks so much like her mother.*

He dropped his face into his hand. "Do you need me to come over?"

Silence.

"Alisen?"

She was crying now. "Derick."

"What is it?"

"I don't think you should. Not right now." She was trying to calm herself. "Rachel is here talking to Dad now, but, Derick." She lost it again. "He remembers it. He remembers *everything*."

What did she mean? "He remembers what?"

She took another gulp of air, and the words tumbled out. "He remembers how it felt to lose her after she asked him to help her but he didn't. And then she fell. He misses her so much. And now he thinks he's losing me, and it's his fault all over again, even though he could have stopped it, he could have been doing something." Her voice trailed off, punctuated by sniffles.

Derick tried to make sense of her words, and though it didn't all cohere, he had the general idea. "Alisen, do you need me to come over?" he asked more firmly this time.

"I wanted you to. I wanted to call you last night, so badly. But Rachel thought that might be the worst thing right now. She thinks you're the reason Dad feels he's losing me, losing my mom all over again."

Derick's jaw tightened. This was insane. Of course, she was right. But alarms were going off all over the place.

"I can meet you somewhere. We can meet at the river or the park. Alisen, let me *be* there for you."

She was quietly sobbing now, but she whispered, "You don't know how badly I want to see you. Last night with you, it was—I felt . . ." She couldn't find the words, and the silence drifted. "But I can't leave my dad. I have to be here for him so he knows it's not too late."

His fist clenched, and his knee bounced up and down. "I'll see you tomorrow at church though, right?"

"Derick, I think we're going away for a few days. That's what Aunt Rachel and Dad are talking about right now." Her voice broke. "I thought we should get Dad away from here for a while. After last night . . ."

He could hear the struggle in her voice. Last night. How different this was from the last night he remembered.

"What about the orchard?"

"I'm hiring some extra help. I'll be back soon."

"I'll help out."

She paused. "Derick, I'm sorry." She was fully crying again. "I'll. Miss. The last. Missionary. Lesson."

Amid all the turmoil he was feeling for her, he had to smile. "Don't worry, I'll let the elders know." He heard her calm just a little bit. "Will you let me know your plans, please? When you'll be home?"

"Of course," she whispered, sounding a little clearer. "Thank you. I wish . . ."

"Yes?"

"I wish you were my home."

Derick felt his chest tighten. "Me too."

Chapter 11

FLOWERS SPILLED OUT OF WINDOW boxes and pockets hanging on the doors. Alisen couldn't get over how many years this street might have been here, looking exactly the way it must have centuries ago. They'd been in motion since the day they'd arrived in Paris. It had been her aunt's idea to fill their days and nights with activity. Sometimes it was restful, strolling along the rivers, making small talk, stopping for lunch at a café, watching people. Sometimes it was breathtaking, like the ride up the Eiffel Tower, when Alisen had felt that the whole thing was actually tipping as they rose, or running to the theater to make the ballet and settling into a private box as the music began.

Now her father took her shopping, and though Alisen didn't ask for very much, she was drawn to the jewelry case in an antiques shop.

A glint of red caught her eye. A bracelet. In the top center, a small round cherry ruby nestled into a pale gold blossom offset by three small diamonds, the cluster enfolded in a delicate curled gold leaf. The band itself was as wide as the blossom, a polished latticework all the way around. The gently worn details glowed with a soft radiance.

"Would mademoiselle care to try it on?" The attentive clerk had followed her captivated gaze.

Alisen looked up at her father, who placed his hand on her shoulder and nodded to the clerk. "Of course."

The clerk removed it from its place under the glass counter and held it out for her. The ruby seemed lit from beneath. She took it and wrapped it around her wrist, snapping it shut. Perfect.

"Happy birthday," her father said. "Sorry it's late."

She nodded, looking down at the bracelet, quickly brushing away an escaped tear.

When they arrived back at the hotel, Alisen eagerly showed Rachel, who praised Keith for giving such a beautiful treasure to his daughter.

Now Alisen looked down at her wrist, turning it in the light, the ruby's facets twinkling.

"Alisen, are you ready?" Aunt Rachel came into the room, fastening on an earring. "I can't seem to find my watch. Do you know where it might be?"

Alisen turned and reached up to the mantel over the tiny fireplace in their room.

"Here it is."

"Oh, thank you."

They were a funny trio: Alisen, Rachel, and Keith. Amanda had not wanted to miss the last weeks of riding camp and the final competitions she'd worked so hard to excel in, and Elizabeth couldn't get the time off. So the three were on their own. It had been awkward at first, but now they seemed to be getting used to each other and were, if not completely comfortable, at least satisfied with the efforts on all parts. For five days, they had been together. They had not approached the subject of the night of Alisen's birthday. Alisen sensed an undercurrent of caution and care between them, as though they were walking through a room full of glass sculptures.

She looked at the clock. As soon as the time difference would work in his favor, she would call Derick.

"Alisen, are you ready?" Rachel asked again.

Alisen yawned and nodded her head. She smoothed out the vivid red dress Rachel had helped her pick out. She had loved the short-sleeved, form-fitting bodice and the way the skirt gathered at her small waist then fell away in soft folds to her knees. It reminded her of the old Hollywood movie starlets.

Rachel gathered up her purse, and Alisen watched her look around. She had insisted that she and Alisen share a room, and the last few nights, she had kept Alisen up late, talking about possibilities and the future and what Alisen deserved out of life.

Last night, Rachel had specifically asked about Derick.

"You know, it's difficult to fall so hard, so young. You think the whole world is that one person, and practically nothing else matters." Rachel had been lying on her side in her bed, watching her niece brush her hair down from the twist it had been in all day. "Then one day, you realize there is so much out there, that you're missing it because you've been so wrapped up in this one person."

Alisen had smiled patiently. She'd put the brush down and walked over to sit on her bed, pulling her feet up beneath her.

"Like this trip, for instance," Rachel continued. "This is the first time out of the country for you. What do you think?"

"It's wonderful." Alisen shrugged and smiled. She'd meant it.

"It is, isn't it? More than you could imagine from books or pictures, right?"

Alisen nodded. Her aunt had been right about that.

"What if you had just stayed home, content with what was there and remained in your thinking that you could make do with movies and posters of other places without ever experiencing them?"

Alisen thought. "I guess I wouldn't know what I was missing."

Rachel had looked knowingly at Alisen. "That's right."

Alisen thought some more. She hadn't missed her aunt's meaning. "So you're saying that even though I'm so happy with Derick, how do I know what I'm missing if I just focus on him?"

Rachel looked pleased with her niece. "Yes, that is exactly what I am saying."

"But, Aunt Rachel," Alisen had said with devotion, "I didn't know what I was missing until I found Derick."

Rachel's eyes had widened, her mouth dropping open a bit. Alisen had crossed the room to her aunt, kissed her lightly on the cheek, then climbed into bed.

* * *

The cruise would take them up the river Seine on one side then turn and come back along the other. The lights of the city dazzled and bounced off the water for a double show. Music played, that distinctive sound of the accordion floating from behind the dance floor.

They had eaten delicious *millefeuille*, and now Rachel danced and Alisen leaned against the railing, watching contentedly. Her father came up and stood next to her, looking out at the city. He leaned forward, his forearms resting on the railing.

She watched him. He seemed hesitant.

"I, uh, am really glad we came here." He stood up and put a hand in his pocket, keeping the other on the railing.

"I am too. I hope it's been good for you." She glanced at him.

He nodded to the shore. "It's been hard, you know, um . . ." He seemed to change his mind about what he was going to say. He cleared his throat.

"But it will be better now. I think it will be." He looked at her quickly then looked back to the lights. "Good to have you here now."

She pressed her lips together in a smile and nodded. She shooed away the little voice shouting that it had *always* been good to have her there. She didn't mention that Derick was part of her now too. She was just grateful for his expression and let it be.

They stood there for a few more minutes before a dark-eyed young man came to ask Alisen to dance. She looked at her father, and he gave her a nod. She hesitated for just a second then smiled and took the man's offered arm.

As the young man took her in his arms and spoke to her in broken English, she thought she caught an exchanged look between her father and Rachel. A look of . . . approval.

"You stay here in Paris long?" the young man asked.

She smiled and shook her head. "No. Not long."

* * *

"Another *week*?"

Alisen leaned away from the phone and looked around, though she was alone. She grimaced, torn. "I'm sorry, but it will only be ten days total." She hoped.

"But, Alisen, school will be starting soon. I'll have to go back in a few weeks." Derick paused then added quietly, "We don't even know what you're doing yet."

She answered him. "I'll go to Missoula, at UM. I'll go with you. It's not that far, and I can come home on the weekends and holidays so I can see my dad."

"Really?"

"Yes, really." She could still hear his mope on the other end. "This really has been good for my dad."

"I don't suppose he's had a change of heart about me?"

"We haven't brought it up. I'm not sure how. I'm afraid it would—"

"Aggravate him?" he finished for her.

"Yes." She decided to change the subject. "I'm almost done with my reading."

"Really?"

She heard his tone pick up.

"Yes. I'm reading in the mornings before the others get up. And, Derick?"

"What?"

"I know it's true."

He was silent for a moment. Then he said, "Maybe this trip, this time with your father, will soften his attitude about your baptism."

She hadn't thought of that but felt a spark of hope at the idea. "Maybe." She bit her lip. "I miss you."

His voice softened. "I miss you more."

She closed her eyes. "I'm sorry."

"It's fine. Really."

"Really?"

"No."

She heard the play in his voice and smiled.

Chapter 12

Derick made his way to the rock, his legs shaky. He needed to be somewhere alone though, somewhere tranquil. This was the first place he'd thought of, but he didn't remember the trail being this long before it opened to the beach. He pushed himself over a fallen tree and brushed a branch out of his way.

Finally, the trail ahead descended to a pebble-strewn crescent. His pace quickened along with his pulse. The rock waited there, jutting out, the water musically making its way around it. His body began to relax somewhat now that he'd arrived.

The sun baked in the western sky, and the canopy of the surrounding woods held the humidity down like a lid over a pot. It was cooler here by the water. He walked across to the rock, took a big step up, and stood above the river, his hands on his hips.

As he sat down, he swung his backpack off and around. First he grabbed the water bottle and took a long swig. Then he reached in the bag and pulled out a fat envelope. His heart started its hard pounding again. He stared at the address for a long time. University of Montana, 32 Campus Drive, Missoula, MT 59812. The sound of the river rushed and played around him. His lips pressed into a line, and he barely breathed.

One thought kept replaying in his mind, becoming rhythmic:

I have to do this, I have to do this. I have to. I just have to do this.

He squeezed his eyes shut and pinched the bridge of his nose.

How will this work? Can this work? With all the complications? Falling for Alisen has been so easy, like ice melting in the sun. And sharing the gospel with her . . . She all but led me. We're cut for each other, a match.

He felt the weight of the envelope and slapped it against his palm then opened it, taking out the contents to read again. He looked up to the sky.

What do I do?

* * *

Derick couldn't wait. She had asked him to, begged him to wait until they got home, and then she would call him. He understood why. Her father coming home to him standing in the drive with his arms crossed, tapping his foot, would not be a good welcome back.

Which was why he sat in his car, parked next to Alisen's truck, up in the orchard. He'd rolled down the windows to allow for any breeze that might pick up—and so he could hear her father's car coming down the drive. He heard a soft meow and looked out his window. "Hello, Jane."

She meowed again.

He opened his door and swung his legs out. "How have you been?" He rubbed the cat's neck. She bunched up her muscles then stretched out long and meowed once more. He narrowed his eyes, looking toward the road. "I know. Thanks for the warning."

He scratched under her chin, then she took off.

Slumping sideways against his seat, Derick ran a hand over his eyes and down around his jaw. He checked his watch then lifted his head.

A car turned off the main road and headed down to the house. His heart beat faster, and his knee started bouncing. He got out his cell phone and held it. He stood and started pacing, watching the roof of the house as if it could give him a sign. He stopped his legs three times from carrying him down the hill. He brought both hands up, still holding the cell phone, and rubbed them through his hair, then placed them on top of his car in an attempt to get a grip. His head dropped down when his phone rang. He jolted and fumbled and dropped the phone, and it landed with a puff in the dirt. Pouncing on it and flipping it open, he breathlessly answered. "Hello? Alisen?"

"Derick?" He heard her smile.

"Yes, hey." He took a deep breath and exhaled. "Whew."

"Have you been running?"

He chuckled. "No, just waiting." He spun around, looking toward the house.

"Okayyy." She sounded amused. "But we're home. I'm home. So . . . when can you be here?" She sounded eager.

"Actually, I'm here." He was glad he hadn't waited like she'd asked.

"What?"

"I'm up in the orchard. I just parked up here and waited."

There was no response.

"Is that all right?"

Still silence. He swallowed.

"Hello? Alisen?"

He looked at his phone. *Call ended.*

Hm.

He wasn't waiting anymore.

He strode down the hill, following their usual route through the trees. He started to run then skidded to a halt.

There she was, running toward him, an open smile on her face, but she was watching the ground in front of her and hadn't seen him yet. He started to call but held back. A thought came to his mind: *This is how she looks when she's thinking of me.*

He took a deep breath and was to her in two leaps. She cried out in surprise as he threw his arms around her and lifted her up, using her momentum to swing her around and set her on the ground in front of him.

She was laughing, and he couldn't help himself. He swooped in and wrapped her up and kissed her and kissed her some more.

He held her out and looked her up and down. Somewhere in the back of his mind he had pictured her coming home changed somehow, wearing tight black clothes and big dark sunglasses and a glossy red pout. But that image had been ridiculous. Here she was, her long, loose curls a little wild, T-shirt and shorts, eyes bluer than the lake behind him, laughing.

Well, she wasn't laughing anymore. Her eyes still sparkled, but she was catching her breath from the run, looking at him just as he was looking at her.

"Hi," she said.

He stepped closer. "Hey. I'm glad you're home."

He cut off her answer, and she let him.

* * *

They were propped up under a tree together. Alisen played with Derick's right hand, his left arm around her shoulders. He toyed with a few strands of her hair.

"Alisen?"

"Yes?"

"I have some news. It's pretty big." He moved so he was holding both of her hands, facing her.

Her eyes widened. "What is it?"

He took a breath. "Last year I applied for a research grant, with a proposal outlining my ideas for improving standards of living through agricultural education."

Alisen gave him a crooked smile. “That was a mouthful.”

“Mm-hm.” He looked down at their intertwined hands. He plowed on. “Alisen, they’ve, uh, given me the grant.”

“That’s wonderful, Derick.” She squeezed his hands.

He raised his eyes and saw her face light up.

He swallowed. “It’s a travel grant. They’re sending me out into the field.”

Her eyebrows knit together as she absorbed that information. “Where?”

“South America, mostly, but parts of Africa and Asia too.”

Now she swallowed. “For how long?”

“Two years.”

Her voice rose. “Straight?”

“No. But I have two years to make contacts, conduct studies, collect data. Actually, two years may not be long enough. Marcus can help with some of that though. I don’t know when I would be back.” He watched her carefully, gauging her reaction. “I really didn’t think I would get it. Apparently they were impressed with my enthusiasm . . .” He trailed off. She had tightened her grip on his hands.

“When?” Her voice was small.

He spoke slowly. “One month, end of September, a week after the semester begins. I already have my initial itinerary.” His hand came up to her cheek, and he brushed away the tear that had spilled there. “I’ll be going to Bolivia first.”

Her breathing deepened. She leaned her head into his hand, and her eyes searched his. He opened his arms, and she came to him.

“I didn’t want to ask you to wait for me.”

Her voice was muffled. “But I will. I will, I will.”

He smiled sadly. He knew she would say that. Most of him believed her. He pictured her face as she’d run to see him. But he had seen too many “Dear Johns” in the mission field. Too many guys so sure, only to be very wrong. She would be at college, and she was such a beautiful creature, inside and out, and so young. She would try, but they would try harder. It was too big a risk.

“I didn’t want to ask you to wait for me”—*I have to do this, I have to do this. I have to. I just have to do this*—“because I wanted to ask you to come with me.”

Chapter 13

Alisen pulled back to look at him with an intake of breath. His eyes bore into hers with intensity. He lifted his hand in front of her, and she looked down. In his fingertips, he held a polished gold band, solid and simple. Her heart raced like she had a helicopter in her chest. He swallowed and tilted the ring to her so she could see inside the band. A tiny inscription in deep, graceful lettering begged her to peer closer.

A. E., I will be your home. D. W.

She exhaled softly, her mouth round.

"Alisen." His voice was husky now. "Marry me."

She looked up into his eyes with all those flecks of brown and gold surrounded in living green, and there was nothing else. No lake, no boat dock, not even the orchard. Only Derick.

She began to nod and reached around his neck. "Yes," she said. "Yes."

She kissed him, and he drew her closer, his arms suddenly strong across her back. Her thoughts swam. She abruptly pulled away and gasped. "But, when?"

He reached and brushed a lock of her hair aside, still looking at her deeply. He held her chin up gently with his fingers. "Before we leave."

"But . . . but my baptism. I wanted to be baptized before school started."

"That can be arranged. I think the elders have had the font filled since I introduced you." He gave her a small smile. "Then, in a year, wherever we are, we can go to the temple together." He stroked her cheek then lifted her hand and slid the shiny little halo onto her finger. He turned his eyes up to her.

She was dazed. It seemed so simple. She let her gaze roam as she pictured them anywhere, together. She could imagine the baptism, Derick there to lift her out of the water. She could picture the simple wedding. She even saw them packing, hauling suitcases to the airport, smiling, bound for their working honeymoon. Seeing the world together. It was so easy to see.

Then her eyes fell on the house.

Slowly, her hand came up to her mouth.

Derick's expression changed from relief to concern. He turned to see what she saw. He turned back quickly. "Alisen," he began, but she stopped him.

"No." She stood up. "Oh no, no, no, no." She started pacing, one hand holding her stomach and the other her head. She supported herself against the tree trunk.

Derick stood and took a step toward her. "Alisen."

She brought her face up to him, feeling reality seep like ice into her veins. She had stopped breathing. Tears came hot now. She took a torn breath.

"Derick," she whispered. "I can't leave. I can't leave right now. I can't leave Dad the way he is."

Derick's hand came to the back of his neck. He gestured to the house. "But he has your sisters. He has friends here."

Her eyes and throat burned. "But he needs me. I'm the one. Because if I'm here, he feels like he has a piece of my mom again and he has a chance to . . ." Though the words were coming, she still felt like she couldn't breathe, like she wasn't breathing. She tried to swallow. "If I leave now, he'll feel like he's losing her all over again. He's only just started to . . . You weren't there. If I leave now, he'll—" Her face crumpled, but she fought the tears and shook them away.

Derick stared at her. Then he squared his shoulders. "We'll talk to him. I'll talk to him. Alisen, we can work this out." His voice wavered in that last sentence. He stepped to her and took her in his arms, speaking over his emotions. "Please."

His cheek pressed against her temple, and she could feel his warm, shaved skin. His breath touched her wet eyelashes, and she could hear the desperation in his voice. For Derick, she whispered, "We'll try."

Her hand rubbed over the ring on her finger, the promise written on it echoing in her mind.

It's my wish, she thought. *My wish.*

She turned in Derick's arms, burying her head in his chest, and tried to numb the dread building there.

* * *

She knocked on the den door, her heart in her throat. She had been going over possible dialogues all night, trying to put together the right words, the right facial expressions. It had given her a headache. The jet lag wasn't helping either. She'd been on her knees, trying to ask the right questions, trying to know which way to go. She wanted to wait, to give her dad more time to readjust to Derick, to find ways to bring them together slowly. But time was not something she had. Her heart tore at the thought of him leaving without her.

"Come in."

Her hand moved to her pocket. She had slipped off the ring and could feel the raised circle through her jeans. She took a deep breath and opened the door.

"Good morning, Alisen. Or should I say, good afternoon." He looked her over. "Didn't you sleep well?"

She shook her head. She sat down in a chair, and her fingers went again to the little shape in her pocket. "I was, uh, thinking about some things."

He looked over the papers on his desk. "Oh?"

He squinted slightly. She allowed herself a distraction. "Dad, maybe you should get some reading glasses."

His head came up sharply. Then he sighed as he nodded his head. "Yes. But I hate the idea."

She chuckled, but the knot in her stomach reminded her that things needed to be said. She took a deep breath and looked out the tall window. The breeze busily chopped the water on the lake while the bright daylight shone into the room. If she looked at the light angling in, she could see tiny specks of dust floating like feathers at the mercy of any air current or rising heat.

Enough distractions. "Dad?"

"Hm?"

"There are some things I need to tell you about Derick."

He brought his head up again from his papers, frowning.

Her hands shook, and she pressed them flat on her lap. Her chin came up. "Dad, I love him."

He breathed out of his mouth, an exasperated sound. She was determined though.

"Since he's been here, I've felt things I've never felt before." Her dad raised his eyebrows. She clarified. "I've been so happy. And more at peace."

Her dad grunted. Alisen bit her lip.

"A lot of it has to do with Derick. He loves me too, Dad. I know it." The space inside her warmed, despite the even, guarded look her father was giving her. Her finger traced the circle again. "But," she pressed on, looking down, "a lot of the peace I feel has to do with my feelings about the Church." She glanced up. Her dad grew very still.

She couldn't tell how this was going, though she was erring on the negative side. He seemed somewhat calm though, so she continued carefully.

"I've decided to be baptized." She looked hopefully into his eyes. "A week from Saturday."

A muscle twitched in his cheek. His nostrils flared.

"I was hoping that you could be there. Or at least understand," she finished quietly.

His silence had her reeling to fill it.

"You're just starting to know me better. I will still be the same person. I've had this planned since that first week with Derick." It was the truth. She had spoken the truth.

* * *

At the last mention of Derick's name, something snapped inside Keith. He stood suddenly and turned away from Alisen. Images of Darrel's red face on the golf course flashed through his mind. The words *cult*, *baptism*, and *fanatical* took turns haunting his thoughts. *Never saw his daughter again. Broken all ties.*

He steadied himself with a hand on his desk. "No, Alisen." He didn't turn around.

"What?" He heard the shock in her quiet voice.

He turned around. She was so small in that chair, blue eyes open to him. Her fingers absently pulled at her leg. She was a child. A child so easily swayed.

"*No*. I can't let you attach yourself to something you know nothing about."

"What?" she repeated. She blinked, and the color in her face rose.

"I will not let you."

"But—" She was struggling. "But I've taken the lessons. I've studied and prayed, and I *do* know, Dad. I know by myself," she whispered with feeling. "Not because of Derick."

"Do not say his name to me. I will not let him do this to you. I will *not* let him."

She stared, fear in her eyes. He didn't like the look, but his anger at her naivety was roiling.

"Won't let him what?" she whispered.

He took a few steps around the desk and stood in front of her, his arms folded in front of him. He tried to calm his voice. It barely worked. "You're so young, Alisen. You have your whole life ahead of you. You could have anyone you wanted. *Look* at you." He threw his hands toward her. "You could do so much better." His voice rose. "Better than some farm boy who wants to baptize you and make you part of his," he clenched his teeth, "part of his *cult*! He's nothing, no one. You could have your pick of *anyone*!"

She looked at him as if he had struck her for no reason. She dropped her head, looking at her hands. Her voice was soft. "But I love him. I love him, Dad."

Keith boiled with the idea of this ridiculous infatuation sure to ruin his daughter's life. "Why?" He threw his hands up and shouted. "Why did you have to pick *him*?" His chest rose and fell with anger.

Alisen began to cry softly. She looked so tired. Worn down. Then she paused. She raised her eyes and wiped a tear away.

"I didn't pick him, Dad. Love picked him for me."

He gawked at her with his mouth half open. He inhaled, then blasted, "*That* is the most *ridiculous thing* I have *ever heard*!"

She wiped her eyes again with the back of her hand. He watched her set her hands in her lap. She nodded and looked up, and the color of her blue eyes against her reddened lids pierced through him.

"It's what Mom said when I asked her about you."

He stared. His breath seemed to whoosh out of him, and he sat back unsteadily on the desk behind him.

Alisen fingered the ring through her pocket again. Cautiously, she asked again, "What won't you let him do, Dad?"

He didn't answer.

* * *

Alisen made her way down to the utility room on autopilot and closed the door behind her. She leaned her forehead against it. It hurt to breathe. She reached into her pocket and pulled out the ring, gazing at it. *I will be your home.* She sniffed and slipped it on her finger.

"Alisen?"

She slowly turned around. She wasn't surprised by his expression. The big mirror had already told her she looked awful. She walked to him, zombielike, and moved into his arms.

She had been away from him so long. But in the last twenty-four hours that they had been back together, she had run the gamut of emotions, dizzily deciding to get baptized, to get married, and to travel the world. Then she had fearfully realized it might not happen. Now she was coming to terms with the very real idea that it couldn't happen. And that she would have to decide it. She had hardly slept or eaten. She was tired of crying. She was tired of everything. She pressed closer into Derick, inhaling his scent, etching it into her memory.

"I didn't even get past the baptism."

He stroked her hair. She felt the weight of his hand.

"You need to sleep."

She nodded her head.

"I'll talk to him."

She looked up at him. "Not today."

He considered that and nodded. "Okay."

"Thank you."

Her hand came up, and she traced the places where the creases appeared when he smiled. She reached up and kissed him.

He pulled her closer and gently started to rock side to side.

She knew he would talk to her father tomorrow.

And she knew it wouldn't work.

But she closed her eyes and swayed in rhythm with him.

Chapter 14

Derick sat in Jay Whitney's kitchen, staring at his hands on the dining table. Jay sat next to him, looking at his nephew with concern. Derick had told him what had happened and what he wanted to do next.

Jay leaned forward. "She'd wait for you, you know."

Derick gave a small shake of his head. "It's not her I'm worried about. It's anyone else out there with eyes, hands, and a heart. She'd be . . . lonely." He turned to his uncle. "I don't want to leave her alone."

"She's been alone."

Derick hit his palm on the table. "I *know*. She doesn't deserve that."

"That's not what I meant."

Derick sighed. "I know."

"You want me to talk to Keith?" After all, Jay had played a part in introducing the kids. And he didn't fear Keith Embry. He just didn't have much respect for the man. He feared what he might say to him.

Derick shook his head.

Jay rubbed his chin. "You've prayed about this." It was not a question.

Derick nodded. "And fasted." His hands came up to his face and pushed up through his hair.

"And what's your answer?"

Derick slowly shook his head. His hands came back to his eyes. "I have to try, Jay. I have to try."

Jay nodded. He put his hand solidly on Derick's shoulder and got up to put his breakfast dishes in the sink.

* * *

Keith stood next to his desk instead of sitting down.

Derick remained standing as well. "Thank you for seeing me, sir."

Keith put one hand, knuckles down, on the desktop. "What is it you want?" His voice brimmed with restrained malice.

"I think you know, sir."

Keith shivered.

Derick continued. "Alisen is unhappy. I would like to change that, but I need your help."

"You think this is *my* fault?"

Derick looked at him steadily. "I think I know what would make her happy."

"You think you know my daughter? You've known her for three months."

"Yes, sir." He wanted to say it felt like an eternity, but that probably wouldn't help here. "I know her better than some though."

His words came out a little more pointed than he'd intended. That probably wasn't going to help either.

Keith's tan face blazed. "I am trying to rebuild a relationship with my daughter that I threw away when her mother died." The tremor in his voice strengthened. He drew himself up. "I am trying to give her the best opportunities, the best situation, the best of *everything*, and I can do that *now*." His eyes were fierce. "Can you say that?"

Derick moved a fraction of an inch. "Maybe not now."

A smug look crossed Keith's face.

"But I will. And I can make her happy now."

Keith made a sound of disgust.

"I love her, sir. Doesn't that count for something?"

"Funny kind of love, stealing away her sense of direction, filling her mind with confusion."

"She's only confused about you. She knows what she wants for herself."

"She knows? *She knows?* She's barely nineteen years old. She doesn't know what she wants, except to listen to your fanatic drivel and follow you into some God-forsaken religion, worshipping the ground you walk on, and forgetting everything she came from."

Derick rocked back.

Keith continued, his lips twisting around the words. "She doesn't know that this *infatuation* will fizzle out after a few weeks away from you and all your attention and careful plans. You have nothing to back it up with, no career, no money. Nothing!"

Despite his growing anger, Derick countered carefully. "I care about her. I have been there for her. I have listened to her." Derick took a step forward. "She has wanted you in her life. You don't know what it's done to her all these years. You just see that maybe it's too late, and now you're grasping." Derick held Keith's gaze, feeling the tension from the man buzz like electricity through a hotwire. He proceeded with caution. "Don't you see? Alisen lost two parents when her mother died." The look of bafflement on Keith's face frustrated him. "All these years, you *chose* this. She just wants to be happy. Why can't you see she's happy?"

Keith laughed derisively. "All I see is your attempt to manipulate and control my daughter."

Derick's control burst at the man's hypocrisy. How could Alisen have stood this for so long? "I *love* your daughter. And the words *manipulate* and *control* have nothing to do with love. But I wouldn't expect you to understand that, sir."

The two men stared each other down as Keith's eyes filled with hate then anger.

Keith clenched his fists, breathing heavily. "I won't let you take her from me. I *won't*!" He stepped toward Derick, both hands reaching for the front of his shirt. His fists balled up, and he shoved Derick back against the wall.

Derick grabbed Keith's hands, and they grappled there, muscles taut, Keith grimacing at Derick and Derick strong but bewildered.

Keith managed to get out through clenched teeth, "You can't give her *anything*. Get out of my house."

Derick suppressed his urge to drive Keith into the ground. "I can give her everything worth having. Everything she needs." Keith shoved at Derick, but Derick held firm. "I've asked her to marry me. She's said yes."

Keith's expression shifted. Dread covered his features. He dropped back and felt behind him. He leaned at an odd angle against the back of a chair, his mouth hanging open.

Derick dropped his hands. He hung his head. How had this happened? He turned to leave, but a movement caught his eye. He looked up to see Alisen standing in the open doorway, grabbing the frame. Her expression looked as though she were being ripped in two, looking back and forth between the huddled figure of her father and Derick's defeated posture.

"Alisen." Her father's whisper was jagged. He swallowed as her eyes stayed on his. "Is that true?"

She nodded, stunned, her hand absently going to the ring around her finger as if to protect it. His eyes followed and narrowed when he saw the gold band.

He stood, his chest rising, his jaw clenching.

"If you do this, you will have no orchard."

Her eyes widened in fear.

"If you do this, you will have no place here."

Derick turned to Keith, stunned.

"If you do this, you will have no father. You will have no sisters."

Alisen slowly shook her head.

"You will have no reminders of your mother."

Derick whipped his head around to Alisen then back to Keith. "You have no right! She's an adult. You have no right!" Even as he said the words, he knew they were feeble against her father's. "Alisen, he can't do that."

Keith ignored him, looking at his horrified daughter. "You will have no home."

Derick lunged at Alisen as she buckled. He caught her in his arms and held her close. She looked at him in disbelief and pain. He turned to Keith.

"How could you do that?" He didn't understand. He had never been a part of anything like this. He had sorely underestimated Keith Embry.

Alisen would leave the orchard to come with him. She'd said so. But would she detach herself from her mother's family? From the father she'd just barely found again?

Derick looked back at Alisen, who was turning away now, and her expression surprised him. It was a look of suffering shame.

Compassion flooded him, and he lifted her gently to stand. He supported her out the door and cradled her next to him. She kept her head down and away. They passed through the living room and were about to head downstairs. He stopped.

"Alisen?" Elizabeth stood dripping wet in a towel.

Was she ever fully clothed?

Elizabeth looked at Derick then back to her sister. "What's going on?"

Alisen just shook her head, the shame in her posture increasing.

Derick continued with Alisen past Elizabeth, down the stairs, and out the front door. He headed in the direction of his car, parked near the fountain that bubbled and splashed as if the world hadn't just been turned upside down. Alisen came willingly, matching her footsteps with his, but when he moved to open her door, she stepped away and put a hand on his arm. Her eyes looked past him.

"No, Derick." Her voice was small, transparent, tired.

He froze.

"I need . . . I need to be alone."

He couldn't move. "This is my fault," he said softly. "I knew what I was asking of you. But I didn't know—I had no idea he would . . ." He looked up at the house.

She closed her eyes. "Please, Derick," she whispered. She let go of his arm and turned toward the orchard.

"Alisen."

She kept walking, waving him away with her hand.

He fought every compulsion to go after her.

* * *

Opening the door wide, Rachel greeted her niece with a hug. Alisen slumped into her arms.

"Rachel—" She couldn't finish.

"I know, honey, I know. Your father called. He was very upset. I'm afraid I only got his version though." She pushed Alisen gently away and looked into her eyes expectantly.

Alisen looked down and shuddered. Rachel had never seen Alisen look so old. Rachel wrapped an arm around her and led her to the sofa. Alisen stared for a few moments. Rachel imagined she was replaying the scene in her head, and from the look of grief that passed over her face, Rachel knew it wasn't a happy ending.

Rachel listened quietly. Alisen started at finding Derick in the orchard when they had arrived home and ended when she approached the open door to the den, drawn by the men's raised voices, listening, helpless. She could barely get through what happened afterward.

Rachel drew Alisen in and allowed her to exhaust the remaining emotions from the scene she had just relived. Alisen wept softly, then it grew into gasping sobs. She quieted, then she let out a strangled cry and looked up at the ceiling with her hands held out. Her face crumpled, and she leaned back into her aunt. Finally, she wiped the hair away from her face. Rachel was ready with a tissue.

"What do I do?" she asked, her voice high with emotion. She blew her nose.

Rachel pursed her lips, thinking. She had been thinking for quite a while. "Your father is having a rough time right now."

Alisen threw her arms out in frustration.

"I know you know that." She rethought. "What I mean is, your announcement was a shock. It's a shock to *me*."

"Announcement? We barely got to the engagement. Derick went to him to ask for his blessing. He couldn't even get it out until my *father* tried to—" The expression of shame returned.

"I know, I know. But, honey, right after the trip? He had barely unpacked. You should have heard him. He sounded wretched."

Alisen grimaced and put her face in her hands.

"I really thought I might have to get off the phone to call the paramedics."

Alisen groaned and spoke through her hands. "Why does it have to be so hard?"

Rachel rubbed her back. "Your first real love always is."

Alisen kept her face in her hands, so Rachel continued carefully.

"I remember my first real love."

Alisen brought her head up.

"It was like we were the only two people on earth. We spent every waking moment together. That was quite a summer." She reached over and rearranged one of Alisen's curls. "He promised me everything." She sighed. "My parents weren't too pleased."

"What happened?" Alisen asked.

"He left for a college out of state. I still had a year of high school." She looked off as she remembered. "Of course, he met someone." She turned and smiled softly at Alisen. "It broke my heart. I thought I would die." She inhaled deeply. "But then I met someone else too, and it wasn't as hard. And I went to college and experienced wonderful things. I got to learn a lot about myself and the world. More of what I wanted out of it." Her smile widened. "Later, I met the love of my life." She looked off again. "I wouldn't trade that for anything."

"Did you ever hear anything about the first boy?"

Rachel nodded her head. "He went to med school, married, became a very successful doctor."

Alisen frowned.

Rachel leaned into her. "But I was happy. I had gone on, grown up, become somebody. And," she shrugged, "I was happy that he was happy."

Alisen turned to stare out the window.

Rachel was quiet for a moment. Then she said, "I have been angry with Keith, what he did to you, all these years. But I see some merit in what he's been trying to do the last few months." She placed a hand on Alisen's shoulder. "I had no idea his feelings still ran so deep over Anne's death. He's always so reserved and cool. The guilt he's been carrying around. I can't imagine."

Alisen remained quiet. Rachel tipped her head to catch her eye.

"He may be going about things the wrong way, but do you think leaving him now, after how far he's come, would be the right thing? For either of you?" She purposely left Derick's name out of the conversation.

Alisen blinked at her. She looked down at her hands in her lap, palms up and open as if she were waiting to receive something. Then she raised her eyes again to the ceiling. She took a small calming breath.

* * *

Meet me at the river. I'll be waiting.

"Aaugh." He winced and shook his head. He'd spent all day agonizing over what she was thinking, what would happen next, wanting to call but knowing she would when she was ready. He kept replaying those final moments in the den and the broken look on her face as she'd turned away from him to walk into the orchard. He kept remembering the way she had kissed him when he had given her the ring and the threats her father had made when he saw it.

His stomach felt like it was full of rocks.

He turned the Camry onto the short road leading to the trailhead. He saw her truck and parked behind it. He couldn't swallow. He got out, and there she was.

He took a step to her, arms held out, and she came to him. He held her tightly, one hand running over her hair. "I'm so sorry. I'm so, so sorry."

She nodded her head. "I know." Her eyes came up to his. Her expression was resolute, determined. He didn't know what that meant. His hand came up to stroke her cheek, and she closed her eyes, her look pained. Then he pulled up her chin and kissed her, and the resolution was gone.

Her grip around his shoulders gradually tightened, and her mouth became fierce on his. He drew his arms tightly around her and lost himself in her intensity, his heart pounding. Then her grip on him began to ease, her lips softening. She kissed him gently now, their breathing mixed together.

Then she eased away, looking down at her hands. There were traces of tears on both of her cheeks. He watched her slowly move her fingers to the ring and pull it off. He watched her as she silently read the inscription one more time and then reached down to place the ring in his pocket. Another tear tracked down her face. He couldn't move. He couldn't breathe. Everything was stuck, caught. He felt like he was choking.

She reached behind her and pulled his hands apart. His eyes began to sting, and she became a blur, but he quickly blinked it away because she was all he wanted to see.

She stepped away, holding his forearms a moment, looking at them like they were the last thing to keep her afloat in a stormy sea.

Then she took a small breath and released him, stepped to her truck, got in, and closed the door. He was there at the open window, his hands holding on to the truck, and she turned to see the pleading in his eyes.

"Alisen, what are you doing?" It was barely a whisper.

Their eyes locked, and the depths there momentarily drove his sudden dread away. He could see her laughing, the way her mouth curved when she spoke, the light inside her, the electricity in her eyes only for him, the look of belonging. But she pushed it away and closed her eyes to his. The choking feeling returned.

Sadness engulfed him. "What are you doing?" he repeated, his voice tortured.

Her eyes remained closed, and the pained look came back. She turned to the steering wheel and started the ignition, scarcely opening her eyes. "Forgetting myself." She shifted gears and pulled way.

Stunned, he let go of the door.

Derick stood there as he scrambled to process her words. He saw her hand come up to her mouth as she turned through the trees onto the main road, and then she was gone.

He reached into his pocket, eyes still on the place she'd left empty, and wrapped his hand around the ring.

Chapter 15

December

Big fat snowflakes fell down at an angle, filling up any space that would hold them. Alisen pulled her hood up over her head. She slammed the truck door shut, and a pile of snow dropped down the window, leaving a clean trail in the dirty slush splashed all over the side. She shoved her gloved hands deep into her pockets and tromped to the curb, ducking under the eaves of the grocery store.

The glass door swung open, and she went in, throwing off her hood and brushing flakes off her shoulders. She grabbed the nearest cart and pushed it forward, almost running over the person she hadn't seen standing there.

"Jay." She swallowed, and her pulse quickened, but his smile brought out hers.

"Hey, sweetie. It's good to see you." The smile was casual, but his eyes were probing.

"What are you doing here?" Alisen looked around as if she would get her answer that way.

"Oh, I had a meeting up here and remembered we were out of a few things I like to have around the house."

She grinned. He held a pack of toilet paper, a box of Ding-Dongs, and a copy of *Football Digest.*

Then she sobered and looked down, feeling her face getting hot.

"How are you?" he quietly asked.

She looked to her right as if interested in the people checking out their groceries.

"Good." She nodded her head rhythmically. "School is good. I'm learning a lot." She looked back at Jay. He hid his concern but not very well.

"How're things at home?"

She kept nodding. "Quiet. Good though." She thought of the morning's breakfast, she and her father sitting at the table as the snow fell on the lake, while Amanda scrambled around frantically getting ready for school.

"You ready for this next season, all on your own?" Jay had completed his time overseeing the orchard. "If you need me, I'm just at the end of the lake."

She smiled. He'd said that a dozen times already. But she knew she couldn't rely on him as she had before. She was the orchard boss. And he was a reminder.

"Thanks, Jay."

"We miss you."

Her throat swelled up. She squinted her eyes and just kept nodding.

He suddenly handed her the package of toilet paper, and though it caught her off guard, she took it from him. He reached into the inside pocket of his jacket and pulled out a wrinkled envelope with red and blue stripes around the edges.

Her heart plummeted as he took back the toilet paper and slapped the letter into her open glove.

"That came awhile go, and I've been carrying it around in case I ran into you. I had strict orders to put it into your hands."

She made to hand it back to him. "But I—"

"Nope, no returns. It's up to you what you do with it."

"Jay, I . . ." Her throat was thick. She shook her head.

He smiled. "I don't think there's anything too bad in there."

She gave him a small smile.

"Aww, sweetie, I hope you get everything you're looking for."

She knew he meant it. He winked at her, and she gave him a quick hug.

"If you need anything, you call me," he said as she released him.

She nodded.

He turned to make his way to the checkout line, looked back, and waved his toilet paper at her. She allowed a laugh to escape.

She looked down at the letter. Derick's face flashed before her eyes, smiling and golden. She'd been holding her breath but now exhaled slowly and shoved the cart back. She went back out into the snow, throwing her hood back on, and wrenched open the truck door.

She stared at the letter as the snow piled up on her windshield.

She pulled off her gloves and tore along the top edge of the envelope. She hesitated then carefully pulled out the paper. It was one thin sheet. She unfolded it, her hands annoyingly shaky.

Alisen,

I don't know where I'll be when you read this. It doesn't matter. What does matter is this: You know the truth.

Regardless of everything, don't deny the truths you know.

They'll lead you home.

Derick

Alisen read it again. Then she stared out at the white, not really seeing.

Chapter 16

May 2005

Rachel and Keith sat in the living room, waiting for the girls to join them for dinner out. Everyone was home for once, and the warm weather had finally arrived after a long, wet spring.

Keith checked his wallet in front of the mirror. He put it in his back pocket then ran his fingers up to smooth his hair, checking for more grays. He furrowed his brow. Then he straightened, patted his firm stomach, and turned to Rachel.

"How was your trip?"

Rachel put her book down in her lap. "It was heavenly. A nice break from that cold spring weather. I can see why people retire there. I may make Florida a habit."

Keith nodded absently.

"How were things with the girls while I was away? How is Alisen?"

Keith raised an eyebrow. He knew what she was asking. "The girls are busy. Elizabeth has been home for a week now. In her room a lot, but she seems to be moving up in her work, so she tells me. She's mentioned taking an apartment in New York. Amanda keeps busy, as usual, with horses, friends, and school, in that order." He smiled wryly.

Rachel laughed softly.

"Alisen has been, uh, quiet, good, I think, not as . . ." He thought for the word. "Emotional."

"Good." Rachel scrutinized her brother-in-law. "I knew she'd pull through."

Keith nodded slowly, placing his hands in his pockets. "Yes, yes you did." He walked over to the window and stared out at the lake. "I, uh, never really thanked you for your help there."

"It was the least I could do, what with you throwing temper tantrums all over the place."

Keith threw her a wary glance. But then he chuckled. "Yes, but it worked. That route seemed to be the means to the end." He turned away from the window and glanced toward the den. "It didn't hurt that he was so bent on marrying her. It forced her hand."

"Yes, well, as long as it was the end. Things got a little dramatic there, thanks to you, but he didn't deserve her, and she is too young." Rachel folded her arms, and Keith checked his watch as he took out his cell phone to call Amanda once more.

* * *

Around the corner, at the top of the back stairs, Alisen stood, her back up against the wall. She was breathing quickly, trying not to make a sound. Had she heard them correctly? She wasn't sure. Was she reading too far into this conversation? Her mind went back to the memories she had pushed aside, retracing conversations, proddings, persuasions, all playing on her emotions, all for . . . for what *they* thought she should or shouldn't have? What *they* thought would make her happy? Wasn't this about her father and healing him?

She tried to shove all of the images away.

But one image lingered: Derick's look of absolute wonder as they sat sharing a heartbeat in front of the fountain, his warm eyes sinking into her own.

His words echoed in her ears. *Alisen Embry, I love you.*

Silently, she made her way back down the stairs. As soon as she was out of earshot, she bolted for the door. Alisen nearly stepped on Jane as she ran out toward the water. She stopped abruptly. Not there.

She turned and ran up to the orchard, winding around, away from where he had asked her, away from the path they'd walked hand in hand. She finally came to rest near the top of the hill, off to the north side, at one of the older trees. Without really knowing why, she grabbed the branches and pulled herself into them. When she could see over the top, she stopped, leaning her legs against the bigger limbs. She tried to catch her breath and think clearly.

I broke his heart.

He's gone.

I was swayed.

And he never hurt me.

Alisen's phone rang. She pulled it from her pocket, letting it ring twice more as she gathered herself.

"Hello?"

"Alisen? Are you coming down? We're about ready to go."

"I, uh, don't think I'm going to be able to make it this time." She hastily wiped tears. "There are some things up here I really should get done before it gets any later in the season." She held her stomach.

Her father paused. "Do you need any help?"

Alisen closed her eyes. He had never offered before.

"No, Dad, no. I'll be fine. It's just some busy work. When I get through this, I'll be more freed up, and then we'll go out."

"Well, if you're sure."

"Mm-hm."

"All right. We'll see you later, then."

She put the phone away.

When I get through this, I'll be more freed up.

Alisen knew things would not be the same. They could not be the same as they had been the last few months. She would stay here at the orchard. She would be her father's reminder of her mother. She would love her aunt.

But she was changed. She knew her own mind.

She knew Derick was her missing piece. She knew she had never been happier than when she was with him. She knew nobody else would come close to filling the empty space beside her.

And she knew she would never again receive Derick's promise or his trust or his love.

Rachel was right. He didn't deserve her.

She sat up in the cherry tree as the sun went down on the lake, and mourned.

* * *

"Hello, Jay?"

"Alisen?" Jay felt that emotional tug he now felt every time he and Alisen met or spoke.

"Yes."

"Is everything all right?"

"I need your help with something."

"Is there a problem at the orchard?" They'd had a late frost, not too bad, but he had lost a few younger trees. "Did you lose any buds?"

"No, I think we're all right up here. It should be a good bloom, just late." She paused.

He waited.

"I want you to do something for me."

"Anything, sweetie."

"I miss the Church. I want that."

He paused. "That's fine, honey. Whatever I can do."

"But I need you to promise me something too."

"Whatever you need, Alisen."

Part 3

Chapter 17

Present Day, June 2008

"I, uh, wanted to let you know that this idea was a good one."

Alisen looked up, surprised. "Thanks, Dad."

Keith nodded and looked away over the lake as he leaned against the low wall surrounding the veranda. "I guess that business degree is good for something."

She half smiled and nodded. It had been two months since the meeting with John Shepherd, and they were moving out. To everyone's relief, her father liked the condo in Kalispell. He'd sold the cars and the boat and bought a used sporty Mazda and a golf cart.

He looked at her and swallowed. "It was a good choice, you staying."

She clenched her jaw and looked at the water. "I've learned a lot. I think you have too, Dad."

He paused. She watched his fingers tap the stucco. "I don't know what I would have done if you'd gone."

She searched his face, wanting to believe. And she did, but not any more than her heart and mind told her to. Her father was healing. Their relationship was still strained, but he smiled more easily with her, and Alisen finally felt some respect from him. But the betrayal of her trust, the manipulation of her feelings, the threats, would always be a barrier between them. Alisen could see no way around that. Not even after four years.

She cleared her head of that and smiled. "Take care of yourself, Dad. I'll see you in a few weeks."

"Are you sure you'll have enough help finishing up here?"

She nodded. "The Michaels family is coming over."

He gave her a dubious look. "Are they bringing the twins?"

"I hope so." She folded her arms. She was counting on the rambunctious duo to help lighten the mood of the occasion.

"Well, good luck."

"Thanks."

He accepted her quick hug then picked up the last of his bags. He looked out at the lake, and she could only guess his thoughts. With a resigned nod, he turned and headed for the condo.

The boat was gone, the garage bays sat empty, and the house was left sparsely furnished. A pale space remained on her wall where the cherry painting had hung. It was now packed, along with the nail, in Alisen's trunk.

She checked her watch and grabbed a box of books then made her way down through the living room and the wide stairway to the open front door. After setting her things in the back of her truck, she put her hands on her hips and looked out at the lake. A gust of wind threatened to ply her hair from its ponytail.

It was such an odd sensation, making this house over for someone else. Every view she took in, she now looked at from the point of view of a stranger. What would Hannah Crawford think as she took in the orchard on an early autumn morning, leaves the color of fire laced with frost? As she sat on the veranda in July, watching the sunset reflecting on the water? As she watched a storm roll in over the lake, snow mounding along the shoreline and on every tree?

Alisen tried not to think of the possibility of Derick's presence in the house after all this time. Why would he come here? But she couldn't help remembering what he had said about his relationship with his sister. Would Derick Whitney come here, to her father's house?

Jay had given Alisen only two pieces of news concerning his nephew. Once, they had run into each other again in town. He and his family had just returned from Missoula, and he let it slip that Derick had earned his master's degree. After that information was out, he went ahead and told her Derick had already formed the basis of his company, utilizing the contacts he had made while conducting his research and his mission. It was unsettling, the pride she felt at this news, as if she'd had anything to do with it. Then, when she'd called Jay for an opinion about new machinery for the orchard, she was sure the news that Derick was not married yet was not a slip. After composing herself from the unexpected rush of emotion that news wrenched from her, she asked Jay not to give her any more news unless it was that Derick *was* married. She didn't need to hear anything else. Jay felt bad but tried to understand. He had not mentioned Derick in over a year.

A sudden push against Alisen's legs, accompanied by loud purring, brought her out of her thoughts.

"All this change, Jane." She had asked John to ask the Crawfords if they would mind a semioutdoor cat at the house. They said they would not mind and requested instructions for Jane's needs. It was a relief to Alisen that Jane would still have her home.

"At least I'll be able to see you in the orchard." Alisen reached down to rub the cat's neck. "If you do see him," Jane looked up, and Alisen whispered, "go easy on him."

The sound of cars floated down from the road, and a light-blue Honda pulled into the circular drive, followed by a white Suburban. Alisen smiled, straightening up. Two young people tumbled out of the small car, and their parents and younger siblings piled out of the SUV.

Dr. Michaels had moved his family from California to Montana three and a half years ago. The valley offered a quieter pace than LA. He'd bought a small dental practice in town, and it had grown rapidly. His reputation for being quick, thorough, and, perhaps most importantly, painless, fueled his popularity. He was now ready to take on a partner, and Amanda's husband, Greg Stewart, had gotten the job.

The family had grown in two parts. Lindsay and her brother, Justin, were the oldest.

"We heard you needed some help." Lindsay Michaels smiled. She was a pretty girl, just twenty, the same age as Amanda. She reminded Alisen of a young colt, leggy and spirited. Her enthusiasm rubbed off on those around her like pollen from a sunflower.

Lindsay pulled her straight, pale-blonde hair back into a ponytail, her sky-blue eyes laughing. "We brought lots of muscle."

Alisen grinned as Lindsay's five-year-old twin brothers ran past, grimacing as they flexed their muscles. These two were the second part of the Michaels brood. Their blond hair stuck straight up in identical crops, and the differing freckle patterns smattering their faces gave Alisen no help in telling them apart. To Alisen, they were Alex and Jack, seven minutes apart. Alex was the flirt.

Lindsay grabbed them by their shirts. "Tell us where to start, and I'll put these little terrors to work." Lindsay filled out the role as boss quite naturally.

Alisen looked at the twins.

"Amanda told me there are some old Game Boys and a pile of game cartridges in her room." Her eyes as grew wide as theirs did. "She just didn't know what to do with them." She shrugged helplessly. "Do you think you could sort them out, see which ones still work, and pack them up for her?"

They grinned and nodded and took off into the house. "Stay in Amanda's room, boys," Lindsay called after them. She looked questioningly at Alisen.

"They'll be fine. I put in fresh batteries. They'll be playing for a while."

"Brilliant."

"Hi, Alisen." Justin stood there awkwardly, a grin on his face. He had grown several inches over the school year, and his voice was just beginning to change, a fact he was well aware of. His darker features were opposite to Lindsay's and his little brothers'. He had his mother's olive-green eyes and nearly black hair.

"Hello, Justin." Alisen smiled as the color rose in his face. "Thanks for coming. My room is full of boxes that need to come down. Could you help with that?"

His shy smile grew. "Where's your room?"

She pointed into the house. "Up these stairs, then up some more after you go through the living room, then down a hall, and—"

"Oh, here, I'll show you," Lindsay spoke up. She started past Justin, tapping him on the face. "Stop gawkin', squirt."

Justin dropped his eyes to the ground, still smiling, and climbed the stairs two at a time to catch up to his sister.

"Stephen, come look at this garden. This is what I was talking about for the beds in front of the dining room windows." Giovanna Michaels motioned for her husband to join her along the walk and waved to Alisen. "We'll just be a minute. I was just telling him about this garden the other day."

Giovanna, or Gia, as she had insisted Alisen call her when they first met, loved the Embry home. She said it reminded her of her own Italy, where she had lived as a girl. The Michaels property was situated on one of the smaller lakes in the area, and they'd built a lovely home there, plus a smaller cabin they were now renting to Greg and Amanda. Gia's garden was a beautiful work in progress.

The home also happened to be in Alisen's ward boundaries. When they'd met at the Church Christmas party, both as newcomers, she'd been taken in nearly as one of their own, and Gia had been Alisen's visiting teacher ever since. The invitation for Alisen to spend her first few weeks at Currant Lake after the Crawfords moved in came without hesitation. With Rachel still in Florida, Alisen was happy to accept.

After the quick garden tour, Stephen walked toward Alisen with a smile. Here was the sure cause of the fair genes overriding the Italian. Stephen stood six foot five inches and sported the same pale-blonde hair, ruddy complexion, freckles, and light-blue eyes as the boys. He even had the same haircut.

"You ready for us, Alisen?"

"You bet. There shouldn't be too much to do." Alisen looked around the garden and sighed.

Gia rested her hand on Alisen's arm. "At least you'll be able to come whenever you want." Gia's calm, laid-back demeanor always created a feeling of assurance that Alisen appreciated.

"I know, but . . . I won't feel at home."

"No, I guess not." Her eyes widened. "But you can feel like the landlord."

Alisen blew out a laugh and shook her head. "So, Amanda didn't come?"

"She isn't feeling well. She thinks she may have eaten something bad. She sends her apologies." Alisen loved the faint hint of Gia's Italian accent. She glanced around the gardens again. "I must make friends with the Crawfords, if only so I can still come here to visit."

Alisen knew Gia would gladly make friends with anyone, no matter where they lived. Gia lowered her voice and looked at Alisen. "Personally, I don't think it was something Amanda ate." She raised her eyebrows.

Alisen looked confused then gasped. "You mean, you think Amanda is . . ."

Gia nodded again knowingly. "She has been so cranky, so tired, so hungry, so sick." She smiled. "We have heard it all."

"Hm. I wonder if Amanda has considered that possibility." Alisen said this with mixed emotions. She was still getting used to the idea of her little sister being a wife. But a mom?

Gia changed the subject. "How is your aunt?" They climbed the stairs as they headed into the house.

"I think she's having a great time. She loves her Florida friends. Sometimes I think if it wasn't for us, she would move there permanently."

Rachel had made a biannual pilgrimage to the Sunshine State for the last three years. She'd left a week ago for her latest trip.

"Well, lucky us that we get you first," Gia said as she linked her arm with Alisen's.

Alisen smiled.

They reached the top of the stairs, and she looked around at the remaining boxes. "We just need to get my things out of—"

Justin came down the stairs, loaded with luggage. He had straps around his shoulders and bags protruding from every direction. He even had a padded strap around his mouth. Lindsay came bouncing down after him with a box.

"I helped him a little," Lindsay said with a smirk.

Justin rolled his eyes.

Alisen finished her sentence with a grin. "And we'll need to clean the kitchen, bathrooms, and floors. All of the windows have been done."

Gia surveyed every lake-facing floor-to-ceiling window and French door on all three levels. "Thank heavens," she said.

Chapter 18

A Week Later

Alisen sat on the front porch of the log cabin. The evening frogs were just tuning their instruments. Currant Lake was much smaller than Flathead, a mile wide, if that, and almost perfectly round. Lily pads, not yet blooming, grew in big clumps along the shoreline. Several old homes and cabins nestled here and there among the trees surrounding the lake, and docks in all conditions jutted out into the water. Rope swings rigged to long lodgepole pine trunks hung out over the deeper water like giant fishing poles stuck in the ground waiting for a bite. Someone had built a floating dock out toward the center of the lake. The mountains rose behind to the south, beyond the woods.

The last few summers on the big lake had been full of reminders for Alisen, and she hoped that this busy, cheerful family and serene atmosphere would help distract her from the underlying pain she tried so hard to avoid. Amanda too was unaware that Derick had been such a part of Alisen's life for one summer, understanding only that Alisen had had a boyfriend and that they'd broken up and her father had been happy to see it end. Alisen was grateful for her sister's ignorance. Though time had passed and she couldn't wish for anything from him, Alisen's feelings for Derick had not faded. She wondered if they ever would.

A few men had tried, and she had tried to see them without Derick's shadow lingering behind them. She'd been frustrated more than a few times, angry that she couldn't shake it. Aunt Rachel had attempted to steer her in the direction of "handsome, eligible" young men, but Alisen would not be steered. She had given her heart, it had been cherished, and she had taken it back—only to have it used and toyed with by her own family.

"It will be so good to have you here." Amanda came out the front door and sat down next to Alisen on the wide front-porch steps. She sighed and leaned her head on Alisen's shoulder. "Ugh. You can take care of me."

Alisen smiled at her sister's dramatics and brought an arm around her shoulders. During Alisen's first week at the cabin, she had urged Amanda to make a doctor's appointment, and it had been confirmed—Amanda and Greg were going to have a baby. Alisen shared in their joy, reassured her sister that this happened all the time, and pushed down the tiny knot of envy that kinked itself every once in a while. The idea of being an aunt thrilled her.

Laughter reached her, and she looked in the direction of their neighbors. The Michaels home was about a quarter of a mile east of the guesthouse. A wide path strewn with pine needles lay between both houses. The family home was also log but more contemporary in design, with large, angled windows covering most of the lake side of the house. The gently sloping lawn led down into the lily pads, and a low dock stretched out long to find deeper water.

The older kids had set up a badminton net and were volleying the birdie over the net while the twins ran back and forth under it.

"Jack, you can't do that. Come here, you little monkey," Justin said.

Squeals of delight played across the water as Justin chased after Jack, one of the twins, with his racquet. When he finally caught him, he retrieved the stolen birdie, and they resumed their game.

"Hey, Alisen!" Lindsay had her hands cupped around her mouth. "Come play with us!"

Amanda sat up and looked over. "Can I play too?"

"C'mon." Alisen pulled her sister up and turned to the screen door. "Greg, do you want to come?"

Greg sat reading the newspaper in the front room, his feet propped up on an ottoman. "Mmm. Maybe later."

The girls hopped down the porch steps without him and walked along the path, veering off toward the lawn and the game. They found more racquets, and each took a side, Amanda joining Justin, Alisen teaming up with Lindsay.

They were just getting a good volley going when Gia poked her head out the door. "Alex Lorenzo Michaels, don't you dare." Her finger pointed behind Alisen.

Alisen turned around to see Alex frozen in place, a racquet poised and aimed right for her bottom. The look of devilish glee on his face made it hard not to laugh, but she tried to maintain a stern image. "Oh, you weren't going to hit me with that, were you?"

Alex's eyes got big, and he shook his head slowly from side to side, still wearing his wicked grin. Then his smile opened, and he nodded. Alisen dropped her racquet and swooped in, grabbing him around the waist, setting him on the ground, and tickling his sides until his tormented laughter turned into giggled begging. "Stop. Okay, okay, I'm sorry. Stop, please!"

Alisen sat back, and Alex got up, abandoning the racquet and running after his brother, who was applauding the whole scene. Alisen took one last swipe at Alex as the two boys ran past, giggling.

"We better watch out for that one," Lindsay said. "He's worse than Justin."

"Hey." Justin hit the birdie at his sister.

It felt good to laugh. Nothing had seemed funny for a very long time, but being around this family, it was inevitable. Alisen was drawn to the family's laughter like a bee to nectar.

Gia came out, wiping her hands on her jeans. "I just got off the phone with Hannah Crawford. They're coming to dinner on Sunday." She motioned to Amanda and Alisen. "You girls and Greg are invited too."

"Oh, thank you, Gia." Amanda grinned at Alisen. "I love it when Gia has company."

Alisen smiled. She'd met the Crawfords yesterday in the orchard. Earlier in the week they were still moving in, so she hadn't bothered them and they hadn't had time to come find her. But yesterday morning, Hannah had walked up through the orchard with a tray of cinnamon rolls. The orchard workers had gathered to meet the new tenant and dig into breakfast. Alisen hung back, allowing everyone else to pass the rolls around.

At first, Alisen had not seen, beyond coloring, much of a similarity between this woman and her younger brother. She was shorter than Alisen and soft around the edges. Silver highlights traced Hannah's blonde hair, and her short layers flipped out at the ends. But then Hannah had turned to look at Alisen.

She had the same startling eyes as Derick, golden browns and green. Alisen had gaped for a few seconds but then had swallowed and introduced herself. She wondered if Hannah knew, and if she did, Alisen wondered if there would be any resentment toward her. But Hannah's smile was genuine, and if she did know any history between Alisen and her brother, she didn't show it.

Alisen had mixed feelings about this: relief, of course, but also confusion at why Derick wouldn't have told her. Hadn't it been important enough to share with his sister? It had been a quick engagement, and Hannah had been out of the country with her husband at the time. Maybe he would have told her, but then after . . . he just hadn't. Maybe time had worked on him the way it hadn't on her.

Marcus came up later in the day to say hello. He was a sturdy man, tanned and muscular, reminding Alisen of a wrestler. His hair was thinning and cut close all around, and he made up for the loss with a tuft of chest hair at his collar.

"You aren't single, are you?" His eyes twinkled.

"Yes, I am."

He shook his head and smiled with his steel-gray eyes and a pleasantly lined face. He offered to lend a hand where needed and asked her questions about how she went about running the place.

Alisen had to conclude after this meeting that, no, the Crawfords were not aware of how close she had come to being their sister-in-law.

"Hannah said her younger brother will be with them, so he'll be coming too."

Gia's words wrenched Alisen back to the present. "What?" The word was out before she could pull it back. Her hand came up to her cheek.

Gia turned to her. "Hannah's younger brother will be staying with them, so I invited him too."

"How much younger?" Eyes turned to Lindsay, and the focus was gratefully off Alisen.

Gia answered. "I didn't ask, but from the way Hannah spoke, I think he is quite a bit younger, no family or anything yet." She winked at Lindsay, who raised her eyebrows up and down.

Justin let out a squeaky, high-pitched, "Ooooooh."

Lindsay whacked the birdie at him. "Watch it, or I'll tell Alisen you keep a picture of her in your dresser."

"I do not. Mom!"

The twins began circling their brother, shouting, "You have a picture, you have a picture."

Alisen wasn't paying much attention to any of it. Her pounding heart had dropped to her stomach, and she looked around for a place to sit. She discreetly walked over to the slate patio in front of the door and sat down on the step, wiping her sweaty palms on her pants.

But Gia noticed. "Alisen, honey, are you okay?"

"Oh, I'm fine. Just a little tired." She took a deep breath and faked a yawn. "It's been a long week." *Long and now just a little terrifying.*

"It has, hasn't it? Emotional for you, no doubt. Why don't you come in and have some ice cream?"

At the words *ice cream*, a small stampede made its way into the house.

Chapter 19

Alisen looked out the window at the rain. The lake danced with drops coming down and bouncing up. A lone rowboat floated out on the water, someone fishing in a green raincoat and hood.

Tenacity. It was what she had lacked.

She turned from the window and threw herself on the bed. She covered her head with a pillow and moaned.

Enough. Stop beating yourself up. What's done is done.

She pulled herself around and walked to the open closet. She stared. She sat down on the edge of the bed then lay back with a flop.

What in the world was she supposed to wear? Was she even supposed to care? Was this really happening, and was she being foolish to place so much importance on this meeting? Did he even know she would be there, and would he come if he knew? She had to think he probably wouldn't. And if he did know and he came anyway, well, that opened up a whole new line of questions Alisen was afraid to ask.

First things first.

She sat back up and stared at the closet, but then her eyes pulled to the right, to her painting on the wall.

The phone rang. A few seconds later, Amanda knocked on her door. She was holding the phone, her hand over the receiver.

"Alisen, it's Gia. She's upset. They're at the emergency room."

Alisen's eyes grew wide. "What happened?"

Amanda handed her the phone.

"Gia?"

"Oh, Alisen. I'm sorry. Alex was playing on the stairs and decided to play pirate, and he jumped all the way down to the landing. He's broken his wrist."

"Oh no. How's he doing?"

"Well, they're putting him in a cast now, but, Alisen, he keeps asking for you."

"For me?"

"Yes. He keeps crying, 'I want my Alisen, I want my Alisen.' So I promised him I would call you, and he calmed down a little."

"What do you want me to do? Do you want me to come to the hospital?"

"Well, I think we'll be finished soon. But I was wondering if you could be at our place when we come home? Then we can tell him you'll be there, and he'll hold still for the doctor."

"Of course. I'd be happy to give him some attention." Then the day's events registered. "Gia, what about dinner?"

"Oh, we still have a couple of hours, and most of the preparation is done. We'll be home soon, and we can get it ready just fine. Broken bones haven't stopped us before."

"Gia, why don't you just bring him over here?"

"Really?"

"Yes. That way you can get things done without distraction. We'll just play, watch a movie. It'll be great."

"Oh, Alisen, he will love that. And so will I."

Amanda was still waiting by the door as she hung up. "Well?"

"Little Alex broke his wrist and kept asking for me." She shrugged and smiled. "So they're bringing him over here to hang out while Gia gets everything ready for dinner."

Amanda looked relieved. "So the dinner is still on?"

"Yes."

"Oh, good. I really didn't want to cook tonight. And Gia is such a great cook."

"Yes, and *Alex* will be just fine." She gave her sister a half smile.

Amanda threw her arms out. "Well, of course he'll be fine." She rolled her eyes and left the room.

Alisen's gaze came back to the closet. She sighed. Of all the choices she had to make in all of her responsibilities, why was choosing something to wear such a mind-boggling hurdle?

* * *

"Will you do this?" Alex looked up at her expectantly.

Alisen looked back at him. They had watched a movie; they'd taken turns reading some books, some more than once; and he had helped while she made cookies. They tried coloring, but Alex made a few slash marks with the crayon and then he was done. Alisen drew a funny face on his cast. Now he was handing her his Spider-Man toy with web-slinging action for the thirty-somethingth time to reload the web, usually a two-handed job.

"Aww, sweetie, I have to get ready for the dinner at your house." She had to admit, Alex had been a great distraction for her nerves.

Alex rubbed his eye with the hand holding his toy and asked once more. "Will you do this?"

"Okay, one more time. Then you watch another show while I get ready." She looked him in the eyes. "Okay?"

"Okay." He sighed deeply.

She loaded the web, sat him down on the couch, and hit the play button on the DVD player. He settled in, and she went to her room. She narrowed her eyes at her closet and grabbed a pair of gray pants and a blue blouse. As she changed, the distraction started to wear off. She looked out the window. The rain still poured outside, and someone flipped the porch lights on at the big house. She went to her mirror and was startled by her alarmed expression. She tried a different one. Now she just looked ill.

Maybe accessories would help. She rummaged through her jewelry.

She came out of her room and passed by the sofa. "Amanda, I need my earrings ba—" She stopped.

Alex remained on the couch, exactly how she had left him, only he'd fallen over sideways.

Amanda came down the hall. "What did you say?"

"Shhhhh." Alisen put her finger to her lips as she looked at Alex. "He's asleep."

"Well, you'll have to wake him up," Amanda whispered as she looked at the clock. "It's almost time to go."

Alisen looked at the peaceful little boy. "I can't wake him up; he's exhausted." She looked out the front windows at the pouring rain and the big house then back at angel Alex. "I'll just stay here."

Amanda's eyes grew big. "What?"

"*Shhhhhh.*"

"Alisen, we can just carry him over. Greg will do it."

"It's pouring outside. He's had such a long day."

"We can drive over. Do you really want to miss dinner?"

Alisen looked toward the big house again. She looked down. Then she squared her shoulders. "I don't want to wake him up. Look at him." She gestured to Alex, whose free hand suddenly flung out and hung straight over the edge of the sofa. He shuddered and sighed. "I'll just eat leftovers and read." She watched Amanda, who studied the boy, her brow furrowed. "We can't leave him, Amanda."

"I wasn't going to say that," Amanda quietly protested. "I just wanted you to come, that's all."

"I know. Thanks. But there will be other times. Besides," she stifled a yawn, "that kid wore me out." She smiled, and Amanda begrudgingly smiled back. "Tell Gia, and let her know I'm sorry, okay? Maybe Stephen can come get him after the Crawfords have gone home."

"Okay. But I'm bringing you back some food."

Alisen laughed softly and agreed to the terms. She was suddenly breathing much easier.

* * *

Alisen pulled the blanket up higher over the boy and turned the main lights off, leaving a small table lamp on in the corner. She went to her room to find the new book she'd started. Before she hit the light switch though, the lights from the big house caught her eye. She walked to the window and opened it. The smell of rain in pines hit her senses, and the air cooled her face. The inconstant drips tapping on the roof proved the rain was slowing down. She watched the big house, half in hope, half in fear of what she might see through the brightly lit windows. But she could see only vague figures moving, gesturing.

She could hear though. Whether it was the water or the night, she didn't know, but she could make out individual voices now and then. She heard a lower voice, then Gia protesting, and laughter. She heard Stephen offer more drinks then murmured responses. Someone asked a question, and Lindsay laughed; then Justin said something teasing—and then she heard it.

His laugh. It was unmistakable.

She caught her breath as her hand came up to her mouth. The tears stinging her eyes angered her.

Four years. Four years, already! And one sound of his laughter does this?

She closed the window hard, trying to calm her breathing.

She sat down on the bed, balling her hands into fists, willing herself to calm down.

"Mama." She heard a soft cry from the other room. Thoughts of herself dissolved, and she went to kneel by her little friend.

She swallowed. "Alex? Are you all right?" She stroked his hair.

His good hand came up to rub his eyes, and he reached for her. "I want my mama." He blinked a few times. "My arm hurts." He wrinkled his forehead.

"Okay, I'll call Mama. All right?"

He nodded.

She got up and went to the phone.

"Hello, Michaels residence."

"Hello, Stephen?"

"Alisen! How's the pirate?"

"He's just waking up and is asking for Gia. He says his arm hurts."

"Okay, we'll be over in a minute. Are you going to join us?"

"Oh, I don't think so. I have to be at the orchard early tomorrow, and I'm pretty beat. Thanks though."

"All right. But we've missed you tonight."

"Thanks, Stephen."

"Be over in a bit."

Alisen hung up and went back over to the sofa. Alex was sitting up, tapping his fingers on his cast. He looked up at her, and she smiled. His blond spikes stuck up even more than usual.

"Where's my mom?" He was still a little drowsy.

"They're coming to get you to take you home. Did you have fun today?"

"Mm-hm."

"Do you want to come back and play again sometime?"

He nodded. "With Jack."

"Yes, with Jack." She ruffled his hair. "Do you want a cookie?"

He nodded again. She got him a cookie and was putting some on a plate for the others when she heard footsteps on the wooden stairs up to the porch. She set the cookies by the door and went to gather up Alex from the sofa. There was a knock behind her, and the door opened. When she turned around with her oversized bundle, Greg and Stephen stood in the doorway, smiling.

She smiled back. "See, Alex? Daddy's here." Stephen moved forward to take Alex, while Greg came in with a plate wrapped in foil. As he set it on the counter and headed for the study, another figure filled the empty space in the doorway.

Alisen inhaled slowly, deeply, but could not breathe out. Her grip tightened around Alex, and she buried her nose in his hair to hide any outward appearance of the turmoil inside her at that moment.

She quickly kissed Alex's temple and whispered, "Good night, little man. No more jumping off the stairs, okay?"

He nodded, quietly munching his cookie.

Stephen took Alex out of her arms, leaving her exposed and vulnerable. She didn't know where to look, so she watched Alex, focusing on his fluorescent green cast.

"Look, Daddy," Alex said sleepily. "Alisen drew a funny face on my cast."

"So she did." Stephen turned to her. "Thanks for watching him tonight."

She was trying to find her voice to respond when Greg reentered the room, walking past them and holding a magazine open. Her eyes followed him unwillingly.

He walked straight to the door. To Derick Whitney.

"This is the one, here. Amanda wants me to get the tandem, but I have a feeling I would be going a lot by myself."

Derick looked down at the magazine and nodded, his hand rubbing his jaw.

He was the same. His sandy hair was a little longer and curled at the ends around his neck and ears. He was broader in his neck and across his chest, but he was the same. His brow as he looked down; his thick lashes; his tan, lean arms; his long fingers set on his hip. He was the same.

It was all she could do to stay in the room.

Suddenly, Greg looked up, and she blinked as his eyebrows rose. "Oh, Alisen, this is Derick Whitney. Derick, my sister-in-law, Alisen Embry."

She dragged her eyes away from Greg and met Derick's. His face was set, but he smiled faintly and nodded once. "Hey." His lips pressed together in a line. He seemed to be breathing just fine.

She couldn't read anything in his eyes, no fire, no sunlit leaves.

Derick turned to Greg. "Actually, we've met."

Greg turned to Alisen, surprised. "Is that right?"

Alisen could do nothing but nod and breathe out a small yes.

Derick looked back down at the magazine. "It was awhile ago. My uncle helped out at the orchard."

"Ah." Greg's attention was diverted.

"Daddy, I want to go home." Alex dropped his head down to his dad's neck.

"Okay, buddy, let's get going. Thanks again, Alisen. We'll make it up to you."

Alisen's fingers came up to her mouth. "Oh, I was happy to help. I, uh, made you a plate of cookies to take back."

Stephen looked down at his son. "Tell Alisen thank you."

Alex was already falling back to sleep. "Fanks, Alisen."

She whispered, "You're welcome, sweetie."

They all turned to head out the door, and Greg grabbed the cookies.

Alisen stood there, watching Derick leave, her heart pounding, her fingers still over her mouth.

Suddenly, Alex cried out, and everyone turned to look back at her. "My Spidey!"

In that brief instant, Derick had caught her watching, and their eyes locked, and she thought she saw . . . But he blinked and turned toward Alex, who stretched his good arm in the direction of the sofa.

She took two steps to the sofa to retrieve the toy. When she turned around, Derick and Greg were already making their way down the porch steps and into the darkness.

Stephen followed, Alex now holding Spidey. The screen door banged shut behind him.

She stood there for several minutes, keeping her breathing somewhat steady.

It was done. It had taken a matter of seconds.

She slowly moved through the front room, picking up DVD cases and crayons, paper and books. She arranged the pillows on the sofa and picked up a few crumbs.

She put things away in the closet and went to the kitchen. She washed out the mixing bowls and spoons, the beaters and cookie sheets. She put the foil-covered plate in the fridge then rinsed the dishcloth in soapy water and started to wipe down the counter. Her chest tightened, and everything went blurry. She kept wiping as the cry came jerking out of her. She blinked as she cleared the last crumbs, rinsed out the cloth again, and hung it up to dry.

She walked into her bedroom and shut the door behind her. She stood in the dark and saw the house lights blur and twinkle through her wet eyes, and then she went to the window and drew the curtains closed. She sat down on the bed and tipped over sideways, curling her feet up beneath her.

It was done. And Derick had shown . . . indifference.

Anything would have been better than that.

Sorrow welled up inside her and escaped in a mournful cry. He had not forgiven her. Another cry escaped. She had been weak and bending. She took in a jagged breath of air. Time had ended his feelings. He was done.

But she hadn't hoped for anything different. Had she?

Chapter 20

Alisen turned away with her clipboard. She had just greeted the beekeepers, who had arrived to maintain the boxes, and caught a glimpse of the old white pickup coming down the dirt road. It beeped twice. She sighed.

It had been three days since the night of the dinner, and she was sure Jay wasn't here to discuss mulch.

Jay parked and got out. He approached her, a cautious smile on his face, and gave her a quick hug.

"You could have warned me."

He drew back and looked at her. "You told me not to give you any news." He lowered his chin. "How're you doin'?" Hidden meanings were laced throughout the question.

She just glared at him.

He looked at the ground and kicked a big rock stuck in the damp earth.

She blew out some air. "I'm trying to be invisible. It seems to be working."

"Now, sweetie, you know I wanted to—"

"I know. But that's not the way I—No. Not that way."

Jay looked at her. Then he nodded. "If you think it's best." He lowered his voice and mumbled, "Stubborn little lady." He gave her a little hopeful smile.

She allowed a corner of her mouth to come up, and he broke into a big grin. But she couldn't hold the smile long.

She looked at the house. "He's just the same. I don't know what I expected." She dropped her head and shook it. "I'm the one who's changed. The last couple of days I've tried to find that girl I was when . . ."

Jay shook his head and started to argue. But she shrugged him off.

"He's over me, Jay." She looked back into his kind eyes. "But that's good, right? I wouldn't want him to be . . ." She trailed off.

"As miserable as you are?" he finished.

She smiled, eyes shining. She nodded.

He looked at the house then back to Alisen. "If you would just let me—"

"*No*, Jay." Her look was solemn again. "You promised."

Chapter 21

"AND YOU SHOULD HAVE HEARD his story about the African village. It was amazing. This whole village coming together for this community farm with irrigation and fencing and having fresh food for the first time in forever. Well, all his stories are amazing." Lindsay kicked her foot, sending a spray of cold water up in an arc.

The exceptionally warm spring morning had encouraged them to sit on the edge of the dock. Glacier runoff fed the small lake, and though it would warm up nicely in a few weeks, the water was still chilly enough to keep Alisen's feet in her shoes.

Tired of hiding in the orchard with Derick so close at the lake house, Alisen had taken the day off to clear her head. But it wasn't working.

"And he taught us some African words, like, hm, something for *garden* and *water*." She attempted some guttural sounds and clicks, and Alisen couldn't help smiling. Lindsay shook her head. "Well, I don't remember, but it was so cool to hear him speak it. He told us about this one village in Peru on a really steep hillside up in the Andes Mountains, and all they grew were hard little potatoes, but the way they prepared them sounded disgusting. I didn't even believe him at first."

Lindsay talked on as Alisen stared at the water, nodding and oh-ing at the appropriate times. Images of a boy in a rowboat flashed through her mind. She'd been pulled right into his dreams. Who wouldn't have been? Of course he was successful. Of course Lindsay was going on and on.

"And I just can't wait until he gets here."

Alisen pulled her eyes away from the water. "What? Who?"

Lindsay laughed. "Derick." Her face opened into a condescending smile. "I just told you he's coming for the day. Marcus and Hannah have a few days off, so we invited them to hang out with us."

"Us?"

Lindsay gave her an exasperated look. "You, me, Amanda, Greg. Greg even took off work."

"He did?"

"Mm-hm, and he never takes off work."

"I know."

"But Derick talked him into it. He is just so . . ." She sighed. "*Amazing*."

Lindsay kept using that word.

Alisen set her shoulders. "You know what? I think I'll try that."

She pulled off her shoes and swung her feet around, plunging them both into the icy water. The shock was exactly what she needed.

Lindsay grinned and kicked up more water. Alisen joined her, and they both kicked furiously until Alisen found herself smiling as she worked the water into a frenzy.

"If you keep that up, this dock'll start moving backward." The mellow voice brought their heads around.

She knew Derick had caught her smile before it had disappeared, but he turned his attention to Lindsay. "Having fun?"

Lindsay smiled up at him brightly, her hand shading her eyes. "Yes. Care to join us?"

"Thanks, but I've already had a shower today."

Lindsay laughed and stood up. Alisen pulled her feet out of the water but remained sitting, wrapping her arms around her knees and looking down the shoreline.

"Did Hannah and Marcus come?" Lindsay looked behind Derick.

"They're up at the house helping Gia with something about the garden. What about Greg?"

Lindsay turned to Alisen. "Are Amanda and Greg up yet?"

Alisen looked up. "Amanda was just eating breakfast when I left. She slept in this morning. Greg is up though." She noticed Derick didn't look at her when she spoke, but maybe that was better.

As if on cue, Greg came around the side of the guesthouse from the garage. He saw Derick and shouted a greeting. Derick raised his hand in reply.

He turned to Lindsay. "So what are we doing?" He flashed her a mischievous smile, and Alisen caught a glimpse of the creases on either side of his mouth. She had to force herself to look away.

"I thought we would go for a hike."

"Sounds good."

"C'mon. Let's round everybody up." Lindsay grabbed her shoes, and she and Derick walked up to the lawn. Lindsay turned back.

"C'mon, Alisen," she called. "You need to get Amanda."

Derick stopped and turned in her direction. She looked at the lake again then stood, grabbing her shoes.

You've got to be kidding me. Her feet didn't move.

"C'mon, Alisen, you have to come." Lindsay flung her arms out.

Alisen squinted toward the sun. She did. She had to go. It would be a beautiful, heart-wrenching day. "Okay, I'll get Amanda."

Lindsay made a little jump and clapped her hands while Derick turned to meet Greg. Alisen watched him and couldn't help but feel that he was somehow disappointed.

Well, too bad. I'm tired of hiding.

* * *

Alisen wasn't quite as sure of her decision when she realized where Lindsay was taking them to hike. She came very close to pulling off to the side of the road and turning the truck around.

"Why are you slowing?" Amanda asked as Alisen's foot came off the gas pedal.

"Oh, um, sorry." She sped back up, taking a deep breath.

"Alisen, are you all right?"

Alisen glanced at her sister. She could usually count on Amanda to be a little too self-absorbed to notice anything like a deep sigh.

"I'm good." Alisen bobbed her head and gave her a forced smile. "Maybe just a little tired."

"Well, it's good for you to have a day off." She rolled down her window, and the cool, fresh air rushed in. "You too, honey." She looked behind her at Greg. "Aren't you glad you both stayed home today?"

Alisen chuckled at the irony of her decision this morning. But she inhaled the sweet air, this time without the sigh. "Yes, Amanda." She looked at the pastures, the pine groves, and the mountains rising to the east, and she almost believed it. Greg didn't answer, but she glanced in the rearview mirror and caught him looking at his watch.

Marcus pulled off where she suspected he would. Her pulse quickened a little as she parked behind the Jeep. Alisen watched Derick out of the corner of her eye as everyone got out. He put his hands on his hips, closing his eyes briefly, then opened them and clapped his hands together, looking around in anticipation.

Alisen turned to get a small backpack out of the truck bed. *Does he feel anything? Does he hurt at all being here?*

She shook her head. *Snap out of it.*

"Are we ready?" Lindsay motioned for everyone to follow, bouncing to the top of the wooden stairs and the steep descent to the trail. Derick followed, then Hannah, Marcus, Greg, Amanda, and Alisen.

This was better. She didn't have to think so much, just concentrate on the trail, the fallen logs and underbrush growing into the path. She could just listen to the birds, the chattering of chipmunks, and the rush of the river, high with spring runoff. She inhaled again, that smell filling her with needed peace. They came to a spot where the trail had eroded over the water, and Greg stopped to give her and Amanda a hand around the steep drop-off.

"Those bear-proof garbage bins at the beginning of the trail, does that mean there are a lot of bears in this area? Or just the occasional nightly visitor?" The nervous tone beneath Hannah's casual voice brought a smile to Alisen's face.

"If we see any bears, sis, you only need to run faster than Marcus."

Alisen let herself chuckle with the others and quickly breathed it away, pressing her lips together. She looked down then stopped, crouching to tie her shoe. Greg waited for her.

"Sorry."

"No problem. You all right?"

She nodded and kept her sarcastic laugh inside.

"You know, Derick knows a lot about orchards and farming."

"Does he?"

"Mm-hm. But that's right, you know that."

She shrugged.

"He seems like a pretty good guy. Decent."

She stood and took a breath. "Yup. Lindsay thinks so."

Greg turned and looked at the group ahead of them, frowning. "Oh."

Alisen walked past him, and he said no more.

They reached Amanda, who was waiting. "Keep up, slowpokes."

They continued, catching up to the others. Coming around a curve, Greg pointed out a nest up high in the trees. Alisen looked up as she walked, searching for the nest.

"Watch out."

Her head snapped around. Derick had braced himself against a tree leaning out over the river, its roots clinging to the edge of the trail. The ground dropped away again, more so than she remembered. He held out his hand to help her across.

She didn't have time to think and found herself looking directly into his eyes. She saw nothing but politeness and patience. She swallowed and placed her hand in his.

Oh, this is insane. What kind of world, what kind of God, would put me through all this? Mom? Are you laughing? Are you having a good time?

His warm grip tightened around hers, and she recognized every muscle, every line, every bone as if they were her own. She held firmly, and the muscles in her arm tensed as she pushed against his arm, jumping over the gap.

He let go and turned to help Amanda. Then Greg jumped over, and Derick followed.

Alisen tried to slow her thrumming heart, tried to ignore that she still felt the heat from his hand in hers. *Well,* she thought, *if I can survive that.* She turned her attention to the others, who were turning off to the right. She closed her eyes. They were headed down to the crescent beach, to the story rock.

Before she reached the turnoff, she had already decided. She stopped a little early and pulled off to the left, taking off her backpack without turning around.

"What are you doing?" Amanda asked.

"Go ahead; I'll be right down," she answered, not looking up.

"Okay." Amanda continued past, followed by Greg and Derick.

She watched his easy stride as he continued down to the beach. She took out her water bottle and drank, watching him stop short of the rock and sit on a log between Lindsay and Hannah. Marcus sat on the crushed gravel against Hannah's knees, and Greg crouched down, rummaging through his pack. But Amanda walked over to the rock and climbed on. She sat, looking at the river, her hands feeling the rock's surface.

No more hiding.

Keeping her eyes on Amanda, Alisen pulled herself up and walked down, past him. He was talking to Lindsay, who she was sure gave him rapt attention. Alisen joined Amanda on the rock.

"I haven't been here for years." Amanda stared over the water.

Alisen put her arm around Amanda's shoulder. "Neither have I."

Only one other person on that beach understood the deeper meaning of those simple phrases. But Alisen pushed him to the back of her mind now.

"Maybe we can bring this little one here and tell him stories," Alisen said.

Amanda looked up at her sister. "Or *her*."

Alisen smiled and gave her a squeeze. "Boys like Cinderella too. They just don't admit it."

Amanda giggled. "We could throw in a pirate or two." Then she rubbed her stomach. "I'm hungry. I'm always hungry."

Alisen smiled at her younger sister. Amanda had grown up a lot in the last couple of years, but she was still childlike in a lot of ways. The pout, for example. Alisen ran her hand over Amanda's lighter brown hair, recently cut in a smooth bob. It fell just above her shoulders. Her eyes were like Aunt Rachel's, soft and bright.

"I think pregnancy looks good on you, Amanda."

Her sister broke into a wide grin.

"Did I hear somebody say they were hungry?" Greg brought over some sandwiches.

"My prince." Amanda beamed.

* * *

Hannah, Marcus, Amanda, and Alisen were the only ones interested in walking to the low falls. Alisen had been more interested in not being left alone with Lindsay and Derick while Greg snoozed on the rock.

"So, Alisen, how come you don't have someone to hold hands with on this hike?"

Hannah swatted her husband's arm. "Shh. Marcus! Mind your business."

"I'm just surprised, that's all. She's nice to look at. And a hard worker to boot. I bet you cook too. Do you cook?"

Alisen smiled and felt her cheeks get warm with his bold assumptions.

Hannah sighed and looked back at the girls. "I'm sorry. He's a work in progress."

Marcus chuckled. "I am. But I also want to know why there isn't someone hanging on her every word."

"Shh! Marcus!"

Alisen shook her head with a smile. "It's all right. I just . . . chased the good one away." Amanda squeezed her arm.

"Oh, honey. Now see, Marcus? You didn't need to remind her of things."

Alisen swallowed. If only they knew how their mere presence was a reminder of *things*. "It's fine, really."

Marcus looked apologetic. "I'm sorry, Alisen. I'm just an old farmer."

Hannah giggled. "He really was born in a barn."

Marcus raised his eyebrows, nodding with a grin, and Alisen had to laugh.

After an easier stretch of conversation, Amanda began to slow down.

"You okay?"

"Yeah, I think so. Just tired all of a sudden."

"Well, let me walk back with you."

"No, that's all right."

Marcus turned around. "Is she all right?"

"Just tired. You two go on. We'll rest here."

"Are you sure?"

"Yes. Go see the falls; they're beautiful."

Reluctantly, Hannah and Marcus continued on.

"I don't feel so well." Amanda held her stomach.

Alisen looked back down the trail. "Do you want me to get Greg?"

"No. Let's walk back though. Maybe if I just lie down for a while."

But Amanda was sick halfway back. Gradually, they reached the trail above the beach.

"Greg!" Alisen called.

When he lifted his head from the rock and saw her, he pulled himself up and made his way over.

"Amanda's sick. I thought we should take her home."

"No, Alisen, you don't have to leave because of me." Amanda brought her hand to her forehead.

"I don't mind."

"It's your day off. You already missed the dinner party. Greg, tell her it's her day off."

Greg had his arm around his wife's shoulders. "It's your day off. I'll take her home."

"But it's your day off too."

He shook his head and held out his hand. "Give me the keys. I have plenty to do at home."

"But—"

"Alisen, you love it out here." Amanda, pale and tired, was begging her to stay behind with Derick so she could enjoy the day she'd taken off to get away from him.

Amanda shook her head. "I'll feel awful if you don't stay."

"Why? Why will you feel awful?"

Amanda leaned her head into Greg's shoulder and blinked back at her.

Finally, Alisen shoved the keys at Greg. "Get some rest. I'll bring the packs home. I have my cell phone if you need me."

She watched them make their way up the trail. And she was alone.

She walked back to the beach but stopped. She couldn't see Lindsay or Derick but could hear them talking quietly. She did not want to be part of that conversation. She walked around to the other side, where they had come in, and saw a smaller boulder under a tree leaning out toward the water. It wasn't part of the beach, but it was close, and she would be able to hear when the others returned. Quietly, she made her way over some shrubs and a stump and ducked under the tree's branches to sit on the boulder. It was a nice spot . . . at first.

She heard Lindsay's voice draw nearer, along with the crunch of footsteps on the rocks. They had walked to this side of the crescent, and they definitely did not know she was there. The tree Alisen sat under leaned between them, but she could see an occasional rock go shooting out across the river, sometimes skipping.

Lindsay spoke low. "Greg liked Alisen first, did you know?" There was a pause, then, "It's true. He said he would bring home bags and bags of cherries from her stand because he kept stopping there to see her."

"What happened?"

Alisen listened harder. She hadn't heard this version.

"He said he was never sure of what Alisen thought of him. He said she seemed uncertain, indecisive. He didn't know if it was him or if she was just . . ."

"Noncommittal?" he offered. He said it like he understood. The term stung.

"Yes. Exactly. Then one day, Amanda was there at the stand, and Alisen introduced them. He said Amanda was so open with him; he couldn't help but switch direction. Did you know they are six years apart?"

"Really?" Derick was smiling. She could hear it. Alisen felt frozen to the rock.

"Mm-hm." Lindsay paused. Then she dropped her voice further. "You know, I really can't see anyone choosing Amanda over Alisen. I mean, Amanda is pretty, a little whiny, but Alisen is—"

Alisen waited, not breathing.

"Beautiful. Inside and out. She's *amazing*."

Alisen sucked her lips in and tried not to laugh. Of course it would have been a sarcastic *I-can't-handle-the-irony* laugh, laced with a bit of anger and self-loathing, but a laugh nonetheless. She dropped her head between her knees and put her arms over her ears.

"Have you ever asked her about it?" Derick asked.

Alisen's head came up.

"About Greg? Yes, once. She just got really quiet. She said Greg wasn't the one for her. She said she was happy for Amanda and him."

"But?"

"I remember her saying something about her father, and Amanda being so young."

There was another pause.

"Her father didn't approve?" Derick asked.

"No, actually. That was the thing. He did."

They were silent for a very long minute. This had to be the longest hike Alisen had ever been on.

Lindsay finally sighed loudly. "I know one thing though."

"What's that?"

"If someone like Greg loved me enough to come buy my cherries every day, I wouldn't be noncommittal. I would choose, and I would be immovable."

After a moment, there was a big splash. Derick had thrown a larger rock into the river.

Lindsay laughed. Derick gradually joined her, chuckling softly. Lindsay's laughter walked away with Derick's, retreating with the crunching rocks.

Alisen sat there on the boulder, her mouth open, breathing as though she'd just run five miles. Then her eyes narrowed.

She'd grown up a lot since that summer four years ago. Out of survival, she'd grown independent of her father but was still able to mend a portion of that relationship. She'd become aware of terms like *breakdown of trust* and *emotional abuse* and used that knowledge to strengthen her own boundaries. To not be so *noncommittal*. She knew her protective walls kept her from trusting in love, but they also made her aware of her strengths. And being easily persuaded could not be one of them.

Her pulse calmed, her muscles relaxed.

Enough.

Chapter 22

Alisen looked in the mirror. She studied herself for a long time. This was not an admiration session. She was looking for the beautiful. Lindsay had said it. Why should she feel it only through him? She was, after all, her mother's daughter. Her lips pursed.

Hm.

She turned on the hot water in the tub and soaked for a long time. Rejuvenated by the bath, she moisturized and sprayed herself with scent. She pulled out some nicer jeans she hadn't worn in a while and a top Amanda had given her for her birthday last year. She hadn't worn heels with jeans in a long time, and she'd forgotten how it made her feel. Strong but feminine.

She toweled her hair dry until it shined. The haircut she'd gotten a few weeks ago had been pulled back in a ponytail ever since. Now it hung in loose, curly layers just past her shoulders. She swept her bangs over with her finger and sprayed the whole thing lightly.

Alisen opened the drawer and pulled out the mascara and lip gloss, still her basics, but even so, she hadn't used them in a while. She applied them and stepped back from the mirror, straightening up. *This is for me. Not for him.*

She gave herself a half smile. It was a start.

When she came into the front room, Amanda let out a whistle.

"There's my girl. Nice top."

"Thank you. You look nice too. The nap did you good."

"You think?" She did a little twirl.

Greg came into the room. "I think." He walked to Amanda and kissed her neck. He turned to find Alisen watching them, smiling. "Alisen?"

"Hm?"

"Just checking. I almost didn't recognize you." He winked.

She shook her head.

Turning back to his wife, he announced that it was time to go.

They walked along the path, Alisen trailing behind. She stopped and noted the sun in the western sky lighting everything up from the side. The greens glowed, and the browns were warm and alive. The dark water shone like glass, with a plop and a ripple now and then from a hungry fish. Her heart beat with the beauty of it.

Magic time. That's what her mother had called it.

Amanda and Greg had reached the house, and she could hear everyone's greetings. She smiled to herself. This was good. She could do this. The hike had been revealing. She had seen herself through someone else's eyes, and though it had been somewhat skewed, it had been a reality check. She had spent a lot of time being what she thought other people wanted her to be. It was time she started being who she wanted to be.

She walked up the slate entry and let herself in. The group was scattered around the room. Gia and Stephen exited the kitchen, Hannah and Marcus sat talking with Justin, and Greg's and Amanda's heads leaned together as they showed Lindsay something under the light of a table lamp. Alisen smiled at the sight of them and shut the door behind her.

"Alisen." Gia came toward her with open arms. "Why, you look wonderful." She gave her a hug and stepped back, smiling. She lowered her voice. "Oh, poor Justin."

Alisen gave a suppressed laugh and rolled her eyes.

Just then, a very small herd came bursting into the room.

"Alisen! Alisen! Alisen!" they chanted as they ran around her and Gia. All eyes turned, and as Gia shooed the little boys away, Alisen looked up, smiling, only to meet Derick's gaze. He must've come in with the twins. She looked away quickly, feeling her cheeks flush. He turned away to Hannah, saying something to make her smile.

Stephen walked toward Alisen. "I don't get that welcome when I come through the door."

"That's because your name isn't Alisen," Gia said as she joined him.

He chuckled then focused on Alisen. "There's something different about you tonight," he said thoughtfully.

"Alisen is always lovely," Gia said.

"I know, I know." But he looked again, scrutinizing her.

"It's the makeup." Alisen dismissed his comment with a wave of her hand, her eyes turned down.

"Maybe. Maybe." He scratched his chin. "But it's something else too. I'll figure it out."

"Great." She shook her head at the thought of him playing detective all evening. Stephen just grinned.

Lindsay's voice lifted above the noise of the small crowd. "Excuse me, everyone, but Greg and Amanda have an announcement to make."

"You're having twins." Stephen guessed.

"No. Please, no," Amanda said a little too insistently.

Gia laughed.

"It's not about the baby. Greg?" Lindsay said.

Greg shook his head, obviously not expecting an audience. "Well, it's our first wedding anniversary tomorrow." Applause went around the room.

"And tell them what you gave Amanda."

Greg looked like he didn't want to do the talking. He looked at his beaming wife.

Amanda took the cue. "Greg had an inscription put on the band of my wedding ring."

"Awww." Everyone in the room moved forward as she held the ring in the light.

"What a beautiful idea," Gia said.

"Alisen suggested it." Greg nodded in her direction, obviously pleased by the reaction.

Alisen froze in her step, very aware that she was not the only person who paused.

Derick had held back from the crowd, and when he heard that, he turned away. She glanced at his broad shoulders, tense, his arms folded across his chest. She took a deep breath and quietly walked away to the kitchen, placing her hands on the counter.

She would not let this get more awkward than it was. If he could be unfeeling, then so could she. She was glad she had given Greg the idea. No, she would not feel sorry or upset. She thought every ring, no matter the expense, should make the bride feel the way Derick's had made her feel. She nodded, turned, and made her way back out into the happy room.

* * *

"Everyone partner up." Stephen set up the game in the middle of the big dining table. The food had been cleared away, and Alisen and Gia were coming out of the kitchen.

Alisen's gaze drifted into the living room. Justin leaned against the back of a sofa, legs straight out and ankles crossed, arms folded across his chest. He looked down but kept glancing at her out of the corner of his eye.

She pursed her lips in a smile and walked over. "Justin?"

He brought his face up. "Hm?"

"Everyone is pairing up. Would you be my partner?"

He broke out in a grin. "Yeah, sure."

Everyone made their way to the table to play Pictionary. Its appearance always elicited a little grumbling when Stephen brought it out, but he heard none of it and everyone played, no excuses. With the arguing and finger pointing, it was a loud, rowdy, laughter-filled game—a family game. Alisen relished it.

It was her turn to draw for Justin.

"A dog," he guessed as Alisen scribbled. "A cat. A cat with a hat. Cat in the hat! No. What's that? A bird. Long neck . . . a goose! The dog. Dog goose, no. A dog with a hat and a beard. Sounds like goose? A—a moose!"

Alisen threw down her pencil and held her hand up for a high five. Justin smiled and slapped her hand. Someone clapped. Others booed.

Marcus grabbed the piece of paper with the drawing on it. "Now that is one ugly moose."

"Yes, but you're losing." Justin grinned at him.

Alisen laughed at the exchange, and Stephen abruptly said, "That's it!"

Everyone stopped and looked at him, amused. His finger pointed at Alisen. All eyes turned.

Her eyes grew wide, and she flushed. "What's it?"

"You. What's different." Gia began to laugh and shake her head, but Stephen continued. "Your smile. It's all the way up to your eyes." He nodded proudly.

Alisen continued to turn three shades of red. Her eyes dropped, and she could barely raise them. But she did, to Amanda.

Amanda had a small smile on her face and nodded encouragingly. Slowly, Alisen looked around the table and met the smiles of these people she'd come to love, some looking confused, some looking harder at her, one who flicked his eyes to her for just a split second then looked down while he played absently with his pencil. She lowered her eyes to his hands and a slow smile came to her lips.

"Well, of course it is," Lindsay said. "She finally has a chance at winning this agonizing game."

There were a few nods of agreement about Alisen and Justin's lead on the game board and about the word *agonizing*. Alisen passed her notepad to Justin, and everyone resumed playing.

It was an all play. Those who were drawing for each couple looked at the same word. Then Stephen turned the miniature hourglass over and shouted, "Go."

The room immediately erupted. The drawers all scribbled clues at the same time while their partners tried to be the first to guess correctly. Some shouted out their guesses, some murmured, and some gave up on their partner's drawing completely and started guessing from their neighbor's pictures.

Alisen watched Justin's pencil until two little hands came up around her face and someone small tried crawling up her back. She grabbed the hands away, but another little someone climbed into her lap, yelling, "Go, go, go, go, Alisen!"

"Alex, I can't see, just—"

"I'm not Alex; I'm Jack."

Justin concentrated on his drawing but glanced at her with a worried expression as she struggled with the boys. The hands behind her came to her face again, and she laughed, still trying to see.

"Umm, airplane, um, bird. Alex, stop!"

Suddenly, there was a soft grunt, and the two boys were stripped away and carried off, squealing with delight. "Help, Alisen, help, help, help!"

She looked at the drawing and yelled out, "Killer whale!"

There were groans, and pencils clattered to the table.

Justin sat back with relief, looking at Alisen gratefully.

She turned to where Stephen sat, his face in his hands, leaning forward on the table. Gia sighed and rubbed Stephen's back. Alisen turned in the direction of the boys' outbursts. There, in the other room, Derick wrestled on the ground, defending himself from the attacks of Alex and Jack. She looked over at Lindsay, whose arms were folded in front of her, her pad and pencil pushed away.

"Thanks a lot, boys!" Lindsay called into the living room.

Derick's chair sat empty. It took a moment for Alisen to understand. Derick had left the game. To help her.

Chapter 23

Alisen looked at her hands. She was filthy. Taking inventory in the storage buildings had coated her with a layer of dust. She headed down to one of the water spigots to rinse off, and Jane met her there.

"Jane. How are you?" She bent down and rubbed the cat all over. Jane's motor started, and she jumped into Alisen's arms. "It's been a crazy last few days." She felt like she was taking steps through a maze, not knowing what waited around the next turn and not expecting much. She put her hand under Jane's chin and lifted her little face. "How's it been here?"

Jane just blinked.

"I know. Crazy."

She let the cat down, turned on the spigot, and washed up.

A Jeep pulled into the drive. The Crawfords were home. Alisen headed back up into the orchard to get back to work.

"Alisen!"

She turned.

"Alisen." Hannah, rosy-cheeked and smiling, hurried up the hill.

"Hello, Hannah."

"Hello. I'm glad I caught you down here."

"Did you have a good drive?"

"Oh yes, it was wonderful, thank you." She was a little out of breath. "I was just on the phone with Derick."

Alisen frowned. "Oh?"

"Yes, he's at the Michaels' today while we've been gone."

Despite the tug in her stomach, Alisen smiled at this golden little woman.

"We've had such a great time with all of you, and we want to thank the Michaels family for making us feel so welcome, so we're going to have a party, and I wanted to invite you as soon as I saw you from the car."

"When is it?"

"In two days. Saturday afternoon, around three o'clock. Marcus will have the boat out, and we'll play and have a barbeque. We'll have a fire in the outdoor fireplace and roast marshmallows."

"Sounds fun." She couldn't help grinning. Hannah's eyes sparked with excitement.

"It's supposed to be a nice day."

"Is there anything I can do?"

"Well, just invite anyone you want. We've met several other families here already, and Jay will be bringing his family."

"Thank you, Hannah."

"Oh, you're welcome. I better get going. Lots to do!" She turned and hurried down to the house.

Alisen smiled after her.

* * *

Derick stepped inside the boathouse and paused a minute, tapping his fingers against his jeans. He switched the light on. After a few steps forward, he stopped again. Above him he read the words *Bowl of Cherries*, but they were upside down. Reaching up, he ran his finger along the bottom of the boat. It hung thick with dust. He wiped his hands on his jeans. His gaze ran along the back wall, over two oars lying across the pegs there. A pair of life jackets hung by their straps. He hesitated and then walked to them, lifting one off the peg. He glanced back to the door then slipped his arm through and brought it around. His other arm fit, and he buckled it up. His brow furrowed. With a quick movement, the life jacket was off again. His hand came forward to touch the other jacket, but then the door opened, letting in natural light.

"Hey," he said.

"Hey, Derick." Marcus looked at his ski boat. "Well, I guess we better get her out, see if she'll float."

"Yup." The two men went to work.

* * *

Saturday's sky shone clear, but a wind had kicked up enough to make the lake choppy. Not great for skiing, but they'd cruise the lake anyway for those who were interested.

"Where's Greg?" Derick asked as Stephen tossed one of the twins into the boat by his life jacket. Marcus was on the receiving end, making an overly loud grunt with the catch.

"You're pretty big, kiddo." Marcus tousled the twin's hair as he set him down. Derick noted the cast. Alex.

"That's 'cause I'm five."

Stephen picked up Jack and paused, leaving him dangling in midair, which made the boy grin from ear to ear. "Greg had a dental convention this weekend." He tossed Jack, and Marcus grunted again. "I sent him to take notes for me. Amanda went with him."

Gia walked up the dock. "Which will be good for her. She needed to get out of the house. Don't throw the boys, *amor mio*."

"I remember when you used to come with me to the conventions." Stephen tried to pull his wife into him, but she resisted, smiling.

"That was when you thought they were boring and you liked me more than golf."

He was stronger than her and pulled her in anyway. "You are so wrong. You know I still think the conventions are boring."

She laughed and pretended to be hurt, hitting him softly as he held her close in a bear hug.

"Okay, you two, break it up; there are people present." Lindsay came down the dock, carrying a cooler of drinks.

Derick smiled and took it from her. He handed it to Marcus, who grunted again.

"What am I, a front loader?"

Derick laughed softly. Justin and a few more kids came down the dock.

Marcus did a quick head count. "I think that'll do it for now. All aboard." He turned to Lindsay. "Are you coming, or are you manning the lighthouse?"

She grinned. "I'm coming. I was going to wait for Alisen, but she might be awhile."

Derick looked up. "Why?"

"She didn't say." She held her hand out for Derick, and he helped her into the boat.

They made an entire circle around the choppy lake, and when they got back, a new group waited. Alisen wasn't part of it. Derick drove this time, allowing Marcus to go up and start the barbeque. Lindsay stayed in the boat.

"So, what do you think of your sister's new place?" she called over the engine and water. She smiled at Derick behind her big sunglasses.

He concentrated on the water in front of him but finally shrugged. "It's not too bad."

She laughed. "You knew Alisen before, right? What was she like then?"

His jaw set. He shrugged again.

Gratefully, she changed the subject. "How long do you think you'll be staying?"

He turned to her. "As long as I need to."

She smiled. He turned back to the water, his smile turning back into concentration.

When they returned, the smell of charcoal and cooking meat whirled in the wind. Derick made sure everyone got out of the boat all right, secured it, and walked up the dock. Lindsay ran up ahead to help the boys with their plates. He saw Jay and his family and turned to join them just as a paper plate blew in front of his feet. He stepped on it and bent down to pick it up.

"Sister Embry!"

His head shot up.

A family he didn't know greeted Alisen, who was just coming down from the cars, and she smiled happily back, shaking the woman's hand. He glanced over to Jay, who was already watching Derick, his mouth in an O, his eyebrows up. Derick turned back to Alisen, who was now shaking hands with the woman's husband and patting a couple of their kids on the head. She turned and headed down toward the gathering. Derick spun, looking for a place to escape. He strode back toward the dock then turned and headed straight up the road behind all the SUVs and minivans. He dodged into the stand of pine trees off the road and stood there, trying to breathe. Footsteps sounded, and he whipped around.

Jay put his hands up. "Easy, easy."

"Jay." He could breathe now, but it was coming fast and hard. He lifted his arm and pointed a finger in the direction of the house. "Why are they calling her Sister Embry?"

Jay looked at him then looked down and shook his head. He brought his eyes back up and put his hand on his hips. "Because . . . she's a member of the Church, Derick."

Words and thoughts whirled like paper in the wind, and he couldn't step on any of them. He turned around and brought his hands up to his hair. He turned back. "When?"

Jay shifted his weight, considering. "May, the year after you left."

Derick calculated. His eyes narrowed. He was still breathing heavily.

"She got your letter, Derick. She read it."

Derick stepped back and ran his hands over his face. "But, why didn't sh—" He looked at Jay. "Why didn't you tell me?" His voice broke.

Jay ran his fingers through his hair. "Because she made me promise not to tell. Would it have made a difference? She didn't want you to . . . to come back because of that." He looked to the house. "She didn't think she deserved you after what she did. After what her father did."

Derick blinked. Would it have made a difference? He shook his head. "But her father. How? How did she . . ."

Jay put his hands up again. "I think you should ask her that. I've already broken enough of my promise."

Derick's jaw tightened. "No, I can't."

"You can't, or you won't?" They stared each other down.

Derick's mind raced. He pictured the way the Michaels family treated her as their own, the way she'd lit up from the inside when Brother Michaels had pointed out her smile. *You knew Alisen before, right?* Lindsay's question had seemed odd. Before what?

Before she was baptized.

They knew she was a member. Of course they knew. They all did. She'd been a member of their ward for three and a half years. Why hadn't they told him? Because they figured he knew. But he had just assumed the connection had come from her sister, from Greg working with Stephen. He'd just assumed.

Why did it matter so much? If he'd returned for her, learning she'd joined the Church, wouldn't that make him what Keith Embry had accused him of?

No. He'd always, always put her happiness first. He'd loved her, Church or no Church. But the Church had definitely played a part in drawing them together quickly. Just as his lack of faith had helped in their undoing. If he'd only been patient. If he'd only . . .

He looked toward the house, his jaw still working. "I can't go back there."

"Derick, she has to know you know."

"No, she doesn't."

Jay took a step toward Derick. "Look, I never wanted—"

"Then you should have told me."

"Do you remember? Do you remember how upset, how *broken* you were?"

Derick jerked his head closer to his uncle's. "Of course I do." His face was hot, and his eyes shone with emotion.

Jay gently laid his hands on Derick's shoulders. "If I had told you, what would you have done?"

Derick's eyes searched his uncle's then searched somewhere beyond him, trying to come up with an answer that could throw all the blame on Jay or her family or her. He dropped his head.

"If Hannah asks, just let her know I've gone to lie down for a while and I'll be out later," he murmured.

"I'll do that." He patted Derick on the shoulder.

"Don't say anything to Alisen. I have to . . . figure this out."

"All right."

Derick moved past Jay and crossed over to the orchard. The blossoms were beginning to drop, that heavy smell blowing in the air. He walked behind the house, came around to the side door, and quietly let himself in. He made his way up the back stairs, slowing to make sure he was alone, then continued up the next flight of stairs and down the hall. He took a left and opened the door at the end.

Her room. He'd been here once before, when she had shown him the painting of the cherries. He breathed a trace of her scent as he walked to the balcony door looking over the lake. Carefully stepping out, he closed the door behind him and leaned against it.

Fatigue overtook him. He slid down the door and sat, his forearms on his knees, his hands clasped together, his head down.

Why, he thought, *why did I push her*?

* * *

The sun had set, and he listened to vehicles pulling away. His head felt clearer after a little sleep. He stretched his back. Voices and the smell of wood smoke drifted on the night air. He needed to get up.

Downstairs, he stepped out through the screen door onto the veranda. Heads turned, but he kept his eyes on the fire. A few sticks bobbed marshmallows around, and bigger figures hovered over smaller ones.

"There he is," someone said through the low conversation.

Hannah came over, concern lining her face, but she smiled anyway. "Are you feeling better, hon? Do you need anything? Are you hungry? I could make you a plate."

He smiled back, and his hand came to his stomach. "Maybe some food would be good. Just a little though."

"You bet. Have a seat." She went inside.

He walked to the nearest chair and sat down. He pinched the bridge of his nose. Something soft and noisy purred against his legs, and he reached down. "Hey, Jane. How are you, lady?" Her purr reached a crescendo, and he chuckled. "Thanks." He sighed and sat back.

"I'm sorry you weren't feeling well, Derick." Lindsay sat across from him in the semicircle of chairs. "Hannah was just telling us her favorite things about traveling with Marcus." She flipped her platinum hair back over her shoulder, a ribbon of firelight running along it.

Derick gave her a small smile. The brighter porch lights were turned off, and only the smaller light by the screen door was on. The large fire glowing in the brick oven built into the stucco wall of the veranda lit everything else, but barely.

"Hannah was telling us about riding a rickety old bus up something we wouldn't even consider a road," Gia said.

Hannah stepped out with a plate, a full glass of water, and some ibuprofen. "Yes, but at the top was Machu Picchu, and that was more than worth the ride with the chickens."

"And the goat," Marcus added from closer to the fire, where he threaded marshmallows onto sticks for the kids.

Derick chuckled and took the plate, piled high. He looked up at Hannah and grinned. "This is a little?"

She shrugged. "Eat."

"Thanks, sis." He downed the medicine and set his cup on the floor.

"What is it about traveling?" Hannah found her chair. "I know Mom and Dad have enjoyed discovering the Deep South. Dad says if Mom cooked like they do, he would be a much bigger man." She smiled and shook her head. "They come home in three months. I can't believe it."

"That *would* be a foreign mission," Derick murmured. He drew a few laughs.

The quiet conversation continued, and he felt better. He was finishing up, wiping his hands on a napkin, when Lindsay asked, "Derick, what have you loved most about traveling?"

He thought a moment, narrowing his eyes. "We were in Bolivia. That was three, almost four years ago, when I had just started." He set his plate on the ground. "We were up in this little village and the place was desolate. Just barren. We were there to do a study on growing quinoa and anything green or orange we could get to supplement the potatoes they grew in the hard, cold ground. But there was another group there building a school. Some of the kids were walking two hours to and from another school every day. So for a few days, we pitched in to help build the new one. When we finished, the village held a celebration." He laughed at the fire. "They had this llama, and some of the American women in the group named it Fred. Fred the Llama. Then this priest said a prayer, took a knife, and slit poor Freddy's throat." A few gasps sounded. "He took a little blood and flung it over the door of the new school, and the village women started to prepare Fred for llama stew right there on the ground. They got the fire going and a big pot and threw in the meat, some potatoes, and some skinny onions."

"That's your favorite story?" Lindsay sounded amused and disgusted.

Derick still chuckled. "Well, that's not the great part. The great part was the kids. You know how I said it was desolate? The kids were so excited about the school and so grateful to us. Their smiles. That was the greatest. And they wore the brightest colored clothes in all kinds of patterns. Sweaters, hats, skirts, pants. Those colors with those big smiles against their brown skin and dark hair—set in that wasteland—it's something I'll never forget." He took a deep breath. "It made us feel the importance of what we were doing for that area, any area we were in after that, keeping those kids in mind. They are the . . . the hope."

He stared into the fire. A sudden movement from the next chair caught his attention. It was pushed back a bit, so he hadn't noticed anyone sitting there. Now he watched as Alisen uncurled her legs, stood, and walked over to the low stucco wall surrounding the veranda. She looked out to the lake as the wind blew her hair around her. She touched her fingers to her eyes and rested against the wall. He pulled his gaze away, back to the fire.

"I think traveling could be the best education." Lindsay was looking at the fire but brought her eyes to Derick's. He nodded and looked down.

"But, Derick, you're here now." Marcus grinned at him, and Derick braced himself. "What next?"

Derick brought his hands together and glowered at his brother-in-law. Marcus had been ribbing him ever since he'd arrived at Flathead. But he took a deep breath and answered. "Well, there's still a lot to do with the company. It's still so new. But, uh." Derick hesitated and looked into the fire. "I guess I'm taking some time off to find a place of my own."

"All your own?" Marcus asked pointedly.

Derick shook his head at his brother-in-law. A trickle of knowing laughter came from the other adults around the fire. He allowed a crooked smile but turned away.

"Heaven help the girl who falls for you, bro." Marcus was done being subtle. "She's going to have to be one committed lady." He turned and winked at Hannah, who smiled back at him like he was the only one there.

Derick stared back into the fire. His jaw tightened.

Chapter 24

"OH, ALISEN." HER AUNT'S SMILE was apparent, even over the phone. "I am having such a good time, but I feel so bad. How are you getting along?"

Alisen paused. "Actually, I'm having a really nice time with Amanda and Greg. And the Michaels family always treats me well. It's been really good to be here."

"That's wonderful. I was worried about you."

"Well, you don't need to be."

Rachel paused. Then she asked, "Have you met anybody?"

Alisen gave her head a shake. "What do you mean, Rachel?" *Here we go.*

"Well, you just sound . . . Well, anyway, if you haven't met anyone, I have a friend here who has a grandson about your age—"

"Rachel," Alisen started.

"Honey, he's a doctor, a pediatrician, and she showed me his picture. What a handsome boy. He—"

"Rachel, stop."

"What?"

"Please don't try to set me up with your friend's grandson." She changed the subject. "When are you coming home?"

"In a week."

"Perfect. Amanda and I and some other friends have been invited to a ranch for a few days. Amanda is so excited, as you can imagine. She doesn't get in as much horse time as she used to."

"You're going to a ranch?"

"Mm-hm."

"With friends?"

"Yes."

Rachel paused again. "Are you sure you haven't met someone?"

"Rachel." Alisen shook her head again. "I'll see you when you come home, okay? I'll move in after you get yourself settled."

"Oh, all right, then. Bye, honey."

"I'll talk to you soon."

Alisen hung up the phone and sighed. The week had flown by. It hadn't been as eventful as the previous week, but she was not complaining. There had been some trouble with the irrigation at the orchard, and then they'd had another big rain, so it had been kind of a mess getting things fixed. She'd come home exhausted every night, but by Friday, things finally dried up. Nope, not nearly as eventful.

But Friday afternoon, Lindsay had come running down the path to the guesthouse, a big grin on her face. Alisen read a book on the front porch step, and Amanda relaxed in the hammock, nearly asleep.

"Guess what," Lindsay asked. Alisen was reminded again of a colt.

"What?"

Lindsay flung her arms wide and blurted out, "Derick has a friend who has a ranch, and he's invited us to stay for *four* days."

There had been an immediate struggle in the hammock, and Amanda had suddenly flipped herself out onto the wooden porch, landing on her bottom, legs out, her hair in disarray.

"Are you all right?" Alisen asked.

Lindsay had just stared, open mouthed.

Amanda sat there, blinking. "I'm good. What was that about a ranch?"

Alisen laughed into her book.

Lindsay explained. "A former missionary companion of Derick's has a ranch in Ronan, and when he heard *Elder Whitney* was in the area, he called him up and invited him and whoever he wished to stay at the ranch. Derick invited all of us. My parents and the Crawfords will come up on the weekend."

"Greg has to work." Amanda had wrinkled her brow.

"Maybe he can take a couple days off. Derick will talk him into it." Lindsay had shrugged her shoulders, carefree. "Fun, huh?"

Fun.

Alisen shook her head to clear her thoughts and brought herself back to the present dilemma. She had packed jeans and T-shirts, night and underthings, her toiletry bag, and an assortment of shoes, but now she was stuck.

"Amanda!" she hollered.

After a minute, Amanda's head appeared in the doorway. "You bellowed?"

"I don't know what to pack for this dance. I think I'll just skip it."

"Oh no you don't. If Greg doesn't make it, I'm going to need a dance partner."

"Well, it's not like a hoe-down, is it?" Alisen made a face, picturing big puffy skirts and bolo ties.

Amanda laughed. "I don't think so. Lindsay said it was just a nice dance they hold out there every so often." She came in and took a look at Alisen's closet. Rifling through the hangers, she paused toward the far end and brought out a dress. "How about this one?"

"The Paris dress?" She had worn the red dress only one other time since that trip. "Isn't that a little too fancy?"

"No, it's a classic. It's all in the accessories." She studied it. "Tie a black ribbon around your neck and wear black strappy heels. You'll look gorgeous."

"You think so?" Alisen was doubtful, but she scanned the rest of the closet and shrugged her shoulders. "Okay."

"Trust me. You just might rope yourself a cowboy, big sister." She winked.

Alisen rolled her eyes. She didn't want a cowboy.

Amanda turned toward the door. "I'll get a ribbon."

Alisen looked one more time at the dress then placed it in the garment bag. She grabbed the black heels, threw them in the bottom of the bag, and zipped it up. The rest she threw in a duffel bag.

Just walking through the maze, Mom.

* * *

On Tuesday afternoon, Alisen found herself driving into Big Sky Country. The ranch house was set several miles off the highway, down a long dirt road under open sky and puffy clouds. The ranch itself sprawled flat, for the most part, but the Mission Mountains rose up behind it, a perfect backdrop to the white farmhouse and bunkhouses, the big red barn, and the stables.

As she drove toward the house, Alisen couldn't help but smile. She loved living in a place with so much natural, simple beauty. She glanced sideways at Amanda, who leaned forward in anticipation.

Earlier in her marriage, Amanda had been eager to have a horse or two on some property somewhere, but Greg had patiently told her they would have to wait. Alisen had admired his firmness with her, and Amanda had eventually given in to the wisdom of it. But she loved horses and missed riding. She would go occasionally, getting together with friends with horses, but it wasn't what it used to be.

Alisen reached over playfully and tousled her hair. "Hey, promise me something."

Amanda turned to her. "What?"

"Take it easy on the horses, okay? You've got a little someone to take care of."

Amanda smiled impishly. "I know. I'll be careful."

Alisen laughed at the similarity between her twenty-year-old sister and five-year-old Jack asking his mom for a second dish of ice cream.

Alisen pulled up in front of the wraparound porch, next to Derick's Rav-4. She wondered for a moment what had happened to the Camry. His "Old Reliable." As everyone got out, the front screen door of the farmhouse opened and a young man came out dressed in a clean white T-shirt, jeans, and cowboy boots. His dark hair had been cut close, and he carried his cowboy hat instead of wearing it. He met Alisen's eyes and nodded, and she smiled. He had a lean, athletic build, and he wasn't much taller than Alisen. Something seemed familiar about him, but she was sure she hadn't seen him before. His overall demeanor was reserved. Likeable.

"Elder Whitney." His voice was quiet and welcoming.

"Ben, call me Derick." Derick grinned, and the two men embraced, patting each other's backs hard.

Alisen watched this reunion and tried to picture white shirts and ties, black pants, and little name tags.

Ben stepped back to look over the group. Derick held out his hand. "Ben Harmon, this is Lindsay Michaels, Amanda Stewart, and," he cleared his throat just a little, "her sister, Alisen Embry." Ben pressed his lips into a straight line, showing a dimple to the left of his mouth. Derick rested his hand on Ben's shoulder. "Ladies, this is Ben Harmon."

Ben shook his head. "Well, Derick, you sure know how to pretty up the place." The girls grinned at the compliment. He stepped forward and shook each of their hands, repeating their names. "Welcome, all of you. We're happy to have you."

The screen door opened again, and a little mess of blonde curls came running out as the screen closed behind her. "Daddy." She stopped suddenly at the sight of strangers and stuck her thumb in her mouth.

Alisen guessed she was two years old. She wore little jeans and a pink T-shirt, with brown cowboy boots, same as her dad's.

Alisen turned, surprised, to watch Ben as he held out his hands to her. "Come here, cupcake." She slowly came down the stairs, one at a time, and walked to her daddy, eyes on all the girls as she walked past.

Lindsay asked the obvious question as Ben scooped up his little girl. "Is this your daughter?"

"Yes." He looked down at the blondie in his arms. "Maisy, these are some friends of ours. They'll be staying for a few days, okay?"

Maisy nodded seriously.

Ben looked up. "I hear a husband will be joining us a little later on. Is that true?"

Amanda nodded at that.

"All right, then. I'll get you ladies some help with your bags and show you to your bunks." He pulled out a walkie-talkie from his back pocket and spoke into it. "Frazier, Eliot, come out to the house please. We have guests."

A couple of cowboys made their way over from one of the outbuildings. They were both covered in dust, but they had big smiles on their faces. The taller one paused in front of Alisen and tipped his hat then looked to Ben.

As Ben gave them instructions on the luggage, Alisen looked the taller one over. He wore a cowboy hat, but she could see his hair was almost black. His eyes were dark as well. Everything about his face was angular: his cheekbones, his nose, even his mouth. It all seemed to have been carved from smooth, brown stone. His chin was gently creased down the center. Even with all the dust, he was one good-looking cowboy.

Ben finished talking, and Alisen looked away just as the cowboy turned. He paused and stepped around her. "Excuse me, miss," he said, his deep voice resonant. She sidestepped him, and he walked around to the back of the truck. He hefted their bags and looked at her again.

She smiled this time. "Thanks for getting those."

The corner of his mouth came up. "My pleasure." She saw a little shake of his head as he took a long step past her. He met up with the other cowboy, who was loaded with Lindsay's luggage, and Ben fell into step behind them, his hat on his head, Maisy on his hip.

Alisen turned and was startled to find Derick watching her. He looked away quickly and walked to catch up with Ben. Lindsay ran ahead, her hair swinging as she talked excitedly, asking Ben about the plans for the day, asking Maisy about her curly hair.

"Alisen," Amanda called to get her attention. "C'mon." She motioned impatiently.

They walked to a low, whitewashed bunkhouse with a covered porch; it sat not too far beyond the main house. The men took their things inside and set them on two of the low beds. The interior walls of the long room were whitewashed as well and lined with three beds covered with white and blue woolen blankets. Three small windows with blue-checked curtains let in light above each bed on the front side of the house, and a long rail of hooks hung above the beds across the aisle. The cowboys turned to leave.

"Thanks, boys." Ben set Maisy down, but she still clung to his leg.

"Thank you," the girls said in unison. Frazier and Eliot turned their heads, touching the brims of their hats. Alisen caught the quick smile they gave each other as they left the bunkhouse.

Ben walked down the center of the room to a door at the end. He opened it and switched on a light. "The bathroom is here. Sorry, ladies, you'll have to share, but you're certainly welcome to use the bathrooms at the main house too."

"I think we'll manage." Lindsay grinned. "Won't we, *ladies*?"

Ben smiled and looked at Derick, who lingered near the front door. "Derick, you'll be staying at the main house in the guest room." Derick nodded, and Ben turned to Amanda. He lowered his voice a bit more discreetly. "When your husband comes, we've got a honeymoon cabin back a ways in the trees."

Amanda broke out in a big grin. "Thanks."

He smiled back and turned to the rest of them. "We'll be meeting in front of the main house in an hour to show you around and talk about what you might want to do while you're here. Until then, feel free to visit the stables, relax, or come to the kitchen to see what you can talk my mom into making for you. Dinner's at six." He gave them that closed grin, and the dimple came back. "Derick, let's get you settled."

He walked to the front door, Maisy holding his finger as she walked with him, staring back at the girls, and Derick turned to follow.

"Derick?" Lindsay flashed him her brilliant smile as he turned to her. "Thanks for inviting us."

He grinned at her and nodded before he left.

Lindsay turned around, still smiling widely. She shrugged. "Yeehaw."

Amanda rolled her eyes, grabbed a pillow, and threw it at her.

Later, after they had utilized every wall hook and shoved what didn't need to be hung up under their beds, Amanda excused herself and headed out to the stables.

Alisen was lying on her stomach, her fists under her chin, watching Lindsay brush her hair up into a ponytail in the bathroom. "I didn't know Ben was married." She didn't know why the news surprised her; he had to be about Derick's age.

"He isn't. I mean, he was." Lindsay finished up and came to sit across from Alisen on her own bed. She spoke quietly. "His wife died a couple of years ago. I guess after the baby was born, she had an infection they didn't catch until it was too late."

Alisen was struck by the news. "Oh no. And so young."

Lindsay nodded. "Derick said she was sick before, during the pregnancy. The baby was too small, and all the focus was on getting the baby through the first week. I guess his wife just kept how she was feeling to herself, and she was home, so nobody noticed until it was too late."

They were silent for a minute. Then Lindsay added, "Derick said he remembers the funeral, how torn up Ben was, and how he held that baby like it was his only possession."

"Derick went to the funeral?" Alisen asked.

Lindsay nodded. "Mm-hm. He flew here from Indonesia. He said Ben tracked him down through his uncle Jay." Then she brightly said, "But he has that beautiful little girl. Did you see that hair?" She shook her head, smiling.

Alisen nodded.

"He seems like a really sweet guy."

"Yeah."

Lindsay got up. "I'm going to find Derick and Amanda. I'll see you at the house, okay?"

"Mm-hm."

The door shut behind Lindsay.

Alisen was still for a while, thinking about Ben's wife. She also considered the meaning of the other news.

Derick had been here two years ago. He'd been here, at Flathead. She took a deep breath and blew it out.

Jay had been really good at keeping his promise.

* * *

The guests' first full day at the ranch consisted of a horseback ride, a breakfast fit for an entire posse of riders, and a few light chores in between fishing, hiking, and a much-needed nap. Alisen had found the kitchen a bright, happy place to spend some of her free time and was now helping make dinner for the guests and ranch hands.

Windows on two exterior walls lit the big room. Tall white cupboards reached up to the ten-foot ceiling. A large rectangular wooden table sat in the center, its surface mellowed with age. Though it was pocked with marks from various utensils, the wood glowed and invited Alisen to run her hand across it whenever she passed. Under the table, pots and pans, baskets, mixing bowls, and crocks sat lined up on two low, wide benches.

"Alisen, honey, will you get out that really big bowl?" Ben's mother stood on a step stool, pulling down jars of canned peaches from the upper shelf. "We'll need the deep lasagna dish too for this cobbler."

Alisen wiped her hands on the towel next to her and started to rummage under the table. After some digging and rearranging, she resurfaced with the needed items.

"I swear, one of these days I am going to have Rick remodel this entire kitchen." Sarah Harmon came down from the stool, arms loaded carefully with bright jars of fruit.

Alisen silently protested. She wouldn't change one board of this old place.

She took up her knife and continued chopping onions then slid them into the simmering pot of cubed beef already on the big stove.

"What now?" she asked with a little sniffle, thanks to the onions.

"We'll let that simmer for a while. Grab that lid and cover it, will you?"

Alisen did and turned to rest against the counter. They had already finished the biscuit dough, and it lay covered until it was closer to dinnertime. She watched Sarah for a moment. Though this woman was slight, she was not frail. And she knew what she was doing, keeping the large ranch fed and in high morale. There were no recipe books out, no fancy doodads or frills, just intuition, years of experience, spoons, ladles, and spatulas, and really, really big pots.

"Sarah? Oh, hi, Alisen." Ben's father came into the room.

"Hello, Brother Harmon."

"Please, just Rick."

Alisen smiled. "Rick."

"Are you having a good time?"

"Yes, I love it here."

"What did you need, sweetheart?" Sarah asked.

Rick focused again on his wife. "Oh, Ben and I just got in, and we're out of WD-40. That window is still sticking at the boy's bunkhouse, and someone is going to rip it clean off. Do you have any in the house?"

Sarah pointed with a long wooden spoon. "Back in the laundry, in the cupboard above the washer."

He leaned forward, bending around the spoon. "Thanks, sugar." He kissed her on the cheek.

The spoon pointed at Alisen now, slicing down with her every word. "Now, Alisen, I am just going to throw this cobbler together, so you go on out and play."

Alisen suppressed a laugh. "All right. Thanks, Sarah."

She washed her hands in the sink and left the kitchen. As she passed through the front room, she slowed at the old upright piano. New and old photographs in all kinds of frames lined the wall above. Her eyes landed on the one that piqued her interest most. She leaned closer.

Ben and his new bride gazed at each other, laughing beautifully. His expression was open and filled with love for the young woman whose blonde hair was pulled back in a high mass of curls, the veil cascading down beneath it. Alisen meditated there a second.

"Hello, Alisen." Ben's quiet voice still startled her.

She turned her head. "Oh, hi. I was just—" She smiled. "This is a beautiful picture."

He nodded, a sad smile forming on his mouth. "Natalie loved that picture." After a moment, he looked back at her, his polite smile returning.

"You never get over it, do you?" Alisen ventured. She had just realized what she recognized about Ben yesterday when she'd seen him for the first time. It was the look of buried grief. She knew that look well.

Now he searched her eyes. "You've lost someone?"

"Mm-hm. My mother." She looked back at the portrait and lightly touched the glass over Natalie's dress. "You never get over it. But," she sighed, "they want us to, don't they?" She turned and looked out the front windows behind Ben, not focusing. "Maybe not get over it, but they want us to find happiness." She looked back at Ben. "Because *they're* happy."

He set his jaw and gave a slight nod. "How long ago did you lose your mother?"

"Ten years. It still aches. But I learned early on to feel her in the things around me." She thought of the orchard, her aunt, the painting. She smiled at Ben. "You have Maisy."

He slowly returned her smile. "Yes. I have Maisy."

"And there have been happy times, very happy times. It comes and goes." She trailed off. Then she lifted her face. "But that's how it is for everyone, isn't it?" She sighed. "That's how life is."

He nodded. "You're right."

She shrugged, suddenly self-conscious about sharing so much with him. "I guess we just need to keep reminding ourselves that the ones who leave us are still pulling for us."

He didn't say anything, just watched her thoughtfully.

"Well, your mom told me I have to go out and play now." She grinned sheepishly. His smile broadened. She turned for the front door.

"Alisen?"

She turned. "Yes?"

He turned back to the portrait then looked again at her. "Thanks for the reminder."

She smiled then turned and pushed through the screen door.

* * *

A few steps down from the top of the narrow staircase in the old farmhouse, Derick stood, his fingers pressed against the walls on either side of him. As Alisen left the house, the squeaking screen door closed behind her, and Derick sat down and put his head in his hands.

The Alisen he'd just heard now, with Ben, that was the Alisen he'd fallen in love with. But she was different too. He couldn't put his finger on it, but he knew she was different too.

Chapter 25

"Look at her," Ben said.

Lindsay had taken to horses like a bird to air. On Thursday morning, she galloped around the corral, her eyes bright with excitement. "Am I ready?" she called out to Ben.

Ben, who leaned against the fence next to Alisen, gave a small nod, dipping the brim of his hat.

"Yippee."

Alisen grinned. Lindsay had earned a white, straw cowboy hat from someone on the ranch and was now wearing it everywhere she went. She brought the horse around and headed to the others, who were waiting.

"Thanks for being patient, guys."

Ben looked up at her. "Just make sure you take a minute to get a lay of the land, take note of the rises and falls, and be aware of any dry beds or pot holes. Follow us, and you'll be fine."

Lindsay had been asking to gallop a horse ever since they took their first trail ride on Tuesday afternoon. She didn't want to mosey; she wanted to charge. So Ben, Derick, and Amanda had spent some time with her, and now they were going to take the horses out for a run. Alisen had declined. Though she enjoyed the trail rides and felt fairly comfortable on a horse, she was not up for letting the creature loose underneath her.

Ben pulled himself up on his horse. He looked down at Alisen, giving her a smile and another nod of his brim. "Stay out of trouble."

Alisen smiled wider back. "I'll try, thanks."

He winked and trotted over to the others, and they all turned out to the flat, grassy fields. Alisen watched them take a normal pace for about half a mile, and then they started to gallop. She smiled, picturing Lindsay's face in the rush of wind. Her eyes then followed Derick until the horses and riders loped down over a low hill.

"Miss Embry?" A deep voice called from behind.

She looked up at the tall, dark cowboy named Eliot. Their paths had crossed a few times, and he had always given her attention in some small, quiet way. He'd made sure her saddle was ready for her when they went riding. He'd retrieved a pile of blankets and set them beside her when she'd mentioned she was cold at the campfire.

"It's Alisen." She shaded her eyes with one hand and stuck the thumb of her other in her back pocket.

He nodded, smiling. "Will Eliot."

"What can I do for you, Will?"

He looked away, still smiling, then brought his head back around. "I saw that you were left behind, and I wondered if you would like to help me."

Alisen leaned her head to the side, still squinting up at him. "What kind of help?"

He laughed at her expression, a deep, soft laugh. "Not unpleasant. I've got some horses in the stable that need some grooming. I'd do it myself, but it's a nice job, and I just thought, if you didn't have anything better to do."

Alisen looked over at the stables. "All right. You'll have to show me though."

He laughed again. "Not a problem."

* * *

"You live up on Flathead?" He brushed the other side of the horse.

He was right. This wasn't unpleasant at all. She pulled her hand down her side of the horse, brushing the saddle marks away and running her fingers lightly through the horse's mane.

"Not right now, but I have a small cherry orchard there."

He stopped and looked at her over the horse. He had removed his hat when they got to the barn, revealing his dark thick hair in an appealing mess on his head. He looked confused.

She caught the look. "What?"

"You run an orchard?"

"Yes, I do." She looked back at the horse, feeling pride behind her smile.

"So you're not related to Elizabeth Embry?"

Now it was her turn to look surprised. "Elizabeth is my sister."

He raised his eyebrows at her. "No kidding?"

"No kidding."

He drew his lips together. "Hm."

"How do you know Elizabeth?"

He looked down at the horse and resumed brushing. "Oh, we had a mutual friend." He looked back up at her. "That was a few years ago though. When I heard your name, I remembered Elizabeth, but," his eyes narrowed, "you don't look much like your sister."

Alisen watched her hand move across the horse. "No, I don't look much like my sister." She chuckled. "Actually, Elizabeth and I aren't that close. She . . . lives her life by different rules than I do." Then she shook her head at herself. That wasn't fair. "She's in New York a lot. She's there now, as a matter of fact." She changed the subject. "Do you like working here?"

"Oh yeah. Good hours, good food, surrounded by mountains and trees. It's God's country." He looked down at her. "What's not to like?"

His low voice vibrated through the stable. The flash she saw in his eyes left her slightly nervous. She set her brush down on a stool behind her and stepped back. "I think my side is done."

He came around and checked her work. "Yup. Good job." He looked over to the next stall. "Only three more to go." He smiled at her.

She found herself smiling back.

* * *

Will was walking her out of the stables, back toward the corral, when he looked up. "Whoa." He rested his arms on the fence.

Alisen followed his line of sight. Two horses raced toward them, still quite a distance away. She leaned forward on the fence next to Will, spotting Lindsay almost at once, her pale golden hair flying out behind that white cowboy hat. The other rider was Derick.

Fifty yards before the corral, they pulled up and slowed, then stopped at the gate, flushed and excited. Derick had that open grin, looking at Lindsay with admiration and disapproval. Lindsay leaned toward him, a taunting tone in her laugh.

Alisen's stomach twisted.

"Alisen!" Lindsay called to her. "Did you see that?"

Derick looked over too, his grin fading.

Alisen flickered her eyes up at Will, then she swallowed and called to Lindsay. "Yes. What was that about?"

"I challenged Derick to a race. I think I won!"

Alisen forced a bigger smile. "Congratulations."

Lindsay laughed, completely carefree. Derick joined her with his mellow chuckle, but his eyes were on Will.

The rest of the group arrived, smiling, shaking their heads.

Will turned to Alisen. "I better go help with that. Thanks for assisting me, Cherry Girl." He smiled again and clucked his tongue.

She watched him walk away. He turned his head back over his shoulder and nodded good-bye.

What am I supposed to do with that?

She looked over to see Derick helping Lindsay down. Alisen turned away, leaning against the fence.

Or that?

The group came around the corral with their horses. Ben stopped next to her as the others walked on. He waited until Will had led the other horses to the stables, then he turned to Alisen.

"I, uh, feel I should warn you," he said.

She looked at him with a small smile. "About what?"

He looked in the direction of the stables then dropped his head and chuckled. "Just be careful about Will Eliot. He's kind of a ladies' man." He brought his eyes up to her apologetically and gave her the dimple grin.

Her smile remained. "Thanks for the warning." She had been right about Ben Harmon. He was likeable.

He motioned for her to get on with the others, and she obeyed.

She caught up to Amanda, who had been lingering behind, waiting for her.

Her sister's eyes danced. "Alisen, you should have come. It was so *incredible*. The Mission Mountains are so beautiful from out here. What did you do while we were gone?"

Alisen smiled thoughtfully. "Oh, just helped out in the stables. Is Greg coming up tonight?" Alisen looked at the setting sun. Oranges and pinks touched the few clouds. Already, a small number of faint stars blinked against the blue sky.

"Yes. I can't wait to see him. Phone calls are not the same." She sighed.

Alisen linked her arm through Amanda's. "How are you feeling?"

"Tired. And I really could not stand the smell of that chili yesterday. I kept putting the biscuits up to my nose to mask it. I couldn't get enough of that cobbler though. It was heaven."

"I know. I had to move away from you, the way you kept looking at my bowl."

Amanda laughed. "Is that why you got up?"

"Well, that, and Ben looked like he could use a little help with Maisy. He was trying to balance his own dessert and help her with hers at the same time."

"He is so good with her." Amanda sighed. "I wonder what kind of parents we'll be."

Alisen squeezed her elbow. "You'll be the best. It'll be a kick to watch though."

Amanda smiled and nudged her sister.

Alisen shivered in the cool breeze and looked toward the bunkhouse. "I think I'll get a jacket before the bonfire."

"Okay. I'll try to save you a seat."

"Just save one for your husband. I'll be fine." She pointed.

Greg's car was leaving a trail of dust down the long dirt road to the big house. Amanda's face lit up, and she started an easy run in that direction.

Alisen watched her and, as she turned to go, caught sight of Lindsay. She walked backward, holding Derick's sleeve, talking animatedly about a possible ride in the morning. He let her pull him in the direction of the fire pit, and from his profile, she could see his smile.

A small ache found its way into her cheeks and across her forehead as she watched him go. There was nothing she could do, nothing she should do. The sunset filled the sky now. She pulled her eyes away from his figure, so familiar to her but so remote. Hugging her arms around her, she walked away to the bunkhouse. Once inside, she pulled her jacket off the hook and sat on the bed.

If there was anyone she would want for him, it would be Lindsay. She took a ragged breath then stood. She pulled her jacket on and made her way out the door and to the fire pit.

"Hey, Cherry Girl."

She turned. Will approached her from a group of cowboys assembled next to a few trucks. She tried to ignore the calls the other boys behind him made.

He turned his head back. "Hold it." They stopped. He gave her a smile and shook his head. "Sorry."

"That's all right." She lowered her eyes, still feeling the weight of her recent thoughts.

"Are you sure?"

Her head came up. He watched her with concern.

She smiled. "Yes."

He grinned and looked toward the campfire. "A few of us are going out tonight." He looked back at her and tipped his head to the side. "I was wondering if you would come?" He gave her a hopeful look.

She glanced behind him at the trucks.

"They're harmless." He got her attention again with his eyes. "I'd look out for you, you know?" One corner of his smile came up higher than the other. He was good.

"Thanks, but maybe some other time?" She looked up at him from under her lashes. She could flirt too.

He watched her for a second then pursed his lips. "Well, you are somethin'." He grinned again and tipped his hat. "That's all right. I'll wait." He put his head down and turned his body away from her. He looked back over his shoulder again as if to make sure she was still watching.

She smiled and shook her head, and he laughed, making his way to one of the trucks. As he opened the door, she could make out faint calls of mock sympathy.

She felt better.

It was nearly dark when she approached the campfire. Benches made of rough-hewn logs surrounded the large pit. Alisen looked around at the group: Greg with his arm around Amanda and then Lindsay, Derick, and Ben. Ben looked up and motioned for the spot next to him.

"Where is Maisy?" She sat down on the bench and pulled her jacket more tightly around her.

"My mom just took her up to the house. She was out."

Alisen nodded. "What did I miss?"

Lindsay smiled at Ben across Derick. "Derick was telling us how green Ben was when he first arrived in Bolivia."

Ben sighed and shook his head. "I think Elder Whitney saved my life a few times. I made some pretty stupid mistakes."

Derick leaned forward, his elbows resting on his knees, his hands folded in front of him. He stared into the fire and smiled. "Oh, I'm sure you would have figured things out. Eventually."

Alisen couldn't help it; she watched the firelight play along his features. It seemed easier now, somehow. Like admiring a piece of sculpture but knowing it wasn't hers.

Ben nodded. "Do you remember when I tried to talk to those gang members?"

Derick rolled his eyes. "Just because they called to us, Elder Harmon walks right over to them, hand outstretched, a big smile on his face."

Ben laughed softly at the memory then sobered. "I remember the tone of your voice when you called me back. There was no denying the power there. I backed away, no hesitation."

Derick nodded into the fire. He turned to Ben and gave him a crooked smile. "You were the best greenie I had. Do you remember the Valenzuela family?"

"Oh yeah. Oh, Sister Valenzuela's conversion was the best. The Spirit was so strong when we were with her. She asked all the right questions, and she would just soak it all in." He started shaking his head. "Brother Valenzuela said, *'Escucharé a qualquiera cosa que hace que mi esposa aparece como angel.'* He would listen to anything that made his wife look like an angel." He shook his head again. "That was my first double baptism."

When Ben spoke of his mission, the grief left his countenance. Alisen felt she had a glimpse of the young man before life had broken his heart. Both men stared into the fire again.

Ben got up, grabbed another log, and placed it on the fire. "Alisen, I heard you're a convert to the Church. I'd like to hear your conversion story."

She froze. Out of the corner of her eye, Derick moved his head slightly but remained staring at the fire. She swallowed, glancing at her sister for reassurance. Amanda just leaned into Greg with a contented look on her face.

Lindsay leaned forward. "Oh, this is one of my favorites."

Derick still hadn't moved. He just stared, his head slightly inclined.

Alisen swallowed again and looked at Ben, who sat back down.

"Is that all right?" he asked.

Yes. It is. Tell it.

She nodded her head and returned his smile. "Of course," she said, but it came out a little hoarse.

What did it matter if Derick knew now? It struck her that it was the least she could do, a thank you.

She turned to the fire, letting the warmth ease her pounding heart. She cleared her throat. "When my mother died, it was like a hole had opened up inside me. Like I was alone for the first time. I felt like I had no one, really, to share those difficult feelings with, no one to comfort me the way I needed to be comforted." Her voice turned quiet and trembling. She took a deep breath. "I knew something was missing, but I thought it was just . . ." Her voice trailed off, and she pictured her father. She shook her head a little and continued.

Her voice became a bit stronger. "Then a friend answered some of my questions." She allowed herself a smile. The vivid flames off the new log were soothing. "I had quite a few, and his answers just made sense. It all made sense. His answers included the possibility of seeing my mother again, that

I had a Father who loved me." She dropped her eyes. "And I didn't feel so alone anymore. He gave me a Book of Mormon, and I read it." She looked out of her peripheral vision. He still sat motionless.

She pressed on, encouraged by the steadiness of her own voice and the warmth she was finally feeling from the fire. "He invited me to church, and I started taking the missionary lessons." She could see Ben nodding his head.

"But then I told my father I wanted to be baptized." Her face turned down. "He was furious. He had heard negative things about the Mormons. Misunderstood, untrue things, but he wouldn't listen. I was devastated." Her eyes blurred, and her throat caught, but she worked through it. "And then my friend left. He, uh, had to go back to school. I was a little lost. I stopped reading, I stopped praying." She paused and looked back into the fire. "I didn't forget though. I knew. All that loneliness from before had come back to me, and I knew that the things I had learned were what I needed to fill that space." Her breathing steadied again, and the only sound was the hiss and pop of the fire. She filled her lungs with night air.

"I got a letter from my friend. It wasn't much, but I started to pray again. I read the Book of Mormon again, looking for scriptures about hope and strength and being . . . *immovable*." She was more sure now.

"One day, I overheard my father. He was boasting about how he'd pulled me away from what I had loved." She shook her head. "I realized I'd been wrong, misled. I had allowed myself to be swayed." She was quiet for a minute, wishing Derick understood her. "I knew I wouldn't be swayed anymore. I called . . . someone I had known for a long time, another good friend from church. I asked him to baptize me."

"Who, Alisen?" Ben asked.

His voice brought her eyes up out of the fire. *Might as well.* "Jay Whitney."

Ben turned his head to Derick, who still did not move, except to raise his eyebrows and look sideways at his friend. Then he looked back into the fire.

"So you were baptized." Ben turned back to Alisen.

"Yes. I realized that nothing my father said or did would change the truth. And the truth couldn't be torn from me."

"Did your father know?"

She shook her head. "Not at first. He noticed I was going to church again, and he was confused because he thought my friend had influenced that. I finally gave him the little program to my baptism. He just stared at it. Then I gave him some magazines—the Church magazines, even the *Friend* and the special edition *Ensign* about Christ. And I left him there, staring at the stack." She turned her head to Ben, smiling a little. "I still don't know if he read them, but he was quiet about it after that."

Ben smiled and leaned back. "That's a good story."

Derick dropped his head down between his arms.

"That's not all," Lindsay said, beaming.

Derick's head came up to look at Lindsay.

She raised her eyebrows, and her eyes twinkled in the firelight. "There's more." She looked at Alisen expectantly.

Alisen saw Derick's head come around, but she looked into the fire again. He was watching her now; she knew it. Her pulse picked up again, but she swallowed.

"There is a little more." She looked down. "Even though I had the gospel and the Holy Ghost and the truth, I still felt lonely. The members were great, and I knew I could call Jay for anything. But my *family*. It occurred to me that I didn't need to do this alone." She slowly raised her eyes up into the fire then above the flames to meet Amanda's gaze. Tears rolled down Amanda's cheeks, but she was smiling. "I asked my sister to come with me."

There was a silence as Alisen's whole being filled with joy, and a small laugh bubbled up to break it. Her hand came up to catch her own tears. She didn't see anything but Amanda's glowing face looking back at her with love and gratitude.

Amanda spoke lightly through her emotions, placing her hand on her husband's. "And what kind of new wife would I have been if I didn't make my new husband come to church with me?"

Greg looked down at her. "I saw what your Brother Valenzuela saw." He reached down and gave Amanda a kiss. "I still do."

"And we're going to be sealed in the temple just before Christmas. Before the baby comes."

Lindsay had her hand on her chest and looked up with glistening eyes, shaking her head. "I told you it was good."

Alisen let out a quiet breath of relief.

"What did your friend think?" It was Ben again. All eyes turned back to Alisen.

Alisen looked at Ben, willing her gaze not to flicker toward Derick. She took a halting breath. "I'm not sure. He was away, out of the country, and I lost track." Her voice became a whisper. "I only just barely told him."

Chapter 26

"I THINK I'M JUST GOING to sit here for a while." Derick looked up at Lindsay.

Lindsay stood in front of him for a moment. "You okay?" she asked.

He nodded. "Yeah, I just want to talk to Ben for a bit."

"Okay. Good night." She turned. "Good night, Ben."

"Good night, Lindsay." Ben smiled as she turned on her heel. She spread her arms wide and looked up. "What a beautiful day!" she exclaimed to the stars. She clicked on her flashlight and hummed as she walked away.

Ben watched her go, chuckling. "She sure is full of energy. Like sunshine."

Derick raised his brow and nodded, poking a stick at the dying embers.

Ben turned to him. "Why didn't you walk her to the bunkhouse?"

"Why didn't *you* walk her to the bunkhouse?" He chuckled at Ben's startled expression at the thought. Ben looked over in the direction she'd gone.

Derick looked over at Alisen, who was saying good night to Amanda and Greg. She was giving Amanda a second long embrace. Then Greg pulled Amanda down the trail to their own cabin, flashlight in hand. Amanda giggled at his murmur, and they disappeared except for the bouncing light.

Ben followed Derick's gaze. He motioned with a raise of his chin. "Did you know that story? She said Jay baptized her."

Derick went back to stirring the coals. "I knew some of it." He looked up to see Alisen returning to the circle. She slowed, realizing who was left. She looked down at her shoes then around at the other benches, back toward the bunkhouse, and at the fire, tapping her hand against her leg.

"Do you need a flashlight, Alisen?" Ben asked. "You can use mine."

Her head came up at his words, her eyes wide. "Oh, um, thanks, I . . ." Her fingers touched her temple.

"Here, I'll walk her." Derick stood up. "I needed to walk some anyway."

Ben threw him a questioning look. "All right." He stood too with a stretch. "Here." Ben handed Derick his flashlight. "Alisen?"

She looked at Ben like a deer caught in headlights.

"Thanks. I didn't mean to put you on the spot like that." He smiled at her. "It was really good to hear how you found your way though."

She broke into a smile, relaxing a little.

"It's like coming home, isn't it?" Ben added.

She paused then breathed out a tired laugh. She only nodded.

"Good night. 'Night, Derick. Don't wander too far."

"Good night." They both answered at the same time.

Ben left them for the house. Alisen turned, her eyes on the ground. They stood there for a long minute, her watching the ground, him watching her.

Finally, Derick took a few careful strides to her side, and they started walking, a small distance between them. Nothing was said, and the longer it was quiet, the more anxious he became.

But he didn't know what to say. Well, he could think of a million things to say but didn't know what he should say or if he should say anything. His mind tossed and turned, everything sounding absurd in his head. What could he say to what she had just shared? How could he . . .

She stopped. "Umm, where's the bunkhouse?"

He looked around. They were skirting the corral, long past the bunkhouse. He looked back, shining the flashlight. Neither of them had been paying attention to where they were going. His hand came up to his hair.

He heard a muffled chuckle and looked at her. Her hand was over her mouth, and she shook her head at the ground. When her head came up, she was trying to stop the laugh.

"Ugh," she softly exclaimed. She closed her eyes and shook her head once more.

The corner of Derick's mouth came up. He swallowed. "Alisen?"

Her eyes locked on his, her expression steady, just watching him.

The corner smile faded. He cleared his throat. He couldn't look away. Even in the dim light, her eyes still held him. He swallowed. Finally, it came out in a whisper. "Thank you."

She searched his eyes. He let her this time. She opened her mouth as if to say something but closed it again and nodded her head. Slowly, she turned her eyes away, toward the bunkhouse. Watching her feet, she slowly started walking in that direction. He turned and followed, shining the light ahead. He caught up to her, still a careful distance but easier. They reached the light of the porch, and she put her hand on the latch. She paused and turned, looking up at him.

She quickly whispered, "I couldn't have done it without you." She looked at him a split second longer then opened the door and disappeared behind it as it closed.

He stared at nothing in particular. Finally, he made himself turn and head up the road, his mind full of new questions.

* * *

Derick furrowed his brow. He'd woken at the break of dawn after a horrible sleep and had found Ben and Lindsay prepping for an early-morning ride. They'd talked him into coming and he trailed behind them, half listening to their conversation, half lost in his own indistinct thoughts.

But now Ben brought up a subject that drew his attention.

"So, Alisen came to this decision that would change her life, that, to her, would make her happier than she'd been in a long time. And then everything went wrong." Ben watched the mountains ahead, and Derick felt a pang of grief for his friend. Everything had gone wrong for him.

Lindsay nodded. "But she allowed herself to be reminded of what was good. She's great at that." Lindsay squinted her eyes at the sun just cresting the peaks now. She smiled at Ben and reached a hand to his arm. "I think it's a hard lesson to learn, especially when things are *so* bad."

Ben's voice softened. "And when you want things to go another way."

Derick knew all about wanting things to go another way. So much so that he'd been blinded to any other possibility.

Ben took a deep breath and turned, smiling at Lindsay. She pulled her horse to a stop, and Ben pulled up too. Derick paused behind them, not wanting to intrude.

"But don't you think," Lindsay spoke carefully, which was unusual for her, "that sometimes the way things go, after pushing through the bad things, can be better than we could even wish for ourselves? I mean, maybe not better but still a different kind of good? I think we're hard on ourselves that way. We can't see any other way to be happy. But it has to be out there, doesn't it?"

She watched Ben a moment.

Ben gave her a nod from under his hat. "Yes, ma'am, I think you're right."

Lindsay giggled. "Did you just call me 'ma'am'?"

Derick took the opportunity to pull ahead. "How'd you get to be so wise, Miss Michaels?" he asked, hiding the emotions her words had drawn from him. He'd been drowning in self-pity, and she'd practically slapped him in the face with Ben's example.

She kicked her horse forward a bit and grinned. "I know some things."

Derick found his thoughts spinning again. Sometimes it seemed they knew everything that had happened. That no matter how hard he'd tried to mask it all, his true feelings were paper thin.

After a couple more miles, Ben checked the sun in the sky. "We should head back. Mom'll have breakfast. Are you hungry?"

Lindsay's face lit up as they turned their horses around, and Derick read her thoughts. Sure enough, as the corrals came into view, he saw the anticipation on Lindsay's face. He waited.

As soon as they left the rockier terrain, she turned to him, a glorious smile on her face. "Race ya!" she cried and kicked her horse forward.

He was ready this time though and kicked ahead of her. He leaned forward and let his horse loose, hearing her laughter behind him. He breathed the air rushing past him and felt the rhythmic beat of the horse's hooves against the hard prairie. The knot in his chest seemed to jostle loose with the movement of the powerful animal beneath him, and his heartbeat hammered.

He let out a triumphant yell just before it was time to pull up.

His horse slowed to a gallop, and he felt Lindsay pull up just behind him. His hand came up to his eye, wiping a tear from the wind or whatever, and he turned to smile at her, laughing. Ben came up close behind them.

She smiled shrewdly. "You think you can beat me, cowboy? I declare a rematch."

"Nope, no way. I'm hanging on to this victory for dear life."

"Can't handle the idea of losing to a girl again, huh?"

He considered. "Yeah, that about sums it up."

* * *

"Hey, boys, how was your ride?" Sarah appeared in the entry to the kitchen across the front room, stirring something in a large bowl she held against her petite frame. The smell of bacon drifted through the entire house. Ben and Derick paused at the foot of the stairs on their way to wash up.

Ben smiled at his mom. "Really good. It's a beautiful morning out there."

"When is it not?" Sarah winked at him.

A voice came from the kitchen. "Sarah, how many eggs do you usually break?"

Both Ben and Derick stopped and peered behind Sarah. She turned and answered Alisen, who was still unseen in the kitchen.

"A dozen per six people, then I throw in another dozen." She walked into the kitchen, working out the math.

Ben and Derick grinned at each other and hurried upstairs.

They came back down as Sarah and Alisen carried big, steaming covered dishes to the front door. Ben jumped ahead to get the door for his mom, offering to take the dish from her. She accepted and, after handing it to him, promptly turned and headed back into the kitchen for another.

Derick took a hesitant step to Alisen. "I'll take that."

"Oh. No, that's all right."

He lowered his eyes.

"But if you would get the door for me, that would be great." She watched the screen door closing behind Ben.

He looked at her as she focused on the door, biting her lip.

"Sure." He walked quickly and held the door for her.

She passed him and walked carefully down the porch steps but then stopped, nearly running into Ben. Derick stopped too.

"Ben?"

Ben had paused halfway to the tables, still holding his dish.

He blinked and looked at Alisen. "Oh, sorry, I just—" His eyes turned back to the table in front of him.

Lindsay sat with her back to them at a table, and Maisy faced her, sitting on the tabletop edge. Lindsay held both of Maisy's hands and was singing a song about a horsey, bouncing and bobbing Maisy's hands as she bounced and bobbed her head. Lindsay's fair ponytail swung appropriately. Maisy's eyes watched Lindsay's every move in anticipation of the next one, her mouth an open smile just waiting for the next giggle to emerge.

"Sorry," Ben repeated, shaking his head with a smile. "It's just fun to see Maisy like that. She looks so much like Natalie."

Alisen studied him. "That's a good thing. A good reminder."

Ben nodded.

"Just love her," Alisen said, a catch in her voice. Her eyes were wet. With a shrug, she shoved her pot at Derick. "Here."

He took it, and she wiped her eyes, whapping Ben on the arm. "What are you doing to me?" She and Ben walked over to Lindsay and Maisy. Ben set his dish down, and they clapped their hands to the song and threw their arms up in the air as it ended.

Derick set the pot down with the rest of the food. He turned and watched as Ben leaned over and Lindsay placed Maisy's hands on either side of her daddy's face. Maisy erupted in giggles.

Sarah came out, carrying two large pitchers of syrup and banging the screen door closed behind her. "Okay, let's bless this food and eat."

* * *

After breakfast, Derick balanced on a ladder. "Marcus, hand me that string of flags."

Marcus came up a few steps with a handful of red flags. He and Hannah had driven up for the weekend, not suspecting that they would be roped into helping decorate for the Friday night barn dance.

From below, they could hear Lindsay giving directions. "I think we'll place those bales back there. That way they'll still be close to the refreshment tables but not sticking out in the path to the dance floor. Oh, and those lights can be strung up with those banner things."

"Who put her in charge?" Marcus murmured to Derick.

Derick laughed to himself. Hannah picked up a box and walked their way. She set it down at Marcus's feet and placed her hands on her hips.

"These go up with those." She gestured to the flags.

Derick looked at the forty feet of flags he'd already hung. "That would have been nice to know." He rubbed his hands over his eyes, thinking of the little sleep he'd gotten the last few days.

Hannah nodded in agreement, smiling at her little brother. "Well, now you know what you're doing."

"Yeah right," he muttered, blowing out a breath of exasperation.

Marcus chuckled. "You'd think Ben's family had never had one of these before."

"I heard that." Lindsay handed a large push broom to one of the ranch hands. "Somebody has to lead this mob." The young man smiled and winked at her, and she looked at Derick with a grin.

Just then, Amanda entered holding Greg's hand. "Hey, this looks great. What can we do?"

Marcus put his hand sideways against his mouth. "Run. Run far, far away."

Derick let his eyes roam over to the refreshment tables. Alisen threw out a tablecloth and let it settle. She straightened out the corners as Ben rolled a couple of big barrels in to stand for conversation tables.

"How many people usually come to these, Ben?" she asked.

"Oh, anywhere from forty to a hundred. It depends on the time of year and the weather, and I guess how bored people are." He winked. "We should have a good turnout tonight though. It's a full moon too."

Alisen looked out the open barn doors. "A full moon?"

"Yup. We might get all kinds of crazies in here tonight."

Lindsay turned. "Who told you my parents were coming?"

Ben laughed, but Derick was watching Alisen. Her eyes had gone to the table, her hand gently smoothing the cloth in swirls. She sighed and shook her head. "It's been a long time since I've danced." She pressed her lips together as if regretting she'd said anything. Her eyes momentarily came up to Derick's, but he made himself look busy with the lights Marcus had just thrown at him.

"Well, we'll just have to reacquaint you with the tradition," Ben said.

She smiled and gave him a small curtsy.

"C'mon, Alisen, let's get the flowers Sarah arranged for the tables." Lindsay turned, and Alisen followed.

Derick watched them, wondering how long it had been since he'd danced. He blinked and refocused.

"Greg, help us move all this. Apparently, we have to start over with these lights." He climbed down the ladder. Greg looked dubious, and Derick gave him a sympathetic pat on the shoulder as he handed him the clump of lights.

Greg turned to Amanda. "Can we go back to the cabin, dear?"

A few minutes later, a truck loaded with stereo equipment backed up to the barn doors. A few of the ranch hands piled out and started unloading. Derick watched one of them in particular out of the corner of his eye—the tall one he'd seen talking to Alisen at the corral and later in front of the campfire. Derick had the distinct impression the guy had asked her out and she'd turned him down. Maybe she'd seen what he saw: an arrogant, swaggering heartbreaker. Not that he was judging. At all.

Derick's eyes narrowed at the tack on the beam, and he tugged on the lights with a little too much force. The tack popped out, and the lights fell a few feet before catching on the previous tack.

"Hey. Watch it, will you?" Greg brushed the string of lights off his head.

"Sorry," Derick mumbled. He pulled another tack out of his pocket, took a breath, and shook his head. What was he thinking? Where was this going? Last night had changed so much, but even before that, he saw . . .

he saw so much of what he had loved in her in the first place. She was the same. Her open heart, her concern. The smile in her eyes. But at the same time, she had changed. Now none of that had anything to do with him. He frowned. And seeing her with family, with her sister . . . His defenses he thought were so strong, unbreakable, were worn thin now, almost pointless. What she had shared at the campfire had been a kick in the gut and a dizzying revelation at once. Yes, he'd been a part of it, but he hadn't shared it with her. Not the way he would have wanted to. So much time had gone by, so much denying any feelings for her.

He'd been so cold to her. He knew he'd hurt her. He had promised he would never hurt her. He couldn't keep up the pretense. He knew she had somehow come around her obstacles and braved them, and that alone was a catapult to his fortifications. So now, as much as he was undeserving, he found himself daring to consider.

"Hey, that sure is pretty." A bass voice interrupted his thoughts. The tall womanizer sauntered toward Alisen as she carried a huge vase of flowers. He took the vase from her and peeked around it. "These flowers aren't bad either."

Derick didn't know what was worse, the compliment or the way she broke into a wide smile. One more complication added to the list. The tack popped.

"Hey, I said watch it."

"Sorry." He pulled another tack out of his pocket. "I've really got to get some sleep."

* * *

There was a knock on his door. "Hm?"

Ben poked his head in. "Derick, were you going to sleep through dinner, or did you want to eat?"

Derick had crashed after the barn had been turned into a countrified disco, complete with mirror ball. He groaned.

"Well, just so you know, Mom made chicken pot pie and cherry crisp, so you better hurry if you want any. The girls have already eaten and gone to get ready."

He brought his arm up over his eyes. "Okay, Mom, I'll get up."

Ben grabbed a stuffed animal sitting on the dresser by the door and flung it at him.

"*Hey.* I said I was getting up." He looked at Ben and scowled.

Ben grinned and left the doorway. Derick chuckled, pleased to see Ben smiling so much. Although Derick knew what it was like to lose someone he loved, he could only imagine Ben's loss.

Derick didn't dwell on his theory of *why* Ben was smiling so much. He'd watched a bond develop between Ben and Alisen. They had things in common. They'd laughed together. There had been a connection for sure. He let out a derisive breath. Of course there was.

He sat up and swung his legs over the edge of the bed. He scrubbed his hair and put his shoes on. Rubbing his eyes, he sat there.

Cherry crisp. He pushed himself up and went down to eat.

Chapter 27

AMANDA PULLED ONE OF THE bobby pins from between her lips and shoved it into Alisen's hair.

"Oww. Amanda, just my hair, not my head, please."

"Beauty is pain."

"That's dumb."

"I know. Sorry." She carefully placed two more bobby pins and stood back. "There. What do you think?"

Alisen turned her head in the mirror. She gave Amanda a smile. "I like it. Thank you."

Amanda picked up the hair spray and gave Alisen a good coat.

"Okay, okay." Alisen coughed.

"Well, you're going to be dancing, maybe into the wee hours of the morning."

"I don't know, Amanda."

"Oh, I think you do." She gave her a knowing smile. "Love is in the air tonight. It's touching everyone."

The corner of Alisen's mouth came up, and she shook her head. "I don't know what you're talking about."

"I'll just say this. I'm glad I have my man all tagged and bagged because you'll be collecting all the others like flies to honey."

"I hope that's not the case, or this dress was a waste of good money." Lindsay appeared at the bathroom door. She held out the skirt of her dress and spun around.

"Oh, Lindsay, you look gorgeous," Amanda said.

She wore silvery blue, the same color as her eyes. Her hair shone sleek and straight down her back, with a single, small, jeweled clip on the side.

Lindsay smiled beautifully. "Why, thank you."

"Girls, do you think I could borrow some of your handsome partners tonight?" Hannah poked her head in behind Lindsay with a mischievous grin on her face. "Marcus dances like a duck."

Amanda giggled. Alisen smiled and tried to breathe away the nerves that kept tightening her stomach.

Lindsay helped Alisen tie the slender ribbon around her neck, and Amanda rifled through the pile of shoes under her bed. Hannah applied her lipstick.

Then Alisen stepped back, smoothing her red skirt. She looked at Hannah in her salmon shift and Amanda in her navy-blue empire waist. "Girls, they're not going to know what hit them."

They made their way to the barn. The bass thud of the music already pounded in Alisen's ears, and flashing colored lights burst out of the doorway and every space and crack of the old barn; she was sure people could see them for miles around. There would be no getting lost tonight.

She felt the flutter in her stomach and shook her head at herself. Wasn't she too old for butterflies? They entered the barn and drew more than a few looks. Amanda squeezed Alisen's hand and left for Greg, who wore a silly smile on his face after spotting his wife. Marcus stepped up to Hannah and took both of her hands, leading her straight out onto the dance floor. Hannah looked back at them with a helpless smile.

Alisen tilted her head. Marcus didn't dance like a duck. "It's more like a chicken."

"We'll say *rooster*; it sounds more manly. Oh, look at her!" Lindsay headed toward Sarah, who had Maisy on her hip. Maisy pulled into her grandma but gave Lindsay a brilliant smile.

Alisen walked over. "What a pretty little cowgirl." Maisy wore a frilly jean skirt and red cowboy boots, a little white blouse, and a red cowboy hat. Underneath her hat were two curly ponytails. "Are you going to dance tonight?"

Maisy nodded her head. She looked behind Alisen and reached. "Daddy."

Just then, Ben brushed past Alisen, smiling. "Excuse me, ladies, but I have a date."

Maisy leaned forward, and Ben caught her up, holding her small hand out and whirling to the dance floor.

Alisen watched them go.

Lindsay shook her head. "He's amazing."

Alisen nodded, having to agree. A familiar face came toward her. She broke into a grin. "Justin. I didn't know you were coming."

"Yeah. Just for tonight." He looked at the floor, shuffling his feet. "You look really nice." He looked up at her, his eyebrows raised.

"Thank you."

"Hey, squirt. I've missed you," Lindsay said.

He looked at his sister doubtfully.

"It's true."

He smiled, watching the dance floor, and then turned to Alisen. "Do you wanna dance?"

"Yes. I love this song."

He grinned, and she took his arm. She looked back at Lindsay, who wiggled her eyebrows up and down. Alisen stifled a laugh and turned to dance with Justin.

* * *

Derick smiled. Justin had asked Alisen to dance. Who could blame him? The kid was braver than he was. He shook his head at himself. Keep a clear head. That was the goal.

At least, he had been clearheaded. He had just watched all of them walk in, and he wasn't the only one. They all looked beautiful, but that red dress. He had zeroed in on that while she was still outside the barn. And it wasn't just the dress. It was how she made the dress. She used to wear her hair that way, loosely pulled back, curls hanging down her neck here and there, some across her forehead. She would have been hard not to watch.

He felt a tug on his arm.

Lindsay stood there, smiling. She made a little curtsy.

He had to smile. "You look really nice tonight."

"Thank you." She looked at him expectantly.

He chuckled. "Would you like to dance?"

She nodded, pleased. He offered her his elbow, and they walked out to the dance floor.

"Oh, hi, sweetheart. Hi, Derick."

Gia danced with Stephen, who looked a little uncomfortable on the dance floor. Gia, though, was spinning and whirling her hands around and stepping with the music.

"Oh. Mom. Please don't."

Gia didn't even pause. "What do you mean, dear?"

Lindsay began to laugh and pushed Derick to the other side of the dance floor. "We can*not* dance by them. Nope."

After the song ended, the music changed and slowed. Out of the corner of his eye, Derick saw Ben walk Alisen out to the dance floor.

Greg shuffled by with Amanda and spoke out of the side of his mouth. "Buddy, you better dance with her, or she's going to clobber you."

Derick blinked, thinking Greg had somehow read his mind, but then he saw light blue and legs, one toe tapping, and realized Lindsay was still standing there from the previous dance.

"Oh. Another dance, miss?"

She gave him a half smile and stepped forward.

He really did need to pay attention. He would hate to come across as a jerk just because he couldn't focus.

"I can't believe it's our last night. It's gone by so fast. But it also seems like we've been here forever too. Does that make sense?" Lindsay looked up at him.

He nodded. Time had seemed to crawl since the campfire.

Lindsay kept up the conversation. "I'm so glad Ben invited you. And that you invited *us*. Is it just me, or does Ben seem to be happier since we first got here?"

She gestured toward Ben and Alisen, who were talking and smiling easily. Derick pushed down that twitch in his chest.

"Yes, I think he's been happier these past couple of days."

"He deserves to be happy. More than any of us, I think."

Derick nodded. He took another look at Ben and Alisen. "He does."

He rocked Lindsay back and forth, leading with her hand in his until the song ended.

"Thanks, Derick."

"Thank *you*."

She looked behind him. "Oh, here he comes."

Ben nodded at Derick then turned to her. "Lindsay, would you like to dance?"

The twangy country song and the stomp of boots on the wood floor announced that the song required special footwork. She grinned. "I would love to."

Derick left the dance floor to lean against a stack of hay bales.

* * *

Alisen watched the couples on the dance floor and laughed quietly as Ben and Lindsay two-stepped past her. Ben grinned at Lindsay's footwork, and she clearly enjoyed trying to keep up with him.

"Hello, Cherry Girl."

She turned, and Will Eliot took both of her hands and held them out. He twirled her so swiftly and gracefully she hardly knew it had happened.

"You really are a cherry girl." He looked her over. "Will you honor me with a dance?"

"Oh." She looked at the couples going around and kicked herself for laughing at Lindsay. "Well, I'll try."

He smiled and took her by the waist, leading her out to the dance floor. He placed her hand on his shoulder and held her other one down near his hip. "Just feel my lead, just a little pressure against my hand." He moved her backward with the flow of the crowd.

She pressed his lead hand, feeling him direct her.

"That's right," he encouraged. "Now I'm going to turn you."

She raised her eyes to look at him with a nervous smile.

"Just relax and feel my lead, and keep that pressure against my hand."

He moved her backward a couple of steps; then she felt his pressure on her hand, and he moved her to his side. He lifted her arm up and led her under his while their feet still kept rhythm, and then she was back again where she started. She let out a nervous laugh, and he winked at her.

"I thought you didn't know how to do this."

She rolled her eyes and shook her head, but she was having a really good time.

He repeated the move several more times until she was able to anticipate it. When the song ended, he twirled her once more and brought her in. She wasn't prepared to be so close to him, but he looked at her and said, "Dance with me again later?"

She nodded and smiled. "Thank you."

"My pleasure." Then he turned and was gone.

Left a little breathless, she made her way to the refreshments and poured a cup of punch.

"How am I supposed to dance with you after that?"

She nearly choked on her drink. "Jay?"

"In the flesh. Actually, more flesh than I like." He laughed at his own joke, slapping his girth.

She had to chuckle. She looked around. "Where's Bobbi?"

He gestured to a small group of women sitting on hay bales, chatting over the music. "I'll drag her out there in a little while. She swears she has two left feet, and I would have to agree. I can feel it every time she stomps on mine."

He laughed again, and Alisen suppressed hers, taking a sip of her punch. She took a deep breath, and her smile faded a little.

"Jay, Derick knows everything now."

His eyes widened. "Everything?"

She nodded. "Ben asked me to share my conversion story at the campfire last night." She shrugged. "What could I do?" She looked over at Derick, who had just redirected his gaze away from where they stood. "But . . . it felt right. I think it was good."

"How did he take it?" Jay was watching Derick now too.

"Well, he didn't keel over, and he didn't seem upset, just quiet." She looked at Jay. "He thanked me."

Jay's eyebrows shot up. "He did?"

"Mm-hm."

"Well."

"Yeah." She took another sip of her punch. The song was ending, and she thought she saw a movement toward her from where Derick had been. She felt the flush in her cheeks, but then she spotted Ben coming from the other direction, giving her that dimpled grin.

"Alisen, would you dance with me?" He looked at Jay. "Hello, Jay, how've you been?" He took Alisen's elbow, and Jay smiled.

Alisen paused long enough to reach up and kiss Jay on the cheek. "Thanks for keeping my secret." She continued with Ben out to the dance floor, glancing at where Derick used to be, but he was gone.

* * *

Derick made his way over to Jay, but his sister stopped him.

"Derick, will you please dance with me?" She was already pulling him to the dance floor.

"Umm, sure, but where's Marcus?"

"He was hungry, and I love this song"—her hand came up over her eyes—"and I need a break from duck-man."

"Uh, sis, he's your duck-man. Forever."

"I know." She sighed. "I knew it when I married him. I was young and naïve, and I just didn't think you danced anymore after you were married."

Derick looked behind her. "Hm."

Hannah turned. Gia and Stephen danced a tango, and Stephen had a flower in his teeth. He seemed to have loosened up on the dance floor.

Hannah covered her grin.

"Looks like there are opportunities." Derick spotted Lindsay pushing her partner to the other side of the room.

After the spectacle, Derick found Amanda and Greg.

"Hi." Amanda smiled at them. "Are you having a good time?"

"Apparently not as good as Gia and Stephen," Hannah said.

Lindsay pulled Marcus over as the next song began. "Switch!" she declared, planting herself next to Derick.

Derick located Lindsay's parents and then directed Lindsay to another part of the dance floor. Alisen was dancing with Justin again. His insides twisted, and he turned his attention to Lindsay.

"Are you having a good time?" He really didn't need to ask.

"Yes. Ben taught me how to two-step. He's teaching me the waltz next."

"The waltz?"

"Yup. Country style." She grinned.

"So, did you see your paren—"

She pushed her fingers to his mouth. "Don't. Just don't." Then she pulled her hand away quickly and looked down.

Was she blushing?

She brought her eyes up and took a deep breath. "So, Amanda and I were talking to Ben, and he doesn't see anything wrong with a morning ride tomorrow before we leave. He says we can ride up the northern plateau to the falls."

"That's a fair distance out." Ben had described the trip to them as one of the more picturesque trails, but it was a full day's ride from the ranch and back.

"Yes, but if we leave early enough, we can drive part of the distance out with the trailers and saddle up the horses there for the best of the ride. What do you think?" She could hardly contain her excitement.

"Won't you want to sleep in tomorrow?"

She shook her head slowly, her smile and eyes wide. "No, I want to ride. I want to win back my racing title and taste victory again."

He laughed. She was so full of . . . What had Ben said? Energy. No, *sunshine.*

The song was near its end. Derick took a quick look over his shoulder. Ben had just left the sound stage and was making his way to Lindsay.

"I think it's waltz time." Derick motioned to Ben, and Lindsay grinned.

* * *

"You know, Justin, you're a pretty good dancer."

"I get it from my parents." He said it so straight-faced, Alisen burst out laughing. He smiled. "Thanks for the dance, Alisen."

"Anytime, Justin." She turned and almost ran into the person behind her.

"Alisen."

Her laughter stopped.

Derick hesitated. Her face was tilted up to him, her chin just inches from his.

"Would you . . . ?" He paused, and she saw him swallow hard.

Alisen tried to answer, but the words didn't come. Finally, she nodded her head, her eyes still on his until she managed to lower them to his shoulder.

Derick took her hand, barely touching her, and pulled her toward the back of the dance floor. He brought her in and placed his hand on the small of her back, holding her hand out gently, curving his fingers around hers, and they began to move with the music.

She watched her hand on his shoulder as they made a slow circle, like an orbiting moon, around other dancers. She was aware of his chin, his jaw line right at her cheekbone, and his scent. It was the same. She dropped her eyes, her mind working to fight any implications of what this dance might mean. What her pounding heart meant.

She didn't try to talk. It would have been pointless because she didn't know what to say. She stopped herself twice from looking up at him. But the third time, her chin came up slowly, and her eyes followed. He was there, already intent on her. He gazed into her eyes as if he wanted to say a million things, but he remained silent. And she saw it. The fire. But he was fighting it, she could tell. And she could guess why.

She'd hurt him. Lindsay would never hurt him.

The song went on, and he held her gaze. Everything else faded out, and she let it. Just this one time, she let it. He was looking at her. They had existed. Once.

He gently increased his grip as the song came to an end, and she had the feeling he didn't want it to be over. He held her for just a moment longer and finally released her. Breathless, they looked at one another. Then he gave her a fraction of a smile. She caught it and leaned her head to the side, wanting to thank him but remaining silent. He nodded his head, then turned and headed back through the crowd and out of the barn.

She stood, watching.

"Having fun?"

She turned her head to see Will. He had come up behind her, leaning down to speak close to her cheek. She looked again after Derick but had lost him in the crowd. She gave her head a little shake and blinked. "Yes." She turned to face him, stepping back.

"Is that something I should be worried about?" He motioned with his head in the direction of the barn doors.

She swallowed and lightened her expression. "Why would you be worried?"

A slow smile spread across his face.

She hadn't meant to encourage him that way, but she had to smile. He was so sure of himself, and he had drawn attention away from the reason her heart was still thumping.

He stepped up to her and pulled her to the center of the crowd. "Dance with me."

She did, but over his shoulder, she watched the open doors. After a minute, she saw a flash of platinum hair swing in the direction Derick had gone. She lowered her eyes and turned her attention elsewhere.

* * *

Derick leaned against the fence just off the barn and took in the night air. Well, he'd done it. He'd had his dance with Alisen. He'd tried to keep his breathing steady, but he'd never been so unsure of himself. And halfway through the song, he'd realized that if he could've held her forever without it disturbing anyone else, he would have. If she would have let him.

But those were big *ifs*. So he'd held her through the song. And that had to be enough.

"Derick?"

His eyes widened. "Hey, Justin, what's up?"

Justin looked up at the full moon. "Not much." He turned back to Derick, who watched the moon now too. "Can I ask you a question?"

Derick sighed. "Sure. Shoot."

"You like my sister, right?" Justin toed the ground, his hands in his pockets.

He swallowed. "Of course I like your sister, Justin. Your whole family is great."

Justin shook his head, still looking at his feet. "Naww. I mean, you *like* Lindsay." His eyes came up. "Right?"

Derick looked back at the moon. He knew what the kid was asking. "Yes, I do. Lindsay is . . . something." He looked down.

Justin shifted his weight. "But you like Alisen too." It wasn't a question.

Derick's head came around quickly. Had it been that easy to see? Derick closed his eyes. Of course Justin had been watching closely with the crush he had on her. Derick looked down but didn't answer.

"Because she talks about you all the time."

"Who does?"

Justin exhaled, exasperated. "Lindsay."

Derick's hands came up through his hair. He *was* a jerk.

"Derick?"

Derick looked over at this perceptive young man and waited.

"You can't—" He paused and looked down. Then he brought his eyes up to meet Derick's, determined. "I care for them both too, you know?"

Derick nodded. "I know."

"So just remember that." He toed the ground again.

Justin had just given Derick a protective warning. One Derick would do his best to respect.

"Derick. Here you are." Lindsay approached them in the moonlight. She looked at Justin. "Hey, you out here having a guy talk?" She fake punched her brother in the shoulder.

Derick spoke up. "Justin was giving me some good advice." He turned and gave Justin a sober nod. "Thanks, bud."

Justin nodded back then gave his sister a half smile as she regarded him. He shrugged and walked away.

Derick watched him go. He looked at Lindsay, standing straight with her hands on her hips. The moon shone silvery on her hair. "How was your waltz?"

She broke into a smile. "Okay. Fun. I think I got it there at the end. Ben's a good teacher."

He nodded. "He's a good guy. The best." He straightened up and took a deep breath. His hand came up to the back of his neck, then he dropped it. "Miss Michaels? May I have this dance?"

She held out her hand to him. "You may."

He looked at her hand then gave her his elbow. She took it, and they went back into the barn-turned-disco.

Chapter 28

ALISEN HAD JOINED THE MORNING riders. Ben's description was too tempting to pass up. Though clouds covered the sky and the temperature had dropped, they had not been disappointed. They had left the horse trailers and trucks off a dirt road on the plateau and ridden up to the foothills of the Mission Mountains, up through a hidden gorge to some spectacular mirrored lakes and waterfalls. Now they were headed back: Alisen and Amanda, Lindsay and Derick and Ben. Greg, who had seen the forecast, had opted to sleep in.

That sadness of an adventure coming to an end hung around them as the horses walked them back to the trailers. Alisen was definitely feeling the effects of the late night before. She looked up at the gray morning sky and smelled rain. It was time to go home, and she felt an underlying urgency to be there already.

She rode up next to Ben. "We've all had such a great time, Ben. I can't thank you enough, or your parents. It's been wonderful."

Ben studied the reins in his hands, smiling, and nodded his head. "I've really enjoyed you all. I've enjoyed myself." He looked up at her from under his hat. "Maisy's had fun too. All you pretty girls. Thanks for everything."

Alisen smiled.

"I hope you come back soon."

She nodded and held her hand out to him. He took it and squeezed. As they let go, they heard a yell and turned.

The whoop had come from Lindsay. She was already flying out in front of Derick. She'd obviously challenged him to one last race. Derick tailed her by a full length. Alisen looked quickly at Ben with a smile, but he was frowning, and without a word, he kicked his horse into a run after them. Amanda joined Alisen, and the girls continued to walk. But something about Ben's expression ate at Alisen's reserve.

"C'mon," she said and tentatively kicked her horse to a gallop.

Amanda followed.

Ahead, Lindsay's hat flew off, her hair whipping behind her, and Amanda went to retrieve it. But Alisen was watching the race, Lindsay barreling on even as Derick slowed, pulling his horse up. He stood in his stirrups and called to her, but Ben still pushed his horse on, passing Derick. Derick followed him, and Alisen tried to make sense of what she saw. Finally, a call reached her ears.

"Lindsay, stop!"

And Alisen remembered. The dry riverbed they'd crossed before they began this unfamiliar stretch of plateau, shallow and full of rocks.

Lindsay was headed straight for the riverbed like she didn't know it was there. Or had forgotten it in the thrill of the race and didn't see. Alisen urged her horse faster, dread in her veins, peering through the distance, even as Lindsay's horse buckled, even as she was thrown from the saddle. "No!" Alisen shouted as Lindsay disappeared over the bank.

Ben reached the bank, pulled up, and was off his horse in one swift movement. Derick pulled up just behind and was off too.

"Oh, please," Alisen whispered, and she finally reached the other horses. She slid off the saddle to the ground and ran down the embankment.

Ben was wadding up his shirt, and Derick hovered over Lindsay as though he didn't know what to do. "I tried," he said, his voice cracking. "I tried to warn her."

Lindsay's leg and arm lay twisted at wrong angles. Her hair, splashed with mud, splayed out in a fan behind her. But that was not what made Amanda gasp as she came to the edge of the bank behind Alisen. The left side of Lindsay's head rested against a rock already covered in blood. Alisen hurried to her side, and Ben shoved the wadded T-shirt in her hands. She carefully placed it between the rock and the wound, holding it there, trying not to shake.

Ben had pulled out his cell phone.

"You have service out here?" she asked. She hoped.

He gave her a nod.

Good. That was good.

Alisen looked up. Derick crouched over Lindsay, fear written on his face, staring at her white complexion and closed eyes.

"Check her pulse," Alisen said. He didn't hear her. "Check her pulse," she repeated urgently. He had to snap out of that fear.

Derick pulled his eyes up to Alisen's then reached over to Lindsay's good arm and closed his eyes. After a few long seconds, he nodded.

Alisen caught Ben's attention, and he motioned to her in a way that let her know help was coming. She found Amanda, who had her hand over her mouth as tears ran down her face. She held Lindsay's hat limply at her side. Alisen looked up again at Ben, who wiped away his own tears. He'd switched briefly to his walkie-talkie but was back on his cell, the dispatcher probably still on the line. He bent down next to Alisen and leaned over Lindsay's face, placing his cheek next to her mouth.

"I can't tell if she's breathing," he said. He shook his head.

The shirt was soaked with blood.

Amanda let out a sob. "Oh no. Oh no, Lindsay." She started to breathe too fast.

Alisen's eyes shot up to her sister. "Amanda, call Greg. Call Stephen, and have Greg head to the hospital to be there for them."

Amanda looked at her and gave a small nod. She tore her eyes away and pulled out her cell phone.

"That stupid race. That stupid race. I didn't have to run it." Derick's voice was strangled, his face twisted.

Alisen watched Derick through tears. He looked broken. She wrenched her eyes away to Ben. "When are they going to be here?"

He shook his head, trying not to look worried. "We're a long way out, but they know right where we are." He watched Derick too for a moment, as if waiting for direction, but then started rescue breathing without a word.

Lindsay still bled from the wound.

"Derick, we're going to lose her if the bleeding doesn't stop," Alisen said.

His wet eyes met hers. His mouth worked, but no sound came out.

"Derick, she needs a blessing," she whispered.

Ben pulled away, grabbed his keys from his jeans, and fumbled until he got to the vial of olive oil. He held it out to Derick so he could resume breathing for Lindsay. But Derick didn't take it. He didn't move.

"Derick," Ben said gently, a tremor to his voice, "she needs me to breathe for her. You give her the blessing."

After half a moment, Derick blinked. He nodded and took the oil. Ben resumed.

Derick applied the drop of oil and placed his hands over Lindsay's bloody hair. He looked at Alisen. His eyes held so much pain she could almost feel it. But she nodded. He pulled in a breath, closed his eyes, and began to pray.

His words shivered in the air, humble and pleading. As Derick continued the blessing, his voice calmed, and sirens sounded from the west.

* * *

Derick blearily watched the flashing lights ahead of them through the swipe of the windshield wipers. He pictured Lindsay on the stretcher, wrapped up, tubes, bags of fluids. Amanda and Alisen had gone in the ambulance. He dropped his head in his hands.

"Derick?" Ben had been quiet as he drove to the hospital.

"Hm?" He put his head down. He was grateful to Ben. He'd been able to help. While Derick had been too . . . frozen.

"I'm so sorry."

"You don't need to be. You did everything you could do. She has a chance because of you and Alisen."

Ben was quiet for another minute. Then he said, "I know how you must be feeling. Lindsay is such a . . . such a bright light. I know how it feels to have that snatched right out of your arms."

Derick slowly brought his head up. He looked at Ben then sighed. "I care about Lindsay. If she doesn't pull through this, I don't—" He pressed his lips together and tightened his jaw. "That stupid race. I should've—" He shook his head. "But I haven't—I mean, we aren't—" He sighed again. "We didn't think of each other that way." He paused. "At least, I didn't." He dropped his head in his hands again.

Ben let that hang in the air. "Does Lindsay know how you feel?"

Derick spoke into his hands. "She does. I told her at the dance last night." He rubbed his face and turned to Ben.

Ben's eyes widened. "But she was so happy all night, smiling. She—" His voice halted, and he swallowed hard.

Derick sat up and leaned his head back against the seat. "I know. She took it really well."

Ben glanced at his friend, confused. "What did you say to her?"

Derick closed his eyes and sighed. "I simply let her know I was the friend in Alisen's story." He squeezed his eyes shut as he let that sink in.

Ben took a breath as if about to say something then shifted positions in his seat a few times and tried again to speak. But he stopped himself, and it was several minutes before any words came. He finally squared his shoulders to the steering wheel, leaning forward slightly, looking at the back of the ambulance.

He shook his head and let out a breath. "Whoa."

Derick, with eyes still closed, nodded his head slowly in agreement.

Chapter 29

Two days later

Lindsay survived her operation and was off the respirator. Her condition was labeled "guarded," which Alisen learned was somewhere between critical and stable. Her head was bandaged and swollen, and her eyes were bruised. They had cut and shaved her hair before the surgery, and now, what was left of it peeked out from under the wrap like fine straw. Her arm and legs were in casts. Tubes protruded from her, and machines and IVs beeped and dripped. Lindsay lay gray and unmoving. But she was no longer in danger of crashing.

Now that Lindsay had been transferred out of ICU to Intermediate Care, where friends were admitted, Alisen had relieved Gia and Stephen so they could get something to eat, see the twins, and make phone calls. Justin remained in the room with his sister but finally slept in a chair.

Alisen touched Lindsay's hand, taking extra care to be gentle. She was so still. So . . . not Lindsay. Alisen closed her eyes and tried to will the light back into her friend. The smile, the laugh, the attitude.

A breathy murmur reached her ears. Alisen opened her eyes. Lindsay hadn't changed. But then her lips moved again, and she whispered something. Alisen followed her instinct to lean forward, her ear right next to Lindsay's mouth.

"What, sweetie? Lindsay, can you hear me?"

Lindsay spoke, hushed, barely a breath. "*Derick . . .*"

Alisen backed away enough to watch her mouth.

"*Derick.*"

Alisen froze, waiting for more, suspended between relief that Lindsay had spoken and the prick of her foremost thoughts.

She swallowed then whispered back, "He'll be here, sweetie. He'll be here soon."

Chapter 30

Two more days had passed since Lindsay's whispered words. She'd stirred only twice more, but her words had been indistinguishable, and she hadn't opened her eyes. And while Alisen had shared the news of Lindsay's first attempts to speak, she couldn't bring herself to tell them what she'd said. She didn't know if the meaning behind the uttered name was meant for general knowledge. She didn't know if she could be the bearer of that particular news. So she kept quiet, telling herself she was respecting Lindsay's privacy.

Still, Lindsay was making some improvements, and everyone else looked a little less haggard. Everyone except Derick, who continued to blame himself for the accident. Ben came with him to the hospital often, and they'd spend an hour or two keeping watch, talking quietly. Ben had begun reading to Lindsay, Barry's *Peter and the Starcatchers*, which made Alisen smile, but she suspected it was for Derick's state as well. The urgency in Derick's expression as he watched Lindsay convinced Alisen of his feelings for her. And she'd stopped visiting during the hours the men came.

Aunt Rachel, in the meantime, had returned from Florida, and as planned, Alisen moved to Rachel's condo in town. Amanda had protested, but Alisen made the point that she wasn't far, and it would be closer to the hospital and the orchard.

Now Alisen sat under one of the cherry trees at the end of a long day of work. She'd come this way for a reason, but when she couldn't remember what it was, she'd just sat down. Jane curled up in her lap, purring until she faded to sleep. Alisen absently stroked her from head to tail, her mind drifting.

She sighed at the tree above her, bare of blossoms, the green berries of beginning fruit already forming. The day's warmth pressed upon her, and she felt an urge to swim, to dive into cool water and feel it slide past her. She closed her eyes. The big lake would be freezing this early in the season.

Her phone rang, pulling her out of her thoughts. "Hello?"

"Hello, Alisen?" The voice was deep and rich, and she knew who it was immediately. A small smile came to her face. "Will."

"How'd you know?" He sounded pleased. "I've been thinking about you." He paused. "How is Lindsay?"

"She's . . ." She thought, her smile fading. "Resting. The doctors say she needs to get through this week, then they'll know more. She hasn't woken up yet."

"I hope she gets better soon."

"Thanks, Will."

Silence fell between them. She pulled at rogue weeds.

"I'd like to see you."

Her heart flopped. She wasn't sure if that was a good or bad reaction.

He continued. "I thought you could use a night out."

She took a deep breath. Yes, she could. "What did you have in mind?"

"Well, dinner, a movie. Get your mind off things."

She considered. "I think that would be great. Thanks."

"How about tonight?"

"Yes. Tonight." She surprised herself at her surety.

"I'll pick you up at seven."

She gave him the address and said good-bye then leaned back against the tree and closed her eyes.

What do I have to lose?

* * *

"Who is this boy?" Rachel called from the kitchen. She walked out with a cup of tea and sat down.

"This *boy* is twenty-eight years old. He works out on the ranch."

"On the *ranch*?"

"Yes, Rachel. It's a job, like a chef or a teacher or a fireman."

Rachel feigned innocence and took a sip of her tea. "Well, you look lovely."

Alisen looked down and smoothed her dress. She had tried not to consider too carefully what she might wear tonight. She'd chosen a simple black dress and was wearing the bracelet her father had given her.

The doorbell rang. She got up and opened the door, lifting her eyes as he filled the doorway. He wore a dark-blue silk shirt and straight-leg jeans. He'd combed his hair back, and his hat was nowhere to be seen.

He read her expression. "I'm not always a cowboy, Cherry Girl."

She dropped her eyes to his shoes then looked up at him questioningly.

"Well, a man has to be comfortable." He chuckled, lifting up a black crocodile Stetson cowboy boot.

She smiled, stepping aside to let him in.

"Rachel, this is Will Eliot. Will, this is my aunt, Rachel Scott."

Rachel blinked. "Eliot?" She set down her tea. "You wouldn't be related to Howard and Patricia Eliot, would you?"

Will looked a bit surprised and swallowed. "Yes, ma'am. Howard and Patricia are my parents."

Rachel stood and extended her hand. "Oh, well, now I see it, of course. You have your father's dark looks." Will smiled and took her hand, and she looked over at Alisen and winked.

Alisen narrowed her eyes at her aunt, recalling the look she'd given her a minute ago about Will's occupation. "How do you know Will's parents, Rachel?"

"Oh, we have mutual friends at the country club in Kalispell. I told you my friend was renting out the condominium there?"

Alisen nodded.

"Well, she and Patricia serve on the committee together for one of the club's charity fundraisers. Will, your mother is one of the loveliest women. Do tell her hello for me."

Will breathed out, relaxing. "Yes, ma'am, I'll do that."

Rachel finally released Will's hand as Alisen pulled his arm, backing out the front door. "Good night, Rachel."

"Oh, good night. You two enjoy yourselves." Rachel gave a little wave.

Will nodded good-bye and shut the door behind them.

He looked down at Alisen. "Small world."

"Yes, it is." Alisen sighed. She held back her curiosity about Will for the moment.

He offered her his elbow, and she followed him to his car but halted when she figured out which one was his.

"This is yours?"

A shiny, black Corvette blinked its headlights off and on as Will brought out his keys.

He stepped forward and opened the door for her. "I told you, I'm not always a cowboy." He looked at her seriously, and then a corner of his mouth came up. He lowered his chin and his voice. "Don't hold it against me."

Her pursed lips turned into a smile, and she shook her head.

He leaned close to her ear. "Thanks. By the way, you look beautiful."

She blushed and ducked into the car, and he shut the door.

* * *

They drove a long time. So long that Alisen worried she hadn't understood his invitation. Dinner and a movie, right? But then they reached the tiny town of Marion out by Little Bitterroot Lake and had dinner at a secluded little grill she'd never heard of. The food was great, the atmosphere relaxing. Will kept the conversation light, and only a few times did Alisen blush under his gaze. She asked about his parents, and he shrugged. His dad was in the oil business, he said, and his mother threw herself into any kind of social event that came her way. Ranch work was his way of escaping their sham of a marriage. He dropped the subject, reaching for her hand.

The movie was also a surprise. Again, they drove all the way to Kalispell to the megaplex and agreed on a romantic comedy. The tone of the movie was just right, not too sad or violent. Will placed his arm around her shoulders with ease.

She looked at him, questioning his move, but he shrugged and whispered, "We're just dancing *real* slow."

She stifled a laugh, and he smiled wickedly.

After the movie, he suggested a drive around the lake.

She considered. "Could I get a rain check?" she asked. They'd spent so much time in the car already. "I've had a great time, but I'm afraid I'd fall asleep, and that would be rude." She covered a yawn.

"Well, it's assuring to know I'm such stimulating company."

She grinned. "It's not you; it's me."

He grinned back. "Your honesty is brutal."

"I was going for alluring."

He laughed out loud and drove her back to the apartment.

He walked her to the door. Alisen felt the drain of the week affecting her energy level. She pulled her keys out of her purse.

He put his hands softly on her arms. "I hope you had a good time."

She watched her keys and nodded her head. "I did." She sighed and looked up at him. "It's been a long week. This was perfect. Thank you."

The way he looked at her, she knew what he wanted. She wasn't sure what she wanted. But as he pulled her closer, leaning in, she turned away slightly. He paused only a fraction of a second then kissed her cheek. He stayed there then moved to her neck, brushing her hair back with his nose.

She took a soft, deep breath and pushed gently against his chest. He came back and watched her mouth.

"Will, I . . ."

His finger came up to run gently along her face. "Alisen, I've known a few of you Mormon girls. I wouldn't keep you from that or stand in your way."

She looked at him, feeling something tighten in her chest.

He continued, stroking her cheek. "But you have to know, I want to see more of you." Without another word, he brought his other hand around her waist and pulled her to him, kissing her lips gently.

She'd missed kissing. She missed it a lot. As she felt herself give in, her phone rang.

She broke away, blinking. Will quickly covered his look of disappointment. She looked at her phone. It was Amanda.

"I have to take this." She turned and put the phone up to her ear. "Amanda?"

"Alisen." She sounded agitated.

Alisen struggled for composure. "What's happened?"

* * *

The hospital doors slid open, and Amanda stepped up to greet her with a hug. Her eyes were shiny, and she took Alisen's hand. "C'mon."

Alisen followed quickly into the elevator. It moved at an achingly slow pace, and they both watched the doors, willing them to open. When they did, the girls rushed down the quiet hall. Four doors down and on the right, they turned into Lindsay's hospital room.

Amanda brushed the curtain aside. "She's here," she whispered.

Alisen timidly stepped past Amanda. She took in a breath, and her hand came up to her mouth as tears sprang to her eyes.

"Hey, gorgeous. You look hot." Lindsay's voice came out in a raspy whisper laced with exhaustion.

Alisen smiled as a tear made its way down her face. "I was on a—" She swallowed. "I was out." She carefully stepped forward, making her way to Lindsay's side.

"Lucky guy. Hope I didn't . . . drag you away from anything . . . important."

Alisen let out a small laugh and bent forward to kiss Lindsay's cheek. She pulled back, shaking her head. Lindsay's head was still wrapped in bandages, but the swelling had gone down. The bruises were fading, and her blue eyes were tired but beautiful as she looked up at Alisen.

"It's so good to see you," Alisen said softly.

"You too. Did you see my cast?" Lindsay made a slight gesture with her hand.

The cast on Lindsay's leg was graffitied with writing and pictures, big and small, in a rainbow of colors. Alisen moved closer, and her eyes roamed over a few jokes.

What time is it when Lindsay wants to race? Time to call an ambulance. She smiled and found another one.

Let us know if you see any signs of drain bramage.

These were terrible.

The vet wanted to put you down.

Alisen let out a soft groan. She read out loud. "We asked the horse if you were all right. He answered, 'Neeeigh.'"

That drew a few chuckles, and she looked up. She'd been so absorbed in seeing Lindsay awake, she'd barely noticed the others in the room. Gia and Stephen smiled. Marcus stood behind Hannah, his arms wrapped around her shoulders. Greg sat with Amanda perched on his knee as she grinned. Ben stood next to Justin at the head of Lindsay's bed, just across from Alisen. Derick sat in the same chair he'd been in the last few days, looking at Alisen as he'd done at the dance. For a moment, Alisen couldn't look away. A sense of belonging rushed through her like warm wind. Then she remembered Lindsay's whispered words.

She blinked and looked around. "Who made up these awful jokes?" she asked, her voice filled with emotion.

Marcus smiled. "It was a group effort."

Gia shook her head, watching her daughter with glassy eyes. The accident could have gone another way so easily.

Alisen turned to Lindsay again. "How do you feel?" It was a stupid question, but it had to be asked.

Lindsay managed a wider smile. "Like Ben hit me with his truck."

Ben protested. "What did *I* do?"

"I heard you . . . kissed me."

Ben flushed. "That was rescue breathing."

A mischievous light came to her eyes. "Is that what . . . you're calling it?"

"That's enough, children," Gia interrupted.

Justin and Greg chuckled.

"Alisen?"

Alisen turned her attention back to Lindsay.

"Thank you."

Alisen came to her side again, sat down on the chair there, and gently laid her head next to Lindsay's arm, taking her hand. She closed her eyes. "You're welcome."

Quiet conversation continued, but Alisen stayed put. She drifted in and out of sleep right there next to Lindsay.

When she woke, the room had emptied somewhat. Greg had taken Amanda and Justin home. Ben and Derick had gone for a walk. The clock on the wall said midnight, though it felt like four in the morning. Lindsay was sleeping again. Alisen quietly excused herself. She needed to use the restroom and stretch her legs. She left her high heels in a corner, slipped on a pair of Lindsay's hospital booties, and padded out of the room.

A visit to the restroom and a splash of water on her neck revived Alisen enough that she felt she could make the drive home from Kalispell. She headed back to the room but paused as she approached the corner, hearing hushed voices and her name.

"Don't you think Alisen should know?" she heard Ben ask.

"Not yet." That was Derick. "I'd like to keep things quiet for now, until Lindsay is stronger."

"But you are going to propose?"

Alisen froze at the question. Derick didn't answer, or maybe he'd nodded.

"I don't think you want to wait too long. The accident is one thing, but—" Ben said.

"I want to do this right," Derick said. "Let Lindsay have the focus of her family. Let everyone catch their breath from all of this. I've rushed things before." He paused. "I'm not doing that again."

Alisen began to back up. She didn't want to hear any more. She didn't need to.

But then Ben said, "Well, she's definitely worth the wait. I hope everything works out the way you want it to."

"Same to you, bro. Same to you."

She heard the sound of a back slap and retraced her steps, escaping to a stall in the women's restroom.

So, now she knew. As much as she'd convinced herself before that Lindsay would be good for him, she hadn't really let him go. But now she could. She had to. He would marry Lindsay. That's all she'd ever wanted to know. Closure.

She placed her hand on the stall door latch and took a deep breath.

By the time Alisen returned to the room to gather her things and say good-bye, those who remained were already saying good-bye to Derick.

Ben shook his hand, drawing Derick in for a hug. "Take care, brother. We'll see you in a few weeks."

A few weeks?

Derick turned to Lindsay, who was awake now. He bent over her and kissed her forehead. "No riding without doctor's approval, all right?"

She attempted a smile, but it faded. She looked at him. "I'm sorry." A tear rolled down her cheek.

He shushed her, wiping at the tear.

The others stepped forward with their farewells.

A lump had formed in Alisen's throat. He was leaving Lindsay, all of them, for a few weeks?

Before she knew what she was saying, she asked, "Where are you going?" She hoped the sudden desperation hadn't sounded as clear as it felt.

He turned to her. Everyone turned. Then they looked at Derick.

But he still watched Alisen, studying her. Then he smiled gently. "I have to go out of the country. The Philippines. I was waiting for Lindsay to make a turn for the better." He turned and smiled at Lindsay. "And she has. But now I have to get back to work. There are some things that need my attention. I'll be back in two, maybe three, weeks though."

She became very aware of Lindsay watching her. She dropped her eyes and nodded. "I just didn't know." She kept her eyes down. It was like summer in the orchard again, and he was leaving without her.

She cursed at herself. So this is how it would be? She'd never get over him? She'd talk it up but never be free of him?

Give yourself time, Alisen.

Time. Yes. He'd be gone. No constant reminders. She'd come to terms and let him go. She would. *Because four years hasn't been enough time already.* She turned and faced the window.

Marcus and Hannah offered to walk with Derick down to the lobby and said their own good-byes. Alisen spotted a tissue box on the windowsill and reached for one. She blotted at her persistent tears and leaned against the window. Before he left, Derick looked at Alisen one more time. She saw it in the dark window's reflection. She lifted her chin and smiled. He seemed pleased and returned it. Then he was gone.

Ben moved beside Alisen. "Are you all right?"

She nodded. "It's been such a long week."

He placed a hand on her arm. "I know."

They both turned and looked at Lindsay, who had fallen asleep again.

Chapter 31

Alisen had promised Will she would call him. He'd been so thoughtful. He'd paid Alisen every attention to make sure she could relax and get her mind off things at the hospital. It had been two days since their date, and now she held her phone in front of her, considering.

It was his kiss that occupied her thoughts now. And though it had been a long time, a *very* long time since she'd been kissed by anybody, she knew his kiss had a lot more intention behind it than she was comfortable with.

She was confused about Will. He was good at his game, but she hadn't forgotten Ben's warning. Will was definitely a ladies' man. He was also kind and sure of himself, and though he was obviously very wealthy, he had chosen to live his life in humbler surroundings. Well, if you could call a Corvette humbler surroundings.

And he'd left a message on her phone, wanting to see her again. What did she have to lose? Nothing. As she pulled up his number, her phone buzzed with an incoming call.

"Hello?"

"Alisen."

"Hey, Dad. How are you?"

"I'm well." Was he smiling? "I'm calling to ask you a favor."

She paused. "What do you need?"

"I was hoping you could come up for a few days. There's, uh, someone I want you to meet."

"Oh, Dad." She put her forehead in her hand and let her hair fall over her face. "I don't want another setup."

Her father chuckled. "No, Alisen. Not everything is about you."

The irony in that sentence alone. "Wait, what?"

He continued to chuckle. "I've met someone, and I want you to meet her, get to know her."

"Her?"

There was a short silence. "Alisen, I know your mom, she . . . I'll always love her. I'll always miss her. But, Sheryl . . . Well, I'd like you to meet her."

"Dad?"

"Yes?"

"I think that's great. And I think . . . Mom would think so too."

He was silent. Then he said quietly, "Thank you, Alisen."

"When do you want me?"

"As soon as you can get away. By the way, how is the Michaels girl?"

"I think she's going to make it. It's a miracle."

"That's good to hear."

"It is. I have some things to do before I can get away, but I can be up the day after tomorrow, all right? Then I can stay through the weekend."

"Sounds good. We'll see you then."

"Bye."

She hung up and shook her head. She let her mind turn things over. A few minutes later, the phone rang again, making her jump.

"Hello?"

"Alisen, I just got off the phone with Dad. *Wow*. Are you going up? I can't believe it. I mean, I know he's dated, but I don't think this is like that. He sounds different. Did you think he sounded different? Greg and I are going up tomorrow for the day. I wonder what she's like. I hope she's not stuffy. Ugh, I couldn't stand it if she was stuffy. Are you still there?"

Alisen muffled a laugh. "Yes, I'm still here."

"Well, what do you think?"

"I think I'm looking forward to finding out what she's like. I won't be going up until Wednesday, so it sounds like we'll miss each other."

"Do you want me to call you and give you the scoop?"

"No, don't call. I want to find out for myself."

"Okay. Are you visiting Lindsay today?"

"I already did, this morning. Ben was there with his parents. Maisy too."

"Oh, I'm sorry I missed them. Doesn't she look better?"

"Yes, yes, she does."

"I hope Derick doesn't have to stay away too long. He's so good for her."

"Mm-hm."

"Okay, well, I need to go. The twins are on the rampage. This is good practice." Alisen heard a loud bang and a squeal. "Bye!" Amanda hung up.

Alisen turned her phone over and over in her hands then stopped. She brought up the number.

"Hello, Will? I'll be visiting my dad up in Kalispell this week, but I'd like to see you."

Chapter 32

ALISEN STOOD IN THE ENTRY of her father's rented condo and smiled.

"Sheryl, I'd like you to meet my daughter Alisen. Alisen, this is Sheryl Camden."

Alisen stepped forward and extended her hand. She hadn't known what to expect—anyone would have been a surprise—but there was something about this woman that put Alisen at ease.

"Alisen, it is so good to meet you. I've heard a lot about you from your father."

Alisen gave her father a doubting look.

"He's very proud of you, you know." Sheryl smiled openly.

"Well, that's nice to hear. I wonder sometimes. He once referred to my work as 'babysitting cherry trees.'"

Keith laughed nervously, and Alisen enjoyed hearing it. This might be fun.

He waved her into the house. "Come on, let's sit down." He offered her a chair and sat next to Sheryl on the sofa. Sheryl offered him her hand, and he took it, interlacing his fingers in hers and resting it on his knee.

Alisen tried to be inconspicuous about her gawking. "So how did you two meet?"

Keith looked at Sheryl, who grinned back at him. She pushed on his shoulder with her free hand. "You tell it."

Her father tried unsuccessfully to hide his look of pleasure.

Alisen watched this interchange with wonder. She looked again at Sheryl. Her light auburn hair fell to her shoulders in a soft, thick wave. Her eyes were gray-green, and her fair complexion had a nice tanned glow to it and a few freckles. Alisen guessed her to be younger than her father but not by much. Her eyes crinkled when she smiled, and her hands showed age and grace. She was beautiful and knew it but wouldn't flaunt it.

"Well," her father began, "Sheryl was out on the golf course, and we ended up playing at the same time. There had been a mix-up with our tee times, and Sheryl just suggested we play alongside each another."

"Why not?" Sheryl added.

He turned to her. "Why not." He continued. "So we were playing, and I noticed she was quite good."

"And I noticed the same thing about him. So I suggested we make a game of it."

He smiled. "And she bet me dinner."

"Who won?" Alisen asked.

"Sheryl did," Keith said just as Sheryl raised her hand.

Alisen's mouth dropped open. Keith was very proud of his winning streaks. "Dad?"

He shook his head back and forth. "I know. It was humiliating. But I had agreed to a bet, so now I had to take this woman to dinner. And to tell you the truth, she had a very unfair advantage."

"What was that?" Sheryl asked.

"I couldn't take my eyes off her the entire game."

Sheryl hit him lightly on the shoulder, smiling her crinkly eyes at him.

Alisen was speechless.

Keith turned to Alisen. "At dinner that night, what else could I do but challenge her to another game?"

"What else, indeed?" Was this her father?

Sheryl looked at Alisen. "And another and *another*. He finally beat me on our fourth matchup, and that's when I decided to tell him I'd played professionally for fifteen years."

Alisen's mouth drew into an O, and then she let out a laugh.

Her father hung his head but then looked up, smiling. "It did make me feel a bit better, actually." He chuckled.

Alisen studied her father and saw what she had not been able to see for so long. She saw why her mother had fallen in love with vain, self-centered Keith Embry. He looked back at her, and they were both smiling, all the way up to their eyes.

* * *

The expansive country club facilities covered a low hill overlooking the course. Sidewalks and raised gardens flanked by concrete benches wove through the buildings. And Alisen was lost.

She'd already come through the outdoor eating area with big red umbrellas and followed signs to where she thought she was supposed to meet Sheryl and her father, but she'd ended up in a small, empty courtyard with a little bench bearing a plaque with someone's name shaded under a young crabapple tree. She went to start over.

As she turned the corner, she bumped into someone big who immediately held her arms, pushing her backward into the courtyard. Almost before she had time to see it was Will, he put his finger to her lips to shush her then moved his finger down her neck and kissed her. She started to protest, then his kiss became harder, more searching, and her objections crumbled.

Why? Why would she push this one away? She threw herself into the kiss. He pulled away briefly, smiling, then brought her to him again.

"Hello," he finally whispered in her ear.

"Hi." She lowered her eyes. "That was a surprise."

"For me too. I saw you out in the dining area. I couldn't help it." He pulled her chin up. "Do you mind?"

She gave him a small smile and shook her head. He looked over her face and then kissed her again, softly this time.

"So, you made it," he said when they came up for air.

She nodded. "And your parents are here?"

"Somewhere. Hm." He looked at his watch. "I'm meeting some people in a few minutes, but can I see you later?"

She nodded.

He smiled, and it was stunning. "I'll call you." He kissed her again passionately then turned and was gone.

She stood there, blinking, then walked over to the bench and put a hand out to steady herself as she sat down hard.

Why didn't she feel better?

If it doesn't feel comfortable, that's your warning.

She shook her head. All they had done was kiss. *No, this is bigger.*

It wasn't the kiss. It was Will. Handsome, seductive, thoughtful, self-assured cowboy Will, who was wealthy on top of everything else, *not* that it mattered.

She raised her eyes to the sky, looking through the red-tinted leaves of the crabapple.

Why. Why do you send me these unattainable, perfect men?

The anger came, and she tensed her jaw and clenched her fists.

Why? Why do I have to be alone? Is that what you want? Mother, is that what you *want? I don't want it. I don't want to be alone anymore.*

The tears came, hot and stinging. She was tired of crying, and it only made her angrier. She stood and paced the small space, breathing heavily, her nostrils flaring. She sat down again, taking a deep breath and blowing it out. Then shame filled her. She thought of Lindsay and Ben and her mother and knew there were worse things out there.

Be still, and know that I am God.

The words came gently, a plea more than a command. She stared at nothing, hearing them again.

Be still.

She calmed, wiping her eyes. After a few moments, she looked at her watch.

"Alisen?"

She looked up, startled. "Oh. Hi, Dad." She sniffled pathetically.

"What happened? We waited for you, but—" His eyebrows came up. "Is it the Michaels girl? Did the hospital call?"

She smiled at his unfamiliar concern, grateful for Sheryl's obvious influence over his softer manner. She shook her head. "No, Dad. Lindsay is good. Doing well. She'll be, uh . . ." Alisen dropped her head, laughing softly, "engaged pretty soon." Her stomach twisted at the words. She couldn't bring herself to tell him who she'd be engaged to.

Her father stood very still. "Oh." He hesitated then came to sit beside her on the bench. He placed a hand on her shoulder and handed her his monogrammed handkerchief. She took it and blew her nose miserably.

"Alisen, I . . ."

"You're what, Dad? You're sorry?" She balled up his handkerchief in her fist. The anger was making a comeback, and she didn't feel any compulsion to hold it in. Her father was right there, and he was going to hear her. "You're sorry I'm alone? You're sorry you pushed away the only real love I've ever known? The one who ruined it for anyone else out there who may want a shot at me?" She was breathing hard again. She stood and resumed pacing. "You're sorry that you ignored me for so long, that when love finally hit me, it blew me out of the water? *Sorry* that you listened to a bunch of lies from your drunk golfing buddy, but you couldn't listen to your own daughter?" Her voice cracked. It was pouring out of her now. She stopped and faced Keith. "Are you sorry that you didn't blink an eye when Greg, the *dentist*, asked if he could marry barely twenty-year-old Amanda?"

He'd grown tense, looking through her.

She narrowed her eyes and sat down again, trying to regain control. Her voice lowered. "Are you sorry for using Mom and your reaction to her death as a way to manipulate me away from the two things I have loved most about my whole life?"

He remained as still as the stone bench. She didn't look to see his face. She didn't have to. It didn't matter. *This* was about *her*.

She dropped her voice to a whisper. "You may have lost Mom, but at least you had her for more than one summer."

The quiet settled so heavily in the sheltered space that she could hear his watch tick. But she didn't know how many minutes passed. Finally, he said, "Yes."

She turned her head a fraction of an inch. "What?" she whispered.

He'd said it quietly but steadily. "Yes. I'm sorry. About all of it."

She turned. A tear trailed down his face, and a muscle twitched in his cheek. He brought his eyes to her. His voice was soft and rough at the same time. "No more games, Alisen. I swear. I'm sorry. I was . . . blinded. I hadn't loved in so long." He shook his head, wiping his eye. "But those are not excuses. No, they're not." He looked back at her. "I could see the change in you, the sadness. Of course I could. You looked like me."

She blinked.

"But after awhile, you got better, happier. Well, more sure of yourself anyway." He sighed. "I told myself I had done the right thing, congratulated myself. But then," he shook his head, "you let me know you'd been baptized into that church, that you'd been going for weeks, even without . . . him. I looked through those magazines you gave me." She released a short breath of surprise, and he nodded. "And although I didn't understand a lot of it, I could see that it wasn't what I had come to believe."

He folded his hands together and leaned forward, his elbows resting on his knees. "Then you dragged your sister with you, and Greg. I could see changes there too." He furrowed his brow. "But I still saw that sadness in you. And I knew *that* sadness had everything to do with . . . what I had done."

She blinked at him. He'd apologized once before, but this was different. Would she allow herself to trust him? She searched his eyes, begging to feel the truth.

He shook his head at the ground. "After all I'd done to keep you from leaving, I had placed a wall between us bigger than any religion or boy could ever do." He swallowed and put his hands over hers. "I'm sorry for the pain I've caused you. Can you ever forgive me . . . for being so selfish?"

She was still a little shocked from her outburst, and now his confession added to it. But Alisen didn't feel sad or confused. She felt relieved. And the relief grew to warmth. Then the warmth became something she hadn't felt for her father in a really long time.

"Dad?"

He looked up.

She leaned into his chest, hugging his waist, resting her cheek on his cashmere sweater. She didn't cry; she didn't even tear up.

He brought his arms around her, and his hand ran from the top of her head down her hair. He leaned his cheek on the top of her head and whispered, "I love you, Alisen Anne."

She closed her eyes and smiled.

After a moment, his phone rang. She released him, and he dug it out of his pocket. "Yes, darling?" He wiped at his eyes with his fingers.

Alisen gave a little laugh, offering his wad of handkerchief back. He looked at her reprovingly, and she kept it.

"Yes, I found her." His eyes softened, and he smiled. "She isn't feeling too well. I'm walking her home. Yes, I'll see you there. Me too. Bye."

She frowned.

"What?" he asked.

"Dad, 'Me too'? When a woman on the phone says 'I love you,' you say 'I love you' back to her, no matter where you are or who may hear you. All right?"

He chuckled and ran his hand over her hair. "All right."

* * *

Derick stood outside the concrete-block building, hoping for better cell service. "What was that? I couldn't hear; you were breaking up."

Ben's voice crackled, but it was better. "Lindsay's asking when you'll be home. And says to tell you she's graduated to eating soup. Very exciting."

Derick smiled. "Tell her I'll be home in two days and to just keep getting better. You sound good too."

"That's 'cause I am. Hey, I don't know if you've tried, but none of us can seem to get h–d of Al–n." The connection broke up again.

"Alisen?" Derick walked farther into the open, frowning.

"Yeah, I thi–k she's w– . . . dad. You might w—" Fuzz interrupted and then cleared. "–d hurry."

He lost the connection. He stared at his phone, trying to attach meaning to those last few sentences.

Nobody could get hold of Alisen, and she was with her dad? Hurry.

Dread hit him in the gut.

Chapter 33

Elizabeth opened the front door and picked her bag back up off the porch. She was exhausted and wanted only to fall into bed. She entered the house and looked up at the sound of laughter.

"Hello?" she called.

"Is that Elizabeth?"

"Yes. Is that my father?" Was it? She pulled the door closed behind her with her foot.

"Elizabeth is home."

"Yes, Dad, we know." More laughter.

Elizabeth dropped her bags and stepped around into the dining room. She placed her hands on her hips. "What's this?"

Her father, Alisen, and a woman she assumed was Sheryl Camden were sitting around the table playing a card game. A card game.

"Hello, sweetheart. Did you have a good flight?" Keith said.

"Yes, *pumpkin*, I did, thanks." What was with the term of endearment?

Alisen giggled behind her hand of cards.

"Umm, have you guys been drinking?" She looked at Alisen. "I thought you didn't do that." She looked at their glasses. Colas and something clear.

Alisen's cell phone rang, but she looked at the number and let it ring.

Keith stood and took her arm. Why was he smiling so much?

"Elizabeth, I'd like you to meet someone. Sheryl?" Sheryl stood up. "This is my oldest daughter—"

"Oh, thanks for that," Elizabeth interrupted.

"—Elizabeth. Elizabeth, this is Sheryl Camden."

The two women shook hands, and Sheryl said, "Elizabeth, you are lovely." She placed her other hand over Elizabeth's. "Welcome home."

Elizabeth felt a smile pull at her mouth, and it spread across her face.

Alisen's phone rang again, and she again let it ring as if she hadn't heard it.

Elizabeth nodded at her. "You're popular tonight."

Alisen shrugged. She reached over and turned the phone off.

Elizabeth watched her. "Did you get a haircut? You're wearing it down again. It looks better that way."

Alisen gave her a small smile. "Thanks . . . pumpkin." Alisen's shoulders shook, and her father laughed.

Elizabeth took a few steps over to Alisen, who cringed a little through her giggle. She picked up Alisen's glass and took a drink. Ginger ale.

She raised one eyebrow. "Well, I'm thinking I'm so tired that this is a weird little dream I'm having. So if you'll excuse me, I'm going to bed."

Her father beat her to her bags, and she paused then walked past him. He followed her to her room.

"Elizabeth?"

She turned, her hand on the doorknob. "Yes, Dad?"

"What do you think?"

"Hm?"

"About Sheryl."

She looked back toward the front room. "She's beautiful, Dad. I'll know more tomorrow."

He smiled at her, and she couldn't help but smile back. She didn't know what was going on, but this was the most *normal* she'd seen her family in a long time, and that was very *not* normal. But maybe that was a good thing.

More laughter came from the other room. She shook her head again. "Good night, Dad."

"Good night, Elizabeth. Glad you're home."

* * *

The clock said eleven. Elizabeth shaded her eyes against the sun shining through the light curtains. Groaning, she rolled over. She sat up and pulled the covers back then stood and put on a red silk kimono-style robe she'd been given during her time in Tokyo. Cranes stood against a big gold moon on the back. She sighed. She had loved Japan. That was a long time ago. She loosely wrapped the belt around her and made her way out to the kitchen. But before she could leave the hallway, she stopped.

Voices whispered urgently. One was low, a guy's voice, very deep, and it carried in spite of the whispering. The other, she was certain, belonged to her sister. She peeked around the corner, keeping out of sight.

Just inside the front doorway, Alisen stood looking up, with her hands on the guy's chest, speaking softly.

"I've just met her. I want to get to know her better, and we have some things planned. It's just not a good time."

He was tall, his back to Elizabeth. He held Alisen's arms, rubbing them up and down softly. She took in his backside with a little smile. *You go, Alisen.*

"I understand. I'm busy too." He touched Alisen's face, and her eyes dropped. "Hey, smile. I just thought . . ." He bent down and kissed her. Whew, it wasn't just a peck either. She backed away around the corner. She wasn't a voyeur, just an eavesdropper.

"Will . . . please."

Elizabeth peeked back around the corner and narrowed her eyes. Alisen pushed against the guy's chest, and he was backing around to the door, slowly turning so Elizabeth could see his face. He grinned crookedly, handsomely, devilishly. Elizabeth gasped then quickly backed away out of sight.

"I promise I'll call you soon."

"All right, Cherry Girl, but don't keep me waiting too long." There was a pause. Another kiss. The door clicked shut.

She peeked again. Alisen stood facing the door, her arms crossed in front of her, holding herself. She shook her head then turned toward the kitchen.

Elizabeth tiptoed back to her room and silently shut the door. She sat on her bed and grabbed the pillow, hugging it to her chest.

Hm. Yes, she was sure it was him. She thought. How long ago was that? Three years? Maybe things had changed. Then again, maybe they hadn't. At all.

There was only one way to be sure. Elizabeth reached for her phone then stopped. She would talk to Alisen first. She didn't want to go ruining anything else for that girl. It could all be harmless. Nothing to worry about.

She stood and walked more confidently out of the room.

"Good morning, Alisen."

Alisen smiled wryly as she looked at the clock on the kitchen wall. "Yes, I guess it still is. How did you sleep?" She set down her book.

"Very well." Elizabeth opened the fridge and started looking for ingredients. She pulled out a peach, some yogurt, and a bag of spinach. "Where's Dad?"

"He and Sheryl go golfing every morning. They'll eat lunch at the club, I'm sure. They might come home after that."

She set her ingredients down on the counter and moved to a cupboard to get the blender. "So, no special plans today for the three of you?" She pulled a banana off the bunch and went to another cupboard for the oatmeal and honey.

"No set plans, but we usually do something in the afternoon. Yesterday we tried to play tennis. It was pretty funny."

Elizabeth looked up as she washed the peach and took out a knife. "Why is that?" She sliced the peach into the blender, threw in a handful of spinach and oatmeal, and squirted in some honey.

Alisen watched her now, a curious look on her face. "Have you ever seen a frog play tennis?"

Elizabeth peeled the banana and dropped it in then added the yogurt. "I can't say that I have." She looked up at Alisen.

Alisen pointed to herself and nodded her head gravely.

Elizabeth had to smile. "Our little tree frog." She added a dash of salt and a cupful of ice, snapped the lid in place, and turned the blender on.

Alisen watched the blender with a little grimace. "What are you making?"

"Green smoothie."

Alisen pursed her lips.

"Oh, you're going to try some," Elizabeth said.

Alisen grimaced again.

She stopped the blender, poured two tall glasses, added straws, and brought them to the table. She sat down and casually asked, "So, little sister, what happened while I was away?"

Alisen looked at her blankly, blinked twice, looked at the beige-green drink, sniffed it, and then took a long draw on the straw. She swallowed, and her brow came up. She shook her head. "You wouldn't believe me if I told you."

Elizabeth held her drink up to Alisen. "Try me."

Alisen hesitated then lifted her glass and clinked it against Elizabeth's.

* * *

The treadmill hummed. Elizabeth had slept too late to make her usual route around the course, and the sun blazed today, so she was in the air-conditioned workout room at the club. Her mind hummed too. Too much information was an understatement. Elizabeth had stared, dull-eyed and openmouthed, as Alisen had related everything, from the beginning, backing up and filling in missing pieces, until Elizabeth's head spun.

Some of it she knew, of course. She'd been there during the summer romance and had been there the night of the big blow-up. She wasn't proud of her inaction at the time. But today she'd gotten way more information than she'd been after. Most importantly, she'd learned that Alisen's relationship with Will was fairly new and that Alisen didn't think she was in love with him but it could easily go that way if she let it. Elizabeth drew her own conclusions about how long Alisen had been without male companionship. No way was she going to say anything more until she knew for sure, but it did seem as though Alisen was shying away from the relationship for some reason. Maybe Elizabeth wouldn't have to do anything. She told herself it would be best if Alisen worked it out on her own.

She hit the button on the console to increase her speed.

* * *

Friday night, Elizabeth sat on Alisen's bed, watching her rifle through her closet.

"I'm going to go to this stupid dance. I told him I wasn't going, but I've changed my mind. I feel like I finally have the nerve to ask him some questions before things go any further in our relationship." Alisen picked up her phone and tried dialing again, but no one picked up.

"Do you want me to come with you?" Even after thirty-six hours, Elizabeth hadn't been able to shake her misgivings about Alisen and Will.

"Why? You don't like these things." Alisen threw clothes on the bed. She paused and looked at her sister. "Europe spoiled you."

Elizabeth sighed, exasperated. "I know." She stretched out on Alisen's bed and made a face at the thought of the bland country club dances. She watched her sister with caution. "I would go though. You may need some backup."

"Backup? It's a club dance, not a stakeout. I need to see Will."

Elizabeth wasn't sure she liked the sound of that. "You *need* to see him?"

"I need to *talk* to him. I have to figure out if his attractive, caring, confident soul is for me."

"In one night?"

Alisen stopped and frowned at her sister. "It's possible."

Elizabeth felt a twinge of sympathy. "Okay, but . . . don't lose your head. Stick to what you feel is right. Men can be very persuasive."

Alisen looked at the ceiling. "I know." She held up a pair of capris and a blouse.

Elizabeth nodded.

Alisen's phone rang. She looked at it then threw it down on the bed without answering.

"Who do you keep ignoring?" Elizabeth was curious about how this little habit of her sister's fit in with everything else.

"Oh, practically everyone except Rachel and Dad. And Will."

"Amanda?"

Alisen sighed. "Even Amanda. Just while I'm here." She looked apologetically at Elizabeth. "She's just too close to them. I need a bubble. I did call the hospital to check on Lindsay and to give her my love. I called late and left a message." She looked guilty.

But Elizabeth nodded. It was more than she would have done. Alisen was hurting over the Lindsay-Derick thing. More space was better. "Have you checked your messages?"

Alisen shook her head. "Not until I figure things out with Will." She sat down on the edge of the bed, dressed. "I just can't handle that right now."

"What about this Ben guy? He sounds nice."

Alisen sighed. "Ben. Ben is a sweet guy. He is."

Elizabeth finished her thought. "He's a *friend.*"

Alisen nodded.

Elizabeth, of all people, looked her sister in the eye. "You know, Alisen, friends can make for great *boy*friends."

Alisen placed her hand over Elizabeth's. "I know."

Elizabeth nodded. Alisen stood and wiggled her feet into her sandals.

She turned to Elizabeth. "You know where I'll be." She headed for the door.

Elizabeth followed her. "How do you know he's even going to be there?"

"His mom is putting it on, and he feels obligated. He actually sounded kind of relieved I wasn't going. Probably embarrassed. If he'd pick up his phone, I'd just meet him somewhere." Alisen paused at the front door.

"Why don't you just wait until the dance is over?"

Alisen folded her arms. "Because if I don't talk to him now, I may lose my nerve. And I want to talk to him where . . . he can't just kiss me the whole time."

"Oh yeah, that's sooo annoying." Elizabeth smiled.

"It is when I'm trying to *talk*."

Elizabeth laughed. Alisen opened the door.

"Keep your phone on."

"I will."

"You're sure you don't want me to come?"

"Yes. I'll be fine. I'll be strong." She headed down the steps.

"Good luck," Elizabeth called.

Alisen looked at her, determined. "Thanks."

With a wave, Elizabeth closed the door. Maybe it was just fine. Maybe Alisen could handle herself. *Maybe I should just mind my own business,* Elizabeth thought.

But after watching mindless television for twenty minutes, the nagging feeling got to her.

She stood for just a moment then pulled out her phone. She walked to her room as she dialed and sat down.

"Hey, how are you? Yeah, I know, it's been a long time. Good, good. Hey, um, something's come up, and I was hoping you could help me out. Well, I hate to do this to you, but have you heard anything at all lately about Will Eliot?"

* * *

Derick tried to focus on the road. His speedometer kept inching up, then he'd glance at his speed and slow down. Getting pulled over wouldn't help anything. He held the piece of paper out in front of him with the directions while his hand tapped on the steering wheel.

He was exhausted, running on adrenaline. His last meal had been on the plane. He ran a hand over his face, wishing he'd had time to shave. It didn't matter. It couldn't matter.

Glancing at his cell phone on the passenger seat, he remembered Amanda's screams on the phone as she'd called over her shoulder, "Greg, you were right! You were right!" And Derick could hardly understand the directions she had given him. At last, Greg had taken over, quite smugly. "I knew it," he'd said then given him the address.

He turned onto the last street, and his heart started pounding. "C'mon, c'mon, c'mon." He watched numbers and pulled off when he saw the right one.

The car door slammed a little too hard as he focused on the front door of the house. He pushed the doorbell and waited, tapping his hand against his leg. *Breathe.*

He heard someone coming, talking loudly.

"I cannot believe—Well, maybe I can." The door opened all the way. "I have to go. I'll talk to you later. Thanks for everything." She hung up.

She stared at him. She blinked. She pointed. "You're . . . you're the one." She looked away briefly, recalling. "You're *Derick.*" She looked at him incredulously. "What are you doing here?"

He'd expected this. "Is Alisen here?" He looked past her into the house.

Her eyebrows came up. "Umm, no, but . . . aren't you supposed to be marrying that girl in the hospital?"

He brought his head back. "What?" He shook his head. "Look, I want to see Alisen. I think she'll talk to me." His voice got quiet. "I hope she will anyway." He looked past her again and called, "Alisen?"

"Oh, you need to get over to the country club right now."

He frowned in confusion. "What?"

"Elizabeth? Who's at the door?"

Keith Embry had rounded the corner from another room. He looked past Elizabeth and right at Derick. Derick lowered his chin and met his gaze. He barely breathed.

Keith's eyes widened. "It's you," he whispered. He paused, then he started toward Derick, taking long strides.

Derick widened his stance and squared his shoulders.

Then Keith slowed and stuck out his hand, a foot of distance between them. Derick blinked, taken back. Warily, he reached for the offered hand. Keith grabbed and shook hard. His other hand came up to grip Derick's shoulder. His jaw tightened, and his chest rose and fell as he whispered roughly, "Please say you've come back for her."

Derick's voice stuck in his throat.

Elizabeth folded her arms. "You better get over to that dance."

Chapter 34

WILL STILL WASN'T ANSWERING HIS cell phone. Alisen walked through the wide entry. He'd probably found something better to do.

People milled around in groups, and a few danced on the parquet floor in the center of the room. A live band played a 70s tune as the small disco ball twinkled weakly. She ventured a little farther in, walking around the perimeter of the dance floor, ignoring some of the double takes a few of the men gave her.

She scanned back to the entry.

A large group was just entering the room. Will was hard to miss. She saw an older, handsome couple, and when the man she thought might be his father turned around, there was no mistaking him.

Will looked around the room quickly but missed her. He turned to the figure behind him, a woman, and leaned down to whisper something in her ear. She looked up at him and smiled then kissed him. He kissed her back, and she pushed him playfully away.

Alisen froze with denial. A friend? With that kiss?

She bit her lip and dropped her head. Will was walking to the dance floor, looking down and smiling, holding the hand of the woman following behind him. Alisen glanced at her quickly. She couldn't help the comparison. Long and tall, black shiny hair straight down her back, chunky turquoise and silver against her dark skin. She was . . . sexy.

Will had turned his back to Alisen and was bringing the woman's bare arms up around his neck, pressing his nose into her hair.

Alisen searched for the best escape route but could see only the main entry and doors to a kitchen.

She looked back just as Will turned again, and with his next step, he saw her. For a moment, their eyes locked. Then he pulled his away. She saw a faint crease in his brow, a small flicker of his eyelids, and then he turned around, not missing a step.

She pushed out a breath then made her way past him and out the entrance. She left the foyer and brought her hand up to her forehead, inhaling the cool air outside. The breeze smelled of water from the sprinklers drenching the course and filled her with longing for the orchard.

Her phone rang. She pulled it out. "Hello."

"Alisen?"

"Elizabeth. Sorry, I just, uh . . ." She was out of breath.

"Alisen, you have to listen to me. Is Will there with you?"

"No, he's"—she looked back at the building—"not yet."

"Listen. I know I haven't been the best . . . well, *any* kind of sister to you—"

Alisen started to protest, but Elizabeth continued. "But I've been watching you these past few years. I've been envious at times, and other times I've seen you so sad." She paused. "And I've seen you change. You're . . . uncompromising."

Alisen chuckled sarcastically as she wandered behind the building. "Elizabeth, I don't—"

"*Wait.* Let me finish. I always felt a little like I was somewhat to blame for the big blow-up with, well, you know, like I made it worse. I didn't realize . . . I promised myself I wouldn't do that again. I'd never seen you so heartbroken. I mean, you were the resilient one."

Alisen stopped abruptly.

Elizabeth continued. "So I'm not going to let any two-faced lying *cheat* send you back to that place again. Alisen, no matter what Will says or promises, you *have* to believe me, all right?"

Alisen braced herself. "What . . . what is it?"

"Alisen, Will is married."

She couldn't say anything.

"Alisen, did you hear me?"

"Yes."

"Honey, I'm so sorry. But he did this to a friend of mine a few years ago. I was hoping, for your sake, that he'd divorced already, but I made some calls to be sure. His wife is an airline attendant, and because she's gone so often, he thinks he can . . ."

Alisen turned at the sound behind her. She wasn't listening anymore. She spoke into the phone. "Will's here now, Liz. Thanks."

In a few strides, he was there, and he didn't even let her speak. He wrapped her up and kissed her thoroughly. She pushed against him.

"Will. *Will.*"

He stopped and held her close, looking fiercely into her eyes. "You said you weren't coming."

His words startled her. She stammered, "Wh—what would you have done if I said I *was* coming?"

He shook his head. "I would have talked you out of it. Heck, *I* would have gotten out of it. We could have met somewhere." He pulled her tighter. "I was going to tell you. I didn't expect . . ." He kissed her again.

She shook her head. "Mm, *no*. I tried to *call* you."

He let go with one arm and pulled out his cell phone. Swearing hard, he shoved it back into his pocket. "It's dead."

She pulled away and spoke through her teeth. "Will, we need to talk."

He furrowed his brow. "I don't want to talk." He leaned toward her mouth again.

"That's obvious." She gritted her teeth as she pushed him away with all her strength. She turned and started walking around to the front, wiping her mouth on her sleeve and fighting the ridiculous tears, but he grabbed her arm and held her tightly. She couldn't shake him. Emotions boiled just under the surface, her jaw still tight. "You *lied* to me."

He walked around to face her and lowered his forehead to hers. He was breathing hard. "I want *you*."

"You. Are. *Married*. And now I know." The tears were making delicate trails down her face. "You manipulated me. *Ugh*. Why do I let that happen?"

"Alisen."

"Please, stop."

"*Alisen*."

"Stop!" She shoved him again.

He glanced in the direction he'd come from. He turned to her and lowered his voice. "Alisen, I was going to tell you. It isn't happy. I'm leaving her." He was close to her again, placing his hands on her arms. "Cherry Girl . . ."

"Don't *call* me that." She let out an angry chuckle. "You don't even *know* me."

He sighed. "Alisen, I want to know you. We could do anything we want. *Anything*."

He pulled her in again, but she'd had enough. "You looked happy to me. You've done this before . . . And I. Don't. Want. That." She wrapped her hands around his arms and kicked her knee up hard.

She heard running footsteps as Will buckled over in pain.

"Do you need help?"

Will groaned. "Uh-huh." He started to get up.

"I was talking to Alisen." Derick cocked his fist back and slammed it into Will's jaw with all the momentum of his run. Will stumbled backward then fell hard on his rear, dazed.

Derick regained his balance and turned quickly, shaking his hand out. "Alisen?"

She stared at Will Eliot on the ground. Then she looked up at Derick, her eyes wide in disbelief. Then her emotions fell apart, and she turned away.

Derick's arms drew around her quickly. "Alisen, it's okay now. It's all right. Everything will be all right."

She shook her head. Her hands came up to grip his arms, partly pulling him away, partly clinging. "No, it won't. It can't."

People were starting to walk in their direction. The woman with long black hair called out, "Will!" She ran and knelt beside him. Will spat out blood and groaned, leaning over. Will's wife looked up accusingly at Derick.

Alisen felt a rise of anger, protectiveness. Derick only shook his head, disgusted. "You might want to keep a better eye on your husband." He pulled Alisen to him and walked her from the crowd, who moved out of his way.

* * *

Derick didn't even know where they were walking. He just followed a paved path, his arms wrapped around Alisen's shivering body. They came to a small bridge over a man-made creek, and he stopped, leaning with her against the wooden rails. The lights of the club faded, and he and Alisen were alone. He still worked to steady himself, adrenaline pulsing through him. He looked down at Alisen, who still gripped his arms, eyes lowered.

He placed both hands on her face and lifted it so her eyes met his. "It's all right now. Everything's going to be fine." He stroked her face with his thumbs, wiping her tears. She looked as if she couldn't believe he was there. "You did nothing wrong. If anyone's to blame, it's me." She looked away, shaking her head. He stroked her hair and leaned to brush his jaw against her cheek.

She whispered, pain in her voice. "No, don't."

He stopped, his brows drawn together, and looked away across the lawns.

She whispered again. "You're going to marry *Lindsay*."

He looked back at her. Why did people keep saying that?

"No, Alisen, I'm not."

"Yes you are. She loves you."

"No, she doesn't."

"Yes, she does; she said so in her sleep." Her face crumpled again, but he continued, desperate to know if this was what she wanted too.

"She also said something about Marcus being a rooster, but that doesn't make it true. Alisen, she had brain surgery," he said.

She shook her head.

"Alisen." He lifted her face once more and willed her to look at him. She did. "Lindsay might have had a crush on me, but that's over now. She's turned her focus, lately, to Ben."

There was a quick intake of breath, and he could see her mind working, trying to make sense, trying to believe. She looked up at him fully now. "What?"

"Ben has fallen for Lindsay. He couldn't help it. He wasn't looking for it. He's as amazed as you are. And with the accident bringing things into focus and learning I wasn't going to be in the way. . . They've spent a lot of time together. It's just the beginning of something, but . . . They've tried to call you. They wanted to share it with you. Amanda tried to call you."

She shook her head in disbelief.

He nodded. "I was wrong too. I thought Ben had feelings for you, but I was wrong."

Her eyes grew wide and focused on his. "Then, you . . ."

"I came back for *you*." His voice dropped to a whisper. "It's always been for you. I had to know if it was possible. I'm sorry it took so long to see. Please tell me I'm not too late." He stroked her face and searched her eyes and felt the thrill of her looking back at him. "Please tell me that when we dance, you never want to let go. Tell me that when you look at me, you want to beg me to stay with you." He wondered if his breathing was ever going to steady again. "Please tell me that your story," he swallowed, "is my story. Forgive me. Forgive me, Alisen." He gathered all the conviction he had. "No games. I love you."

He held his breath and waited.

Slowly, she brought her hand up and pressed it over his chest, feeling his heartbeat. She met his anxious gaze. "I thought I'd lost you," she whispered. "You're my missing piece."

He finally exhaled and drew his arms tighter around her as she melted into him. He kissed the top of her head, smelling her hair. She pulled back and reached up, tracing her finger slowly along the sides of his mouth.

They looked at each other, familiarizing themselves again. No hidden glances, no withholding expressions. He curved his fingers around hers and kissed them.

She gave him a small smile and drew her face up to his, watching his mouth, her lips parting close to his. "I love you," she whispered. "I love you, I love—"

He rushed to meet her, crushing her gently, remembering, exultant.

Chapter 35

THEY WALKED HAND IN HAND through the orchard, the slope of the earth beneath their feet. Emerald leaves and blushing berries glistened in the sun. Alisen reached for a branch and pulled herself closer into the limbs, and he followed. She had no inclination to climb.

She hesitated. "You came back?"

"Yes." He looked a little confused at her simple question.

"You came back two years ago for Natalie's funeral."

He dropped his head and nodded. "Yes, I did. I . . . I stayed at Jay's."

Alisen felt a tightening in her chest. But it didn't matter. Nothing mattered anymore, and she squeezed his hand.

He raised his eyes, shaking his head. "I didn't know. Jay didn't say anything. Although, now that I think about it, maybe he did say something."

"What?"

"We were driving up to Bigfork, and he asked if we could stop by your place. He said you'd made some big changes he thought would be worth checking out."

She repressed a smile at the thought of Jay's attempt and swallowed. "You didn't stop."

He shook his head and leaned his nose against her cheek, closing his eyes. "I wouldn't let him. I didn't care about any changes you'd made to the orchard. I was angry at him for even asking." He shook his head. "He wasn't talking about trees, was he?"

She placed her hand on his face and shook her head, wondering if she would have asked Amanda to church if Derick had come back into her life then. She'd have liked to think she would have. But she wasn't sure.

He brought his finger up to trace her smile. "I'll have to make it up to you."

She nodded and stepped past him, pulling him along until his step matched hers. Jane made an appearance, winding between their legs as they walked then chasing off after some other movement. They wove through the trunks, speaking little, not having to.

As they reached the base of the trees, Derick pulled Alisen around to face him but continued walking carefully so she wasn't rushed, their hands swinging between them.

She smiled. "I always said I could walk around this place blindfolded. I never thought about doing it backward."

He laughed. "You're doing very well." He glanced toward the house as they passed and sobered. "It was really strange staying here, living here without you, glimpsing you working in the orchard when I was too proud to offer help." He shook his head. "I don't want to do that anymore."

Alisen knew there was no use in calming the beat of her heart. Her feet touched the wood of the dock, and he kept guiding her, holding her hands.

"I came across a few things during my stay. Reminders."

She blew out a short breath. "Tell me about it."

He caught her tone and nodded. "There were good reminders too."

They stopped.

"Like what?" she asked.

He looked down to the water beside the dock. She followed his gaze.

Her voice came out in a whisper. "My rowboat." She stepped to the edge of the dock, looking over the polished exterior, the seats and oars ready to go.

His voice softened. "I noticed it hadn't been used in a while. I'm just self-centered enough to think I might have had something to do with that."

Alisen bent down and ran her hand along the edge, remembering his first touch, that first day. "I put it away. It wasn't your fault." Her emotions pushed at the surface.

"Well, I was part of it."

She stood to face him, to tell him she had never blamed him, but she had to take a step back. In his outstretched hand, something glinted in the sun.

"Let me make it up to you."

Her eyes moved between the object in his fingers and the fire in his eyes.

"Marry me, Alisen." He reached for her hand and brought her closer, his eyes never leaving hers. He tipped the ring, and she reached for it, reading the inscription: *I will be your home.* Tears surfaced, and she brushed them away, looking up at him.

"I will, always," he whispered.

Her wish.

She composed herself. The orchard shimmered green behind him, the sky opened blue above, and the lapping water soothed any efforts her heart was making to completely undo her. Alisen wrapped her hand around the ring. She shook her head, meeting his hopeful gaze. “No. I’ll be yours.”

He caught her up in his arms, and as his lips found hers, the scent on the breeze surprised her.

Cherry blossoms.

Are you happy, Mom?

About the Author

Nearly every one of Krista Lynne Jensen's elementary school teachers made a note on her report card pointing out that she was a "daydreamer." It was not a compliment. So, when Krista grew up, she put those day dreams down on paper for others to enjoy. When writing, she fuels her creativity with chocolate-covered cinnamon bears and popcorn. When she's not writing, she enjoys reading, hiking, her family, and sunshine. But not laundry. She never daydreams about laundry.

Krista is a native of Washington State and now lives in the northern Rocky Mountains. Through her stories she places characters in settings she loves, brings them to life, and challenges them to fight for what they want. *The Orchard* was inspired by Jane Austen's *Persuasion* and Flathead Valley, Montana, a favorite family vacation spot. If she had a cat, she would call it Jane.

She is the author of *Of Grace and Chocolate*, 2012.